Long ago, the Gods came back to earth and banished all science from Earth. When Prome finds an amulet in the ruins of an ancient city, he doesn't expect it to take him and his friend Malia on a quest to discover the long forgotten secret of the Technologists, to meet someone who awakens feelings of love in him, nor to defy the Gods themselves.

I0623981

Published by
NineStar Press
PO Box 91792
Albuquerque, New Mexico, 87199
www.ninestarpress.com

SunFire Press Imprint

Warning: This book contains scenes of violence and death.

Print ISBN # 978-1-945952-57-9
Cover by Natasha Snow
Edited by Elizabeth Coldwell

THE GAIA PROTOCOL

Alec Nortan

CHAPTER ONE

I'm crouching behind the wall of a half-collapsed building. I usually don't taunt the Fates like this, but my hiding place seems safer than the arrows of my pursuers.

I hear footsteps outside. I take a peek, just long enough to see a dozen hoplites marching down the street, their bows at the ready. They're scanning, surrounding, searching. As they come nearer, my heart beats faster. I flatten myself on the ground. If I could sink into it, I would, but the only thing sinking is a painfully sharp stone into my ribs.

The Goddess Tyche has blessed me with her luck: I hear them move away at a brisk pace.

When I'm sure they're far enough away, I sit, propping myself against the wall in a more comfortable position. I massage my ribs to ease the pain. Only then do I muster the courage to look at my leg. It's still shuddering from the electric arrow, but luckily, the arrow missed, only grazing the flesh. Had the arrow really hit me, I would already be dead. I know how it works. I've seen it before.

A few years ago, during a search, a Technologist hiding in our village tried to run away. The hoplite shot him in the arm. The man jerked but kept running. He snatched the arrow out of his limp arm. The hoplite then shot several arrows as fast as he could without even aiming. The arrows flew, veering toward the Technologist midflight. None missed.

Though the arrow missed me, it still hurts like hell, from both the wound and the aftereffects of the jolt. I take off my neckerchief and improvise a bandage to stop the bleeding.

Why did the legion attack me? Scavenging in the old city isn't forbidden.

I used to come here as a child and climb inside the deserted skyscrapers, looking for objects to trade on the market. Today, I've found some kind of amulet. It's a small, flat, metallic rectangle with geometric signs on it. It's probably not worth a bowl of soup, but it looks nice. I've put a leather string through a small hole and kept it around my neck to offer to Malia. She'll like it.

I look at the sky. The sun is already halfway down the horizon. I have to move if I want to make it home before nightfall. My leg doesn't feel much better. I take a tentative step and wince at the pain. I won't be able to run, but I can walk.

Walking back should usually take me a couple of hours, but not today. I have to move carefully between the buildings, hiding at suspect sounds, checking for movement in every direction before crossing a road. Two hours walking only brings me to the outskirts of what used to be a great city. Here, the last remnants of houses are swallowed by the first trees of the forest.

"Fuck!" My outburst sends a few scared birds flying away. It has taken me far too long. The sun is already sinking behind the highest ruins. Now I really have to hurry, despite my leg.

I scrutinize the nearby trees. I don't see anything moving. I walk to them and find a broken bough to use as a crutch. I come back swiftly to the safety of the road.

During the day, traveling on the road is usually safe enough. But the forest... Only parties of adults enter it. Sometimes, one goes in alone. And sometimes, they don't come back.

During the night, forest or road, no one goes out. Too many things lurk in the dark.

***

I'm still hobbling along the road. The sun has set and darkness is growing everywhere. Walking in the middle of the road, as far away from the forest as I can, I pay more attention to the lines of trees than to the road. As I take a right turn, I hear a shout. About half a mile ahead of me, on the road, a warrior starts running toward me. I don't think. I just throw my crutch away and dart into the woods. Adrenaline helps me run, but soon feet pound the ground not far behind. The warrior won't be able to throw his spear with all the trees between us, but he's gaining on me.

I jump over a small stream and keep running as fast as I can. The ground around me is flat, and I can't see any escape: no tree big enough to conceal me; nowhere I could hide. My leg is burning. I won't be able to run much longer.

Another shout, this time much closer. Too close. He's almost on me.

Something moves noisily to my right. I don't have time to turn my head. Something big collides with me and throws me ten yards away. I land against a tree. The air rushes out of my lungs with the impact, and dark spots dance in front of my eyes. It takes all my willpower not to pass out. I barely register loud sounds around me: hooves trampling the ground, feet running, shouts.

As I recover my sight, I look up. The warrior is there, spear at the ready. But he's paying no attention to me. In front of him is a gigantic boar, as tall as him, with tusks as long as my forearms.

I cower against the tree.

Everything blurs together: the lightning bolt escaping the spear and the shouts of the soldier, the blood marring the animal's fur and its enraged grunts. They charge at each other, turn, move around in a ferocious choreography. The boar falls once, then again. But each time it stands up again. And each time a fresh bolt hits it.

Its fur is soon completely red. Its front legs threaten to give way. In a final assault, it runs toward the warrior. At the last moment, it moves to the left, evading the spear.

The warrior is visibly unprepared for such a move and reacts too late. A tusk impales him. The boar shakes its head. The limp body falls to the ground.

I can't believe what I've just witnessed. Beasts and warriors are supposed to be on the same side. They're all obeying the Gods. And warriors are supposed to be more than human. I've never heard of one getting injured, let alone killed. How could this happen?

The boar turns its head, and for a moment, all I can see is the blood dripping down its tusk. I'm paralyzed by this sight, as if the blood were mine.

The tusk moves toward me. It keeps getting closer and bigger. It's all I can see.

I can hear the beast breathing. I can even smell its breath and blood. I see every detail. Small chunks of flesh and viscera torn from the guard; every single indentation on the ivory under the gore.

The tusk suddenly stops and lowers itself. I can still see its tiniest details, but I can't hear breathing anymore. Only the metallic smell of the blood lingers.

I stay frozen like this, unable to think, until the cry of an owl shakes me out of my torpor.

I blink and look around. I'm still alive! I realize that the beast must have died just before reaching me.

I look again, but I can't see the warrior's body. It's too dark for that. Night has fallen.

I stand up.

Now my ribs ache with each breath I take. At least my leg still holds my weight. I walk carefully toward where I think the warrior is. I see a faint light reflecting on something. His bronze helmet. I kneel beside it and grope around. My hand falls on something cylindrical.

It's the spear. I won't be able to send lightning with it. Only Heavenly Phalanxes can do that. But it still is a weapon. And a pointy stick is better than no stick at all.

***

I'm completely lost.

I try to backtrack my steps, but I can't be sure I'm heading in the right direction, toward the relative safety of the road. I walk even more deliberately than I did among the ruins. I try to see where I'm putting my feet, to make as little noise as I can, and at the same time, I strain my ears for any suspicious sound.

Advance is slow and tiring. After a few hours walking, turning back, walking again, I'm about to give up. My leg's hurting so badly, even using the spear as a crutch doesn't help much. I take one last step and stop.

Maybe spending the night in a tree is my best option. As I stand here, pondering this idea, something cold engulfs my feet. Surprised, I jump to the side and hear a splash. I look down to see that I'm standing in a little stream. Water has permeated through the leather of my boots.

I feel hopeful again. If this is the stream I crossed when I was pursued, then I'm going the right way to get back to the road. I kneel and cup my hands. The fresh water tastes wonderful! I hadn't noticed how thirsty I was, but here I am, drinking and drinking as if I had just crossed a desert. I feel better, but now hunger gnaws at my insides. There's nothing I can do about it. All I brought with me this morning is long gone, and I wouldn't go back to the boar to eat some of its meat even if I hadn't eaten for a week...

I grip my stick and start again.

Progress is still slow and painful, but at least I now have a chance to find the road again. And after what feel like hours, I reach it and let out a sigh of relief.

My pace gets faster, although I still stay alert to my surroundings, listening to the forest sounds and keeping an eye on the road. During the night, things come out of the forest. Even the road isn't safe anymore.

***

I'm getting closer to the city. Suddenly, I become aware of a noise coming from farther down the road. I immediately hide behind a tree.

After a minute during which nothing happens, I'm about to stand up when a movement attracts my eyes. A hundred yards away, a head appears between the trees. It's about as big as a horse's head. But it looks like a snake. The creature moves forward, and a second, then a third head appear, each one scanning the area in a different direction, forked tongues slashing the air.

I hide behind my tree. It's the first time I've seen such a monster, but I already know what it is and what it's capable of.

A few years ago, one of those monsters terrorized the city. People disappeared, even during the day. More than a dozen vanished. One day, one of the missing came back. They died shortly after describing the animal to stunned villagers. The nobles refused to send a phalanx, proclaiming that the hydra was Zeus's punishment, and that all beasts are holy. A party of villagers took off to hunt it, though. Fifty men, all brave and strong, went after it. None ever came back. Only a few bones were found.

How could they have prevailed with only crude weapons when it took all Hercules's might to kill the ancient hydra in the first place? But, after that, the attacks stopped.

I don't know if it's the same hydra, and I don't care.

I check the road. The beast's still there, in the middle of the road, its three heads moving around on their long serpentine necks, its bulging trunk moved by four short legs, its tail trailing behind it. It's as long as four horses and half that high.

I stay hidden until it disappears. I wait ten more minutes before moving, just to be sure that it's not coming back.

***

After another hour of walking, I finally see the shape of the ochuroma, my city-fortress. No fire burns on the fortification; it would attract monsters. But, in the moonlight, I spot the shapes of a few sentinels pacing on top of the defending wall. Being out during curfew is forbidden, and the doors to the city are closed. Luckily, I used to be a very disobedient kid.

Very young, one learns not to linger in the forest. But exiting the fortifications without the guards noticing is quite a popular pastime. I hope I haven't grown too much...

I move into the forest again to stay hidden, and follow the stone wall to the right. It's not long before I discover what I've been looking for: a small drain opening near a shallow pond.

Such drains go under the fortification every few hundred yards. They are too small to allow any dangerous monster or beast to enter, but a kid can easily crawl through them. The smell of all the feces and garbage flowing through them is a powerful deterrent, though.

I discovered this one when I was about ten. I was trying to escape some older kids who wanted to punch me. Cornered, I decided to jump into the gaping hole. They didn't follow me. I was surprised to crawl through an almost clean drain. Only rainwater flowed through it from the streets. I exited, clean and unharmed, near a small pond.

When my tormentors saw me the next day, they were awed by my courage at jumping into the sewers and surviving. I didn't tell them it didn't take courage. They nicknamed me Rat, but never hassled me again.

Tonight, for the first time in years, I have to crawl back into the drain to enter the city. I hide the spear under some moss and go in arms first. I have to kick with my legs to get my shoulders in, but don't get stuck. A few minutes of crawling, pulling, and kicking get me to the other end. Getting out of the drain is much easier. I enjoy breathing freely as my chest comes out.

Footsteps catch my attention. They're coming my way. I barely have time to get back into the drain when a whole phalanx erupts from a nearby street and crosses the square.

I wait a little before crawling out again, but then another phalanx arrives from another street. I wait again, but no one else comes by. The place looks completely deserted. Not even a night prowler.

I can't believe this. I've never seen phalanxes marching down the streets in the middle of the night like this. Something's wrong. I decide to wait in my hiding place for morning.

***

I'm worn out, but I can't sleep. The drain is too small to be comfortable.

I wonder what life was before the Purification, before the Gods came back. At school, we were taught that, long ago, the Gods didn't live on Earth. They looked upon humanity from afar. But time passed, and men forgot. They replaced the Gods with technology. Those who still believed perverted their faith to kill and enslave in the name of their God. When humanity was about to destroy itself, and the Gods could no longer let mankind follow its own path, they came back to Earth. They destroyed technology, banning it and punishing without mercy anyone trying to use it. They led man into a new age of freedom and peace.

I understand that the monsters and beasts were sent to punish us. But what's the reason behind the sacred armies? They're supposed to protect us, but they also abuse us. For me, they are just monsters in human disguise.

***

The tumult of the market shakes me out of a dream full of Gods made of metal, and giant boars chasing me.

I come out of my hiding place and mix with the crowd. My back and arms are killing me from my poor night's sleep, but I almost don't feel my leg anymore. Groups of three or four hoplites are walking everywhere. Another sign that something's going on. After yesterday's events, I decide to avoid them.

***

I enter Malia's bedroom through the window, but she isn't here. As I look around, I catch a glimpse of myself in a mirror. I take a better look. I brush the dirt from my face and clothes, and try to comb my black hair, without much success. My light-gray eyes look tired, but I can't do much about that, either. At least, I'm half-decent now. I open the door and go down to the living room.

There she is, offering food to the Gods on the family's altar. All I can see is her light-brown hair, worn in a ponytail. I pluck an apple from the table and bite into it ravenously.

"Training to become first priestess again?" I ask with my mouth full.

She doesn't turn around, but keeps doing the offerings. Only when her task is finished does she stand up and look at me. She's half a head shorter than me, but her hazel eyes bore into mine with disapproval.

"If I become one, I'll ask the Gods to forgive you, infidel!" Her face is serious.

I clutch my heart and open my eyes wide in mock horror at what she's just said. "How can you call me infidel when I've learnt all five hundred million names of the Gods of Saintbanana?"

"It's 'Sanatanadharma,' stupid, and there are only three hundred and thirty million Gods... Besides, they rule another continent. You don't have to learn all their names, though you really should pay more respect to them." Her tone is somber, but I notice the beginnings of a smile twitching the corner of her mouth.

I try to look unconcerned, gazing up at the ceiling, waving my arms around. "I don't see why I should even bother. As you said, they dwell on another continent. Besides, I was too busy finding the perfect birthday present for a girl I kinda like..."

She comes closer. "Who's the unfortunate girl?"

"Just someone I know." I stare into her eyes.

"And did you find your gift?" she asks, her nose almost touching mine.

"I don't know. I wanted to ask a girl's opinion first, but there's just you here..."

She punches me in the arm.

"Ouch! That was totally uncalled for!"

"Yeah, sure. I know you only found a lame stone anyway." She pouts.

"Okay. Close your eyes."

I take out the amulet and let it hang in front of her face. "Okay, now you can open them."

"By the Gods!"

We both snap our heads toward the entrance in surprise.

CHAPTER TWO

Malia's mother, Archelia, is standing there, eyes open wide, both hands on her mouth.

Malia and I look at each other, not understanding her reaction.

"What have you done, Prome?" She half runs over to us. "Hide this immediately. Follow me, both of you. Hurry, but stay hidden from the guards."

"Mom? What's happening?" Malia's voice is higher than usual.

Her mother looked at her. "There's no time for that now. Your boyfriend has brought the Gods' wrath upon us."

"But, Mom…"

"I'm not her boyfriend."

They both glare at me.

"What? I'm not."

Malia's about to retort, but her mother speaks first. "Haven't you noticed all the guards in the streets? You're the one they're after. And now we're all in danger. If you love her, follow me."

"They're after me? Why? I didn't do anything wrong!"

She runs to the kitchen without answering and takes a look through the rear door before calling us with a gesture of her hand.

She leads us through the city, using narrow passages; sometimes going through houses, sometimes mixing with the crowd to cross a street. Whenever she spots a guard, she changes her path. Malia and I do all we can not to lose her. We don't dare say a word as we follow. With all the unfamiliar alleys she leads us through, and the detours she takes, I'm not sure what part of the city we're in anymore.

After what seems like hours, she opens a small wooden door and walks into a little room. She stands in the middle of it, still as a statue, eyes closed.

Malia and I look at each other, perplexed.

"Mom? Wha—"

"Shh. Don't move, don't speak."

After a few seconds, I hear a soft buzz, like a bee but much more regular, unnatural. The noise stops with a clank that surprises me. Archelia opens another door. "In here, quick."

The door closes behind us. We're surrounded by tables covered with pieces of metal and plastic. On one of them is a gray metal box.

"What's—"

This time, Malia interrupts me. "Mom! This place belongs to a Technologist!" She sounds appalled.

"Indeed it does." The voice comes from behind the metal box. A man stands up. He has white hair and the blanched skin of someone who doesn't go out much. He turns to Archelia. "Why did you bring them here?"

"I'm sorry, Ekon, but it's an emergency. Prome, show him your amulet."

As soon as it's out of my pocket, the man runs over and takes it from me. He goes back to his metal box and puts the pendant on top of it. The box immediately emits a short beep and a small green dot appears on it.

"By Goibniu! Do you think that's...?"

"A key. Yes, I think so." Archelia finishes for him.

I turn to Malia and whisper, "Who's Goibniu?"

"The Celtic god of metalworking! Ekon must have come from the South." She turns to her mother. "Mom, what are we doing here? That's technology! The guards could kill us for this!" Her breath is ragged.

"I'm sorry, my dear. I suppose it's time you knew. I'm a Technologist too."

"What?" Malia's shouting. "You can't be! You pray to the Gods! You..." She takes a step back, away from her mother.

"You're right, Malia. I pray, but I don't trust them. The Gods are hiding something about the past. Our past. The monsters, the legions... They're restraining us. I'm trying to find the reason, and technology is the only way to get it."

"You... You're not making sense! Why did you make me study the Book of Gods if you don't trust them?"

"To protect you, Malia. To protect you from them, from their lies. To hide you." She tries to brush Malia's cheek with her hand, but Malia takes another step back. "I'm sorry, my dear. I should have told you earlier. I hope you'll forgive me."

A loud bang echoes through the door. The man and Malia's mother look at each other. He picks up the pendant and gives it back to me.

"Prome, keep that safe, whatever happens. Go to Kurea. Find a man named Veron. He'll help you. Look for the fish." He pushes a shelf aside, revealing a door. "Now, go through there and exit the city. Quick. Archelia! The door won't hold long! Destroy the documents!"

Another bang.

"Mom!" Tears glisten on Malia's cheeks.

"Go, Malia. Stay with Prome. You'll find your answers. Don't trust anyone and stay away from the soldiers at all costs. Go!" Archelia gives her daughter a quick hug. She rushes to a stack of papers and begins shredding them.

Another, louder bang.

The man pushes us through the door and then closes it behind us. We're in a narrow corridor. There is a crash behind us, Malia shouts, "Nooo!" I take her hand and pull her along. We start running. After a few minutes, we emerge into a busy street.

Still pulling Malia, I make my way through the streets. The only guards we see are running toward the house we've left, not taking any notice of us. I soon recognize a street that leads us to the square with the drain. The market is busy. As we rush by the stalls, I snatch a satchel and fill it with whatever is close enough: food, clothes, medicine... I don't like to steal, but we're leaving, and we'll need more than a strange piece of metal to survive.

"Malia, get into the drain, quick." I shove her toward it and then look around.

"What? No! It stinks!"

"This one doesn't. Now get in!" She stands there, looking at me as if I were raving mad. "For your mother's sake, Malia! You've seen what happened. Move if you don't want to die!"

I see shock on her face as if I slapped her. But at least she obeys and gets into the drain. I look around one last time to make sure no guard's looking at us, then follow her.

Malia's waiting for me at the side of the pond. She's embracing herself and looking at her feet. I walk over to her and hug her.

"We have to go, Malia. We have to move away from the city. We have to go to Kurea."

Malia doesn't say a word. She just starts walking.

"Wait, I almost forgot." I return to the pond and retrieve the spear from its hiding place. It will be too recognizable once we're on the road.

I take off my already torn shirt and make some strips out of it that I wrap around the spear. With the help of a little mud, it doesn't look like a spear anymore. I put on a shirt I've stolen and walk back to Malia.

She hasn't moved.

We walk through the forest until we reach the north road, far enough from the city gates not to be seen. The road is deserted. We break into a slow-paced jog, one that we can sustain for a long time.

***

The sun is high. It must be almost noon, but we keep running. I want to put as much distance between the guards and us before slowing down. I glance at Malia. She's looking straight ahead. She no longer appears lost. Concentrating on her breath and her pacing prevents her from thinking about her mother. She doesn't look as if she's about to crumble anymore, but I still keep an eye on her.

Suddenly, my foot bumps into a stone. I feel the shock run up my leg, up to the arrow wound. I fall forward, and as I touch the ground, darkness engulfs me.

***

Something drips on my lips. I part them and swallow the cool water. I open my eyes and see Malia above me.

I try to stand up, but she pushes me back down. "Lie down and drink. When did you eat last?"

I hesitate. "I ate an apple this morning."

She rolls her eyes. "When did you last have a real meal?"

"Hmm... Probably yesternoon."

Her face relaxes. "Then you just passed out through hunger. Eat this." She hands me some dried fruits and cheese. "By the way, when did you plan on telling me about your leg?"

I look down at it and see a bandage on my thigh. "You didn't have to do that. It's only a graze."

"Yes, I had to!" She almost shouts at me. "I had to take some pus out of your wound. I've gone through your bag and found some ointment. I hope it's enough."

"Thanks."

I sit and eat my food. We're in the forest, though I can see the road not far away. She must have carried me somehow, just far enough to hide us in case a phalanx walks down the road. When I don't say anything, she takes some food too, devouring it ravenously.

"So, what happened?" she asks when she's finished.

I should tell her about yesterday—the forest, the boar, the fight—but I just mumble something about finding the spear.

She looks at the spear and her mouth tightens. I know she sees my taking of it as another crime against the Gods, but she refrains from lecturing me.

I stand up. "We have to move on." I pick up my satchel and then go back to the road. I don't wait for her. I know her too well, and I don't want to see her face when she realizes that I'm the one who caused all this. I don't want to see the pain. And I don't want to see the disappointment.

My leg hurts again. It's not too bad, but I can't run anymore. I can walk fast with the help of my spear.

Although the road is never very busy, today it's eerily empty, and it's making me nervous. I can't help watching the forest surrounding us and listening for every noise.

Nothing. I only see the leaves moving in the warm breeze and hear birds singing. But even they don't sing as loud as usual, as if they too feel something's wrong...

From behind us comes a low, thumping noise, growing louder fast. I catch hold of Malia's arm and pull her toward the forest. Safely hidden behind a bush, we watch a dozen hoplites galloping by, spears in hands. They quickly disappear.

Malia's first to come out of our hiding place and walk back to the road. She doesn't even look at me.

As the sun begins to drop, I increase my pace. "There should be a station not far away. I want to reach it before nightfall."

Malia doesn't answer. The only sign that she's heard me is her matching increase in pace.

***

As the sun's about to disappear, we see a wooden fortification down the road. I signal to Malia to slow down and take cover among the trees. We walk more cautiously now. Soon, we see the closed gates.

Malia doesn't say a word, but the glance she shoots at me is enough to convey her surprise.

"Yes, they've closed the gates although it's still daytime. Come with me but stay hidden."

As we creep closer, I see first one hoplite, then a second one, appear at the top of a tower. "By the Acheron! We can't go in there. We'll have to spend the night in the forest."

Malia looks at me, shocked. "Are you crazy? We'll die in the forest. We have to go there. They may not even be looking for us." She starts toward the gate.

I catch her arm and pull her so hard she falls on her back. I put a hand on her mouth to muffle her cry. She tries to throw me off.

"Sorry, I didn't mean to hurt you. We can't go there. You heard Archelia."

She stiffens at the name of her mother and looks at me, anger burning in her eyes.

"I've already spent a night in the forest. We can spend another one. But you have to trust me on that, and do what I say. Okay?"

She nods, and I gradually release her.

"We have to move while there's still some light. Then we'll find a tree to sleep in." I hope that setting a goal will help her, even if I feel just as scared as her.

✳✳✳

We follow my "plan." When it gets dark, we walk into the forest and find a tall tree. We climb as high up it as we can and install ourselves on a bough big enough not to break under our weight. I sit with my back to the trunk, and she sits in front of me.

"I'll tie us to the trunk with some bandages to keep us from falling while we sleep."

She doesn't say anything as I tie us in place. Even when I'm finished, she stays silent.

The tree is very uncomfortable, but after a sleepless night and a day spent on the road, I soon fall asleep.

✳✳✳

Something hits me in the ribs.

A whisper. "Prome."

I'm too tired to open my eyes.

Another blow.

"Prome! I hear something," Malia whispers urgently.

"Okay, I'm awake. Shh." I open my eyes and see that the night's almost over. The sky is already lighter in the east. I can see the ground and the trees around us pretty well.

I hear something coming our way. A big animal, by the sound of it. The sound stops and then starts again. It isn't approaching us anymore. It's turning around us, pausing every few paces.

I feel Malia's getting nervous. All her muscles are tense. I hold her tighter, but at least she doesn't make a sound.

A soft hissing makes Malia shiver. The animal paces again, circling our tree, much closer this time.

After a few nerve-racking minutes, something moves between some trees, a few paces from where we're hiding. Six heads appear on long necks. Malia gasps, and I put my hand over her mouth. She's trembling.

This hydra is about half the size of the one I saw before. It walks toward our tree, each head looking around.

It is directly under us. Malia's shaking now. I hug her even tighter to try to calm her down.

The hydra sniffs, hisses, walks a few paces, sniffs again around our tree.

Please, don't look up.

The hydra unhurriedly circles our tree three times before moving away. Malia relaxes, and I loosen my hold on her. We stay like this until the first rays of sunshine appear. She immediately unties us before climbing down the tree. I follow her to the safety of the road.

"There's a hydra in the forest!" she shouts at me.

"Yes. But at least this one was small." She glares at me, and I immediately regret my words.

"Small? How do you know it's small?" As I look silently at my feet, she continues. "What are you not telling me, Prome?"

"Well... The night before last I... kind of saw one. From very far away," I add quickly, to try to play down the incident. "It was twice as high as this one. But it had only three heads."

She looks stunned.

"You... It..." She turns her back to me, fists closed, and stomps her foot. She breathes deeply and speaks again, more calmly this time. "Why didn't you tell me?"

"I just forgot about it."

"You forgot?" Her shouts make my ears ring. "How can you forget a hydra?" She faces me again, hands on her head.

"I just saw it cross the road. It didn't see me. And I had other things on my mind..."

She begins pacing nervously. I know she will calm down. In the meantime, I take out some food so we can have breakfast. After a few minutes, she sits in front of me and starts to eat in silence.

"Prome? Do you think Mom..." Her voice falters, but I know what she's thinking about. My thoughts are the same as hers.

"Yes, Malia. She's still alive. She didn't fight or try to run away. They'll just imprison her." I certainly hope so, but my words sound empty to my own ears.

"Do you think they're looking for us?" Malia's face is a bit white.

"Maybe."

Silence again.

"I'm sorry." Her voice is low. She's looking at me.

"Why?"

"I know it's not your fault. It's just... It was easier to..."

I interrupt her. "It's okay, don't worry. If you're finished, we'd better get on the move again. I'd like to get to Kurea as soon as possible."

She comes closer and kisses me.

CHAPTER THREE

Her lips are soft and the kiss gentle. She breaks away after a few seconds, smiles at me, and walks off.

I stare at her back, dumbfounded. I know that most people think we're a pair, even her mother, and say we'll get married one day. We've grown up and spent so much time together that we're closer than most couples. But we've never dated. We just... are together. I never thought she wanted us to be... And this kiss! Our first one. It should have been special, but I didn't feel... I don't know how to tell her.

I've never been able to tell her.

"Are you coming?"

I come out of my reverie, pick up everything, and then join her.

We walk in silence for a while.

"Do you know why they were pursuing you? Is it really the amulet?" Malia asks me out of the blue.

I think about it before answering. "I think so, yes. Your mother's right. I didn't understand why they shot an arrow at me when they saw me. I just ran. But if it's a key or something important for the Techs, I bet that's what they were after."

"You could put it back where you found it. They'll find it, and they wouldn't be after us anymore." It sounds like a plea.

"I don't think that would work. Besides, I was there when the giant boar and the warrior killed each other."

"The what?" she shouts in alarm.

This time I have to tell her about the fight, giving her the real story.

"But you didn't do it."

"Have you ever heard of a beast attacking a heavenly warrior before? They would sentence me to death because of it. They wouldn't even try to understand. Especially as I stole his weapon."

She looks at my walking staff. "Why did the boar attack the warrior in the first place?"

I shake my head. "I don't know. The warrior was running after me when the boar attacked. Maybe it thought he wanted to steal its prey..."

"Maybe." She doesn't sound convinced. "You were quite lucky that the boar didn't impale you on one of its tusks."

I remember the pain as I collided with the tree. "Yeah, it was feeling merciful, and just wanted to get me out of the warrior's way and save me..."

She doesn't answer, but she makes that face—one brow lowered, lips pressed together—she always does when she's thinking hard. I stare at her, waiting for her to share her thoughts.

I can't help thinking about her idea. What if I dropped the weapon somewhere, along with the amulet? We could walk back and tell the guards that Malia's mother isn't a Technologist. I don't really believe it would work, but the other choice, walking to Kurea, repels me so much, I am seriously tempted to try it.

Too late, we hear the noise coming from above. As we look up, I see a harpy plunging, talons first, long, steellike claws ready to kill us.

Without thinking, I hold the spear above me, trying to protect us. A blinding flash erupts, and a thunderous crack fills the air, deafening us.

It takes us a few seconds to regain our sight. The harpy is sprawled, lifeless, on the road in front of us. It's bigger than I, the body of a bird of prey topped by a human head. It lies there, blackened and smoking. The stench of burned meat and feathers fills the air.

I look at Malia, too afraid to move.

"Look at your spear." Malia's eyes are bulging.

I lift my gaze and see that the strips of fabric we wrapped around have vanished around its head. The steel point's smoking; a red glow progressively dissipating as it cools down.

Surprised, I release the spear, and it falls to the ground with a metallic clang.

"How did you do that?" Malia stares at me.

"What? No, I didn't do it." My mind is buzzing.

"Prome, you saw it. You fired the spear and killed the harpy."

"No. No, I didn't." I take a step back, away from the spear, heart racing, breath short, panicked that it might still do something on its own. I can't take my eyes off it.

Malia wraps her arms around me and tears me from the sight. She holds me like this for several minutes before my heart slows down and my mind clears.

"We have to hide the corpse in the forest and move away. If anyone has seen or heard it, they'll be coming."

The body has stopped smoking, but pulling the monster by its feet is still nauseating. We hide it as best we can under twigs and fallen leaves.

Whatever chance to walk back we had has definitely vanished. I don't want to linger and begin to walk away. Malia doesn't move. She keeps staring at the spear, lying on the road.

I don't want to take it, but we have nothing else to defend ourselves with.

"Prome, please. Leave it."

"Malia, it's our only weapon."

"But it killed the harpy. You're a murderer now!"

"Without it, we'll be dead by nightfall."

I see the conflict on her face. She's always been the one who chastised me when I broke the rules. I've never done anything so serious, though. Stealing the spear from a dead guard could already get me thrown into jail for a few years. Killing a holy beast means death.

Her practical instinct finally wins. She doesn't say anything but starts walking silently at my side. I know that's the most she can do.

Just to be safe, I leave the road and walk in the forest for a while, to make sure that no one sees use, even if it slows us down. Malia follows me without a word.

✳✳✳

"What do you think happened?" I ask when I can't hold my tongue anymore.

She doesn't look at me. "We killed a harpy."

"Yeah, I got that. But why did the spear act like this? And that bolt! It was more like an explosion."

I can barely hide the awe in my voice and get a reproving look in response.

After a few seconds, she says to me, "You shouldn't have been able to fire the spear. Only heavenly warriors are granted that ability by the Gods. And I've never seen one throw off such an explosion." She stops. "Put the amulet on the ground."

I look at her, perplexed, but she seems serious. I shrug and obey.

"Good. Now, try to fire the spear."

I can't believe I heard her right. "What?"

"Fire the spear."

"Hmmm. Okay. What should I shoot?"

"It doesn't matter. That tree, for example." She points at a small tree in front of us.

I bear the tip of the spear, which I'd wrapped in more strips of cloth, and aim at the tree. I have no idea how to trigger the spear, and, unsurprisingly, nothing happens.

I look at Malia. "How do I do it?"

"I don't know. Is there a switch of some kind?" She inspects the spear. "No, nothing. Try thinking about shooting a bolt."

Still nothing.

I look at her. She crosses her arms, usually a sign that her patience is running thin. I concentrate on the spear.

"Shoot!"

Nothing.

I jerk it.

"Shoot!"

Still nothing.

"Okay, stop it. Now, pick up your amulet and try again."

"But you told me…"

She cuts me short. "I know what I told you. Now I'm telling you otherwise. Do it."

I do as she says, but the spear remains still. "Did you think it was the amulet that triggered the spear?"

She shrugs. "I thought so, but I was wrong. There must be something else."

As we walk, I look closely at the shaft of the spear, gliding my hand along it to try to find something that will bring it to life.

To no avail.

"You know, sometimes I wish I were born in the old world, before the Gods came back."

"Prome!" She gapes at me, alarmed. "How can you say that?"

"I bet the world was much simpler when they weren't around. No Gods, no Technologists, no armies…"

"Plagues, wars, atheists, miscreants, and technology… Sure it was much simpler… to die. We're lucky the Gods came back and brought order with them, otherwise, humanity would have eradicated itself."

"How do you know that?"

She starts reciting with a singsong voice.

Dark ages came, dark ages went, but none as dark as the Last Age
For humankind was led astray by false prophets and miscreants
The believers ignored their Gods; they lied and stole, hated and
killed
Engineering and Chemistry, Physics, Electricity, and Mathematics
Such were the names of their prophets, their religion was cold as
steel
Earth, air, water, all polluted. Hence came the plagues that bore
their death.

"I really don't know how you can quote the Book of Gods like this."
"It's called memory," she says and walks off.

✳✳✳

The rest of the day is uneventful. After a few hours, we go back onto the empty road. We don't want to meet any soldiers, but there should be at least some light traffic passing by. The deserted road is making me nervous.

Malia's getting edgy too. She looks over her shoulder more and more often.

We don't talk anymore, too busy scanning the road and the forest around us, so tense that a bird flying off too noisily makes us jump.

In the afternoon, I almost wish for a phalanx to come running down the road.

By the end of the day, we're both glad to leave the road again and look for a tree to sleep in during the night.

Finding a tree that's capable of hiding us from both the beasts lurking on the ground and those flying in the sky takes longer than I anticipated. Malia falls asleep almost immediately at my side, worn out by the stress of the day. Sleep doesn't come as easily to me. Feeling her so close to me is a reminder of the kiss.

I love her, and I can't imagine my life without her. But it's not that kind of love. How I wish it were. But it isn't.

✳✳✳

The road leads us out of the forest, into a patchwork of fields cut in two by a glistening river. In the middle spreads the city of Kurea.

Its defensive wall is twice as tall as our city's and shines in the sun.

It's an optical illusion; just an ornamentation of polished granite, found in nearby ruins and fixed on the cruder stones of the wall, but it gave the city its nickname. The Northern Diamond.

From afar, we can see that the majestic southern gate is closed, but the roads coming from the east and west seem to be crowded.

"Do you think we can mix with the travelers and get in?"

"Not looking like this." Malia opens the bag and takes out some of the clothes I stole from the market. "We'll have to change first. We don't want to look like we've spent a night outside. Let's cut through the fields to that small stream over there, clean ourselves, and change. I'll pray the Gods that it will be enough."

I refrain from pointing at the irony of her last sentence.

We walk through several fields, hidden among tall corn, or hunched like peasants through lower-rising crops. We wash quickly in the stream; I tie new strips of fabric around my spear until it looks like a walking staff, and make sure that the amulet hanging around my neck stays hidden. We then head for the crowd on the east road.

✳✳✳

The road is busy with the end-of-the-day crowd. Carts pulled by oxen carrying food, clothes, or raw materials to the city mix with small groups of travelers or workers in search of a job. No one looks at us, and, hidden in the middle of the crowd, we begin to relax.

Malia stops me abruptly. A woman, surprised by our sudden halt, bumps into me. I excuse myself before looking at Malia. "Why did you—?"

She cuts me off. "Look at the gate."

I can see the heavy oak doors open, people moving between them, and... "Guards. They're looking at everyone entering the city."

My heart drops. Even in the crowd, they'll spot us.

Malia looks around and pulls me to the side of the road. She scans the crowd as if looking for a relative. I do the same. We won't look suspicious. Just a young couple who has run ahead to look at the city and are waiting for their family to catch up...

"What are we going to do?" I ask her. "Buying time won't be enough; we'll have to get in."

"Shh, just keep acting as if you were looking for someone."

We stay like this for several minutes before she speaks again.

"Just play along," she whispers urgently, then louder, in the tone she uses when teaching kids history, "and they carved this door in honor of the seventh miracle. You remember what that miracle was and which God did it?"

I rack my memory... The seventh miracle rings a bell.

"Just look at the door, it should help."

I look up and see all kind of plants: trees, corns, wheat, and some that I couldn't identify, carved in such detail that it was obvious they were dying.

"The plants' plague," I almost shout out.

"Yes. The Gods sent a plague on the crops to punish the atheists from the Last Era. People were starving."

"Crops were indeed dying, but I must correct you, young miss. It wasn't the Gods, but the men's own fault. They had used science to change them and altered God's creation." A group of a dozen people have just stopped. An old woman, her face wrinkled as the bark of a tree, now faces a surprised Malia.

"Oh really? I'm so stupid! I've read the Book of the Gods several times, but I still keep forgetting some important things. I'll never be able to become a nun if I can't even teach my cousin Oli properly..." She looks abashed.

The old woman smiles warmly. "Oli? I'm Edama. And you are?"

"I'm Cassie."

Edama smiles. "You're still young, Cassie. You have your whole life to learn the Book of Gods. I trust you're going to Kurea for the Blessing of Demeter?"

"Yes. I wanted to see it, and Oli agreed to accompany me. Are you going to the Blessing too?" She looks absolutely thrilled.

"Indeed we are. Why don't you join us? We'll talk about the seventh miracle if you want."

We began moving again, Malia speaking with Edama, and I among the other devotees, singing prayers.

As we approached the gates, I get nervous again, and judging by the way Malia's back straightens, so does she.

We're getting closer to the guards. I see Malia turn to Edama and point at a carving. The woman gestures in turn at several statues, probably answering Malia's question. The closest guard looks at the carving the old lady is pointing at. His eyes widen as he stares at it.

I don't dare to look up and make myself noticeable. I hold my breath.

When the guard looks down again, we're through. I breathe again.

***

"Oli and Cassie?" I ask her as soon as we're alone.

"I didn't want to give our real names."

"And since when do you have problems remembering the Book of Gods, or make mistakes about what's in it, hmmm?"

She smiled. "Well, my mistake got us into the group and into the city, didn't it?"

"By the way, how did you manage that? Passing the guards so easily?"

Her grin widens mischievously. "I asked Edama a question about a carving near the youngest guard to draw us there. Then I asked her about another carving above the portal. I hoped that the guard was new enough not to know its story."

"It certainly caught his attention."

"That's usually the effect naked women have on young men."

"God! And I didn't look at that carving!"

We both laugh aloud.

"Do you have a plan to find Veron?" I ask hopefully.

She shakes her head. "No, and I don't think it would be wise to go asking everywhere about him so late. Edama invited us to spend the night with her party if we haven't found a place to sleep. We'll begin our search in the morning."

CHAPTER FOUR

Kurea makes our city look like a tiny village. Commerce, here, is thriving; the streets overflowing with buyers, merchants, and carts, as soon as the sun rises. Every square holds a market. People shout, kids run. There is too much tumult for the phalanxes to find anyone, and we don't have to hide anymore.

In the afternoon, when the Blessing begins, everything will close down for the festivities and the crowd will gather around the temple. If we want to find Veron, we have to find him this morning.

"Ekon told us to find the fish. Should we go to the docks?" I don't feel especially smart, but I don't have any better idea. "If we don't find anything, at least the docks seem like a good place to ask questions without raising too much suspicion."

"I'm not sure about asking questions, but I guess we have to start somewhere."

***

Finding the docks is easy enough, but the crowd slows us down tremendously. When we eventually reach the banks of the river, a myriad of boats wait for a place to unload their goods. The bank is just as crowded.

Malia sighs. "Let's go and try to find that fish, wherever it is..."

We dive into the mayhem.

The street is one giant, uninterrupted flow of people going right and left, carrying crates, bumping into each other, trying to shout louder than everyone to be heard. I'm afraid that if we get separated we'll never find each other again. I lock Malia's hand in mine and try not to get stampeded.

Walking proves difficult enough, looking for anything next to impossible. After what feels like hours, Malia pulls me into a bar.

It is barely less crowded and noisy than the street, but we manage to find two seats in a corner. We sit on the wooden stools with relief.

I go to the counter and come back with two cool ales that we sip with delight. "We can forget the docks. We'll never find anything here." I look down at my glass.

"Our only chance to find Veron is to ask. I'd ask the bartender; she's the most likely to know him."

"I'll ask her, then. A boy looking for someone might be less suspicious."

She's about to retort, but she looks at the counter, frowns, and closes her mouth.

I finish my drink and walk to the counter. A bulky woman is serving drinks behind it. She's red-faced and sweaty, a bit disheveled, but still finds the time and energy to give each customer a smile.

As I approach, I get a smile too.

"What you'll have, cutie? Same thing? Two ales?"

She sure does have a good memory for customers...

"No, sorry, I thought that maybe you could help me."

"I'm in a bit of a rush, right now..." She turns to fill a glass and then give it to a man next to me.

"I'm just looking for someone from the city. Veron. Do you know where I could find him?"

"Sorry, cutie, never heard that name before." She turns again, holding three empty glasses.

"Thanks anyway. Have a good day."

✳✳✳

"We had to try..."

We're trudging away from the docks. The streets we first thought crowded now seem almost empty in comparison.

"Where else are we likely to find a Technologist? They can be pretty much anybody. I could have one in front of me and never know it. Is there a special sign to recognize one?"

Malia looks down, eyes glistening with tears. I immediately feel stupid. I hug her and she hides her face in my chest. "I'm sorry, Malia. I didn't mean that. I..." I don't know what to say. I still can't believe Archelia is one, and she isn't my mother.

"I know." She sniffs and breaks the embrace.

I look up. Right in front of us, on the other side of the square, two gray towers rise into the blue sky, relics from a temple of the past.

Between them, above the columns of the peristyle, the sculptures of the triangular pediment represent Demeter in the middle of thriving crops.

"We should try looking in another part of the city. I don't think Veron would live near the temple."

We cross a bridge over the river and reach a completely different part of the city. Here, the streets and houses are dirty and the shops few. Most of the buildings are workshops.

I try to ask a shoemaker working in front of his house about Veron. I have to ask the question twice before he looks at me and tells me he doesn't know him.

We begin strolling the streets haphazardly, looking for a fish. We don't dare ask anymore.

$$***$$

When a bell strikes noon, we are no closer to finding Veron than we were when we woke up. We buy two sandwiches in a shabby bakery and go back to the river. We sit on the stone balustrade of the bridge and eat tiredly.

The activity on the docks is slowing down. The last boats are unloading.

"How are we going to find that fish? Ekon could have given us more information on how to find Veron," I say grumpily.

"What he gave us should be enough. We know what we're looking for; we just don't know where to find it."

I snort. "Then he should have told us to look for a statue of Demeter, or a cross. They are everywhere!"

Malia snaps her head toward the roofs of the city.

"Malia?"

She doesn't answer. I look in the same direction. All the roofs look the same to me. Every here and there, a tower rises higher than the surrounding buildings, still topped by a cross, a remnant of the God that used to be worshiped in this part of the world.

Malia jumps down and turns to me abruptly. "I can't believe I missed that!"

I'm baffled. "Uh? What did you miss?"

"The crosses!"

I still have no idea what she's talking about.

"Prome, the Book of Gods says that the miscreants used to kill those who believed in God."

"Hmm. Yeah, sure..."

She heaves. "You really should pay more attention at school. The cross had become too obvious, so the believers chose another sign to identify themselves."

"Let me guess... a fish?"

"Yes. And it's still used nowadays to show where a scholar can find shelter."

"Great. So now we're looking for places where future priests can rest? How many can there be in this city? Hundreds?"

Malia smiles. "We're not looking for a fish, we're looking for *the* fish."

She's lost me again. I stare blankly at her, waiting for an explanation.

"We're looking for the biggest place where they can stay."

"Which is?"

Her smile widens. "The residence where all the future priests and priestesses live while studying the Book." She turns her head and points at the two tallest towers.

✳✳✳

We stand in front of Demeter's temple again. People pour into the square from everywhere. The Blessing will soon begin, and everyone will be here.

I still have some doubts about finding Veron here. "What do we do now? Go to the temple and ask the High Priest if he knows Veron?"

Malia looks up and shakes her head slightly. "We'll ask, yes, but there." She indicates a huge building next to the temple.

As we approach the entrance, I try to look for a fish but don't see one. "Malia? I don't want to burst your bubble, but I don't see any fish."

"Look above the door."

I look up and see a sculpture of Demeter. At her feet, all kinds of food are growing. I turn to look back at Malia. "I see Demeter, but no fish."

"Look, right in front of her right foot."

There it is: a sculpted fish swimming lazily in a small stream. "Wow, they could have made it bigger. How's anyone supposed to find it?"

"The fish used to be a sign for people in hiding. It had to be as inconspicuous as possible. But if you knew what to look for, you would be able to find it."

She knocks and enters.

**

I don't know what I expected to find, but certainly not boys and girls running everywhere and shouting.

A girl, a couple of years younger than me, rushes past us, her blonde hair flying in disarray after her. She waves her hand. "Tilya, I can't find my..."

I'll never know what she's looking for, as her words are lost in the surrounding brouhaha. She disappears around a corner.

A man, a little shorter than me, his hair graying, comes down the stairs, holding a student by the shoulder. When he sees us, he releases him and comes over to us.

"May Demeter bless us all. If this madness goes on much longer, I'll seriously think about joining Hades's worshippers."

Malia gives a small laugh, but the joke is completely lost on me. I just smile politely, to pretend it was mildly amusing...

"How may I help you?" he asks, surveying all the students running around.

"We're looking for Veron."

The man breathes out loudly, relieved. "Thank Demeter and all the Gods! You must be the new aides-de-camp my cousin sent me. The Blessing's about to begin, and we still have so much to do. Come with me." He walks off briskly before we can say anything. All we can do is run after him.

"To the right is the kitchen. You'll have to be there as soon as the Blessing's over, but for now, the most urgent matter is the dressing of the valedictorian." He runs up some stairs and takes several turns, never letting us say anything. "Here's his room. Help him prepare; he has to be ready in ten minutes." He opens a door, pushes us through, and then leaves us.

We look at each other.

"Help me! I can't find the neck!" A headless body's turning around in the middle of the room, trying to put on a white ceremonial dress, but clearly lost in the fabric.

"Stop moving!" Malia pulls on the dress here and there, and after a little effort, a red-faced head appears in the folds.

The boy's a few years older than us. He's about my height, with black curls falling on his shoulders. He's a bit overweight, and has a pleasant, open face. It's the first time I've seen him, but his face already feels comfortably familiar.

"Thanks. I thought I'd never get out of it."

"I thought you were trying to get in, not out," I say jokingly.

The boy's face gets even redder. Although I feel guilty for teasing him, I find his shyness adorable.

Malia glares at me, then lifts the boy's arms. "Stay like this, and don't move. Prome, come and help me."

I drag my eyes off the boy reluctantly as Malia gives me a fold of the dress to hold. She finds some pins on a table and spends ten minutes folding, pinning, unfolding, folding again, ordering me around and snapping at the poor boy to stay immobile whenever he tries to move.

My hand brushes the boy's skin inadvertently. The furtive contact makes my heart beat faster.

Mali asks me to move again. Looking at her, I feel a pang of shame. The boy is a complete stranger. I shouldn't be drawn to him. How can I allow myself to have feelings for him I don't have for Malia? How can I possibly fall for him, when I haven't told Malia the truth?

Eventually, Malia takes a step back and smiles. "There you are. Now we'll need the food."

The boy points to a table. "It's over there. The kitchen has already prepared it."

On what looks like a big plate are several types of fruit, some corn, and a fish.

Malia looks at the food carefully, then begins arranging it. "Oh my God! Who prepared that?"

She runs out of the room and comes back several seconds later with a sheaf of wheat. She takes a few ears and adds them to the plate.

"What are you doing? You're ruining the offering!"

She ignores him. She takes the six pomegranate grains and throws them away, under the gaze of the dismayed valedictorian.

"You've ruined everything. I'll have to do it again!"

The door opens, and the old man who brought us here enters. He looks at the boy, turns around, and smiles.

"Perfect. You can't dress alone, but at least you can give good instructions. Let me look at the offerings... I see you haven't added any pomegranate grains like your predecessor did, five years ago. The High Priest almost collapsed when he saw that! Now, take your plate and off you go, or you'll be late."

The boy rushes out, throwing a quick glance at Malia then at me.

"Thank you. You can go to the Blessing now, but come back right after, there's still plenty to do."

I can't take part in this deception any longer. "I beg your pardon, sir, but we weren't sent by your cousin."

The man frowns at me. "Who are you, then?"

"We're looking for Veron."

"I am Veron," he answers harshly. "What do you want of me?"

"Ekon sent us."

Veron's mouth drops. He runs to the door and closes it. "Who are you?"

"I'm Prome, and this is Malia. Ekon wanted us to show you something." I pull out the amulet. As soon as he sees it, Veron orders me to put it back. "Not here, follow me."

Veron leads us to an office. Without saying a word, he pushes a bookshelf aside and leads us through to a hidden staircase. We descend it, finding ourselves in a vaulted room full of barrels.

"This is just a precaution in case they find the hidden staircase in my office. The barrels are full of wine. It isn't legal, but it's just a minor breach of the law."

He leads us behind a barrel higher than me, and pushes a stone aside to reveal a door.

We go down another long and narrow flight of stairs, and arrive in a dark room. I hear a click and, a second later, the room is lit by thin lines of light, the like of which I've never seen before.

The concrete walls are hidden by bookshelves containing more books than they can safely hold. In the middle, several tables are covered with the same kind of metal pieces we saw at Ekon's.

Veron finally stops and faces us. He looks at Malia. "You are Archelia's daughter." It isn't a question. "You look so much like her."

"Do you know what happened to her?" Malia's voice fills with tears.

"I only know that they didn't kill her. They took her to Parthenos."

The city of all Greek Gods. Why did they take her there?

As if he has read my mind, Veron answers my unspoken question. "Usually, when they catch a Technologist, they kill them. If they didn't, my only guess is that they want information from her. And my guess is the information is about you. Can you show me your amulet again?"

I take it out and give it to him. He examines it, turning it over in his hand.

"When Ekon put it on a box, it beeped and produced a small, blue light," I say matter-of-factly.

Veron stares at me. He seems excited, though I can't figure why. "Did it? Did he tell you anything?"

"No. He didn't tell us what that box is, nor why it beeped."

He jumps out of his seat and dashes over to a wall. "No one knows that. But it's an ancient artifact. It's a miracle it's still working. We could get precious information from it. I wish I had seen it." He sounds wistful.

He pushes a shelf aside unceremoniously. Behind it, the wall isn't made of concrete but of metal. Veron touches a small metal panel on its side with the amulet. The wall immediately slides open, revealing another room.

He slowly turns around to face us, wide-eyed and openmouthed, the amulet clutched in his hand. He looks like a kid who's just been given a new toy.

I look at Malia and frown questioningly.

She shrugs.

"Veron? Sir?"

"You found it!" he blurts out and collapses.

CHAPTER FIVE

Malia takes care of Veron, who at long last comes back to his senses. I can't help her, and to tell the truth, I'm still a bit uncomfortable about hiding from her what I really am. So, instead, I surrender to my curiosity. I select a book from one of the shelves. Its battered cover has been repaired several times. The title is *A Tale of Two Cities*. I can't read the author's name. I quickly scan through it but see nothing of importance. Another one is titled *L'Encyclopédie Diderot et D'Alembert*, with drawings of monkeys and birds on its cover. I open it and see many drawings of animals, some of which I've never seen. I can't find any monsters or beasts, though. I can't read any of the text, as it's written in another language.

I put the book back and then walk toward the room that was hidden behind the metal wall.

The air is stale, but as soon as I step inside, a low humming begins and fresh air flows in.

I'm surprised to find a room so neat. The books on the shelves are neatly aligned, all the same size and color. Another wall is covered by the smoothest panels of glass I've ever seen. I can't see anything through them, though. The glass is completely black.

In the middle of the room is a simple white table on four thin metal legs. A wheeled chair faces a small metal box. This one is a bit different from Ekon's, shining black and slightly smaller.

I wonder if that box would beep too if I put the amulet on it. I take out the amulet and approach the box with it.

"Prome! Come!"

I look at Malia. She's helping Veron to stand. I drag myself away from the box, still staring at it.

With Malia's and my help, Veron hesitantly makes his way to the room containing the black box. I can see his hands shaking slightly. He stops on the threshold as if he were too shy to enter.

A book falls to the ground on his left. He jumps and stares at it. I recognize the book with the drawings I looked at earlier. He picks it up. Suddenly, his eyes widen and he drops the book.

"My God! The Blessing! We're late!"

He walks out, and we follow him.

"Malia," I whisper, "why do we have to go?"

She doesn't look at me. "Everyone has to go to the Blessing. It's an offense not to go."

"Oh. Okay."

We walk through Veron's office again, and he replaces the shelf carefully behind us.

As we walk down a few stairs and into the entrance hall, we hear a loud knock on the door.

"Hide! Quick!"

Malia and I hide around a corner while Veron brushes his robes and then walks to the door. He opens it, and a hoplite comes in.

"Veron. We didn't see you at the Blessing." He's smiling, but his tone barely hides the threat under the pristine comment.

"Yes, I've had an emergency. The valedictorian's attributes for the opening of the festivities are missing..."

Veron is hesitant. It's obviously a lie, and the hoplite doesn't look like he's ready to buy it. Malia noiselessly runs up the steps, leaving me alone.

I look back at the entrance. The hoplite is trying to come in. Veron does his best to keep him out, but the hoplite's voice is getting louder and more authoritative. I doubt Veron will stall him much longer and I prepare to run away.

Hurried footsteps sound from behind, and Malia runs past me toward Veron, shouting his name.

She stops abruptly a few steps from him, feigning surprise to see a guard.

Veron turns to face her. "What is it, Malia?"

"I found it! I found Demeter's cup! But there's no one in the kitchen to prepare the sacred beverage." She holds an empty cup.

Veron suddenly looks imperious. "There's a list of ingredients on my desk. Get it and meet me in the kitchen. We'll have to brew it ourselves, and it will take time." He turns to the hoplite. "Will you excuse us? My cousin sent me this girl to help, but she doesn't know much. I'll have to prepare the beverage myself. I doubt the High Priest would appreciate having less than a perfect one for the opening of the banquet."

The guard mumbles something, clearly unhappy, and walks out.

"The ceremony will soon be over. I'll have to attend to the banquet," Veron says. "You'd better stay in the kitchen. You'll sleep in the bedroom next to my office. In the morning, the festivities will still be going on, but I'll find an excuse not to attend."

✳✳✳

After spending the past few nights sleeping in trees, sleeping in a bed feels incredible. When Malia wakes me up, I feel like staying in it for the whole day.

"Wake up, Prome! The sun's already up, and the festivities are about to begin. We'll soon be alone with Veron."

We walk to the kitchen to get breakfast, Malia light-footed and smiling, me still sleepy eyed.

We pass students, already running and shouting as they get ready, but today the shouts are not ones of stress but of glee and impatience. Everyone's dressed in white. So is Malia. I'm the only one dressed as usual, but my choice of clothes is quite limited.

When everyone has left for the festivities, we meet Veron in his office.

As we're walking down to the secret room, he tells us more about the Technologists. "Before the Gods came back, science and technology were taking a great place in our lives. They weren't good or bad in themselves, though. What people did with them was. They were used for the best, but also for the worst. Healing people in hospitals and killing them with bombs during wars..."

"But the Book of Gods says that men were using them only for the worst."

I can hear in her strained voice that Malia is barely refraining from quoting the book and calling him a miscreant.

"When the Gods came back, humanity wasn't ready. They hadn't been seen for millennia, and men thought they were higher beings, without physical existence. It was too sudden, too fast. Some men tried to resist, but it wasn't a war. Not when one side was so superior to the other. We don't know what really happened. The Gods took great care to destroy everything and rewrite history. Some people managed to save a handful of books, like the ones you see here. Over the years, they found other books and artifacts in forgotten places. They became the first Technologists in this new world. But most of the knowledge had already been lost. That's how we know about the Last Age. I'm afraid the Book of Gods is very partial and doesn't tell the whole truth..."

Malia clenches her jaw and doesn't retort.

Veron keeps talking. "We believe that something made the Gods come back. Something so important, such a threat to their superiority, that they couldn't ignore it any longer. Something men had found or created. We want to discover what this secret was. Then, maybe, we'll be able to create a society where everyone's free, where Gods don't oppress us anymore.

"They don't oppress us!" Malia objects.

"Oh really? Yesterday, a boy, barely younger than you, was flagellated because he wasn't at the Blessing. What do you call that?"

She doesn't answer.

"What is this amulet?" I ask, trying to move the conversation to safer ground.

"It's a kind of key, to access the Last Age's technology. We thought that something like it existed, but we had no proof."

We enter the secret room, and Veron almost runs to the small black box. I give him the amulet.

As soon as it touches the box, we hear two short beeps and a blue light appears. Other lights appear above it, floating in the air, forming a picture. It looks like Earth, but the continents are all wrong. Under it, are the words *GAIA PROTOCOL.*

Veron tries to touch the picture, but his hand goes through it, unharmed. He tries to touch the box, and move in front of the picture; nothing happens. After a minute, the box beeps again and the lights disappear.

Veron falls on the seat, stunned. "It works... It works."

"What is that Gaia Protocol?" Malia asks.

"I don't know." Veron shakes his head. "I'll probably need years to learn how to operate that thing. I wish your mother were here. She has a knack for finding how things work..."

"Why didn't she tell me?"

"To protect you. You were too young to become one of us. She hid you until you were old enough, in the best place she could find. Under the priests' noses." Veron chuckled. "Just like I'm doing here. She wanted you to be old enough to understand the truth." He puts a fatherly hand on Malia's shoulder. "She would be proud of you."

A tear glitters in Malia's eye, and I give her a hug. "We'll find her. I promise you."

As we break the hug, Malia dries her eyes with the back of her hand. She points at the amulet. "Does it work with the heavenly warriors' weapons?"

Veron stares at us. "I don't think so. Why do you ask such a question?"

Instead of answering, I take the strips of clothing off the spear.

Veron looks at me, appalled. "Where did you get this?"

As he's my best chance of getting some answers, I tell him the truth. I describe how I got it and how I killed the harpy.

He creases his brow. "I don't think that the amulet has anything to do with the spear. But you shouldn't have been able to shoot it. Only the heavenly warriors can do that, and even then only after a long training."

A loud bang resonates through the walls. Veron looks up, alarmed. "Quick, you have to go!"

We all run up the stairs. When we exit his office, we hear soldiers' voices coming from the entrance hall.

"Go down that hall," Veron shouts at us. "Turn right, second door on the left side. Jump through the window and get out of the city. I'll try to slow them down. Go!" He runs toward the voices.

Malia turns to follow him, but I grab her hand and make her come with me. "We have to go now, if we want to save your mother."

She looks at me and nods. She goes into our bedroom and retrieves the bag. We both run down the hall. We open the door and jump out of the window. It's just a short fall into a narrow passageway.

***

Everyone has to attend the festivities taking place around the temple. It's easy at first to hide in the middle of the crowd. But as we move away from the temple, toward the gates, the streets become eerily empty.

We hide in every recess we find, try to take small alleys, and cross the roads at a run. So far, we haven't seen any warriors.

The narrow alley we're hiding in opens onto a park. A low hedge runs around it. In the middle, a dozen guards are talking. I signal to Malia to lie low. On the other side of the park, I see another alley. "We need to make our way over there," I tell her.

She goes first, and I follow her.

She stops suddenly. I bump into her, but we both manage not to fall. She shows me that the hedge stops here. It starts again a little farther along.

I take a cautious look. The guards are still in the middle of the park, their backs turned to us. I push Malia, and we both start running, eyes on the guards.

Time freezes when a guard turns around and spots us. I see him purposefully lift his bow and aim at us. I push Malia hard and then plunge to the ground.

The spear emits a loud crack and a violent flash. When I look at the guards again, they're all sprawled on the ground, unconscious or possibly even dead.

"Run!" With the noise the spear created, we don't have time to be careful. We have to move away before more guards arrive.

Sure enough, I soon hear shouts and footsteps running after us. The gates are probably closed, but I can't think of another way to escape the city. I run as fast as I can, Malia running at my side in her white gown. I don't have a plan that will help us escape, but another one is taking shape in my mind, in case things get ugly. I take off my amulet and put it in one of Malia's pockets. She's too busy trying to keep up with me and looking for guards to notice. I take her hand and keep running.

We turn around a corner and see the top of the gate above the roofs. We're nearly there.

We're both out of breath, but we keep running.

When we round another corner and arrive in front of the gate, we both stop dead in our tracks. Guards are blocking the gates, and others are coming from all around us.

I pull Malia into a tight grip in front of me. She shouts in surprise.

"Play along," I murmur in her ear. "Stop, or I'll kill her!" I shout at the guards. I put the tip of the spear under her neck.

The guards freeze.

I tighten my grip on Malia's arm and twist it. This time she shouts not as much in surprise as in pain. I have to make it look real. "Let me go. I just want to leave. If you let me go, I'll release her." I move us toward the gates.

One of the guards lifts his spear.

Sorry, Malia.

"Stop!" I shout and I push the spear.

The point breaks her skin, and a few drops of blood fall on the white dress. The guard freezes again.

We move toward the gate. The guards blocking it step aside, but from the corner of my eye, I see movement. They won't let us through.

I throw Malia to the ground and make a run for it.

I feel pain in my whole body, and darkness engulfs me before I touch the ground.

CHAPTER SIX

I'm lying on my back, eyes closed. I feel like my whole body's on fire. A hundred drums are beating in rhythm inside my head.

My stomach's about to throw up everything it contains. As I turn on my side, I fall flat on a stone floor, hands and face in my own vomit.

"Fuck!"

I barely manage to pull myself into a sitting position. My body's reacting with reluctance, and every part shoots a warning of pain as I force it to move. I will my eyes to open.

The room's spinning so fast around me that I have to close them again.

I hear laughter.

"Looks like the taste of a heavenly sword didn't suit you much. You're lucky not to be dead."

Another voice. "That will change very soon."

The owners of both voices leave, laughing.

When my head stops spinning, I open my eyes again. In front of me, behind thick iron bars barely an arm's length away from me, is a dimly lit corridor. The only furniture in my cell is a bench behind me. It takes up most of the cell but isn't even long nor wide enough for me to lie down comfortably.

I close my eyes and put my face in my hands to recover enough to be able to stand and move a little.

***

I hear footsteps and look up. A man approaches with a plate and a glass. He puts them in front of my cell and leaves.

The glass is small enough to fit between the bars, but not the metal plate. I have to take the gruel through the bars with my fingers to eat.

Soon after I'm finished, the man returns to take the plate away.

The food has settled my stomach. My brain is clearer than it has been since I woke up.

I call out, but no one answers. It's almost a relief. I take it as a sign that my plan worked and they didn't arrest Malia too, thinking she was my hostage.

My future's looking bad. I've killed guards with a stolen weapon. For that alone, they should have killed me on the spot. No need to add Technologist activities. I wonder why I'm still alive. Probably because I managed to use the spear. They probably want to know how I did it.

I've heard of their interrogation methods. Torture comes first, questions next, if the prisoner's still alive. I really don't think they'll let me survive.

With a little luck, I'll be wrong on that account. My only solace is to think that Malia managed to leave the city.

✳✳✳

Footsteps.

"Are you sure you want to be left alone with him?"

"Yes please." The feminine voice is familiar.

I look up and see Malia, standing with a guard in front of my cell. My body freezes in shock. What is she doing here? The guard smiles at me cruelly. He's much taller than me, and probably twice my weight, all muscles.

"Do you want a spear? I'll be glad to help you if you want to avenge yourself. Just don't kill him."

Malia shakes her head. "No, thank you."

The guard leaves us, disappointed by her answer.

Only when we hear the door close does Malia come closer.

"What are you doing here? You should have left!"

"Shut up! We don't have much time!" She shoots a quick glance to where the guard disappeared. "I'm safe enough for now. They think I'm your victim. They told me that you'll be tortured to learn how you fired the spear."

I was wrong about Malia's being out of the city, but right on that account... I swallow hard.

"They're waiting for someone to come from Parthenos to interrogate you. He'll arrive the day after tomorrow."

We hear the door open. I step back and then sit on my bench.

"I'll be back. I'll find something," Malia whispers urgently.

"No! Run away!" I whisper back before the guard arrives.

***

I have too much time and nothing to do. The brief meeting with Malia has set my mind on fire. I can't help worrying about her. I have to escape before she does anything stupid.

The boy keeps intruding into my thoughts too. I realize I don't even know his name. I know nothing of him. Still, my mind wanders into wishful futures that bring us together.

I shake myself out of them. They'll never come true. Malia needs me. She needs the Prome she knows and trusts, not someone who's kept secrets from her for years. Not the Prome she kissed but who can't kiss her back. I wreaked havoc on her life. I have to set everything right. I can't let feelings for anyone lead me astray.

I have to escape.

It's easier said than done, though.

I'm alone. No one comes to keep an eye on me. Without a window, there's no way for me to even know if it's day or night.

Hours after Malia left, the same man comes to bring me the same gruel. He won't look at me nor answer me. For all I know, he could be mute, blind, and deaf. I can only guess that it's the evening meal.

My guess is confirmed when, a bit later, my eyes want to close.

***

The night is uneventful, but I'm woken up several times by guards passing through the hall and rattling something on the bars. Preventing me from sleeping is probably a strategy to break me. Even when they don't come, I'm woken by my fears for Malia. Sometimes, her mother, Ekon, and Veron appear in my nightmares too.

When the man appears to bring me a plate of the same gruel, I try again to talk to him, without any more success. When my plate's empty, I pull it through the bars. The only reaction I get when he comes back is that he looks for a few seconds at the ground then leaves.

Hours drag on indefinitely. After the almost sleepless night, I feel like sleeping again, but I want to find a way to escape. The bars of my cell are solid, and the lock isn't something I could pick even if I had a pin. The stones of the cell wall and floor won't move. My only chance to get out of that cell is if a guard lets me out, and I seriously doubt they'd do it willingly, except maybe to clobber me.

A crazy idea pops into my mind. What if I had a guard come into my cell to hit me? I'm not that much of a fighter, but I've noticed that all the guards have a sword. If I could put my hand on one...

Gradually, a plan takes shape.

The first difficulty is getting a guard to come into my cell. I bet they already want to beat the crap out of me and won't need too much incentive to act. A little annoyance should do the trick.

Fighting will be my biggest problem if I want to get out of my cell. I have no idea what to do about that for now.

Once out of my cell, I'll have to leave the building. Night will be the best moment; when most of the guards will be asleep.

Even once I'm out, my problems won't be solved. I'll have to find Malia and a way out of the city. I'll take care of this if—no! *once*—I manage to escape.

I still have a few hours before my evening meal, and try to sleep a little. When the man comes, I'm suddenly nervous. I take my time to eat, and then wait for a few minutes after he's cleaned up.

I pull the bench to the middle of the cell. It won't help me, but it will impair the guard.

I pick up the plate I haven't given back and rattle the bars as loudly as I can, and shout.

It doesn't take long for a guard to storm in. He comes to a stop in front of my cell.

"Shut up!" he barks at me.

He's about my size. Stronger, but it's no time to be picky. I put on my nicest smile. "Hey, stupid, it's a bit too quiet for me here, so I'm just making a little music. Too bad I only have one instrument." I rattle the plate on the bars again. The movement hides my shaking hand.

The guard tries to snatch it, but I pull it away. The rattling resumes.

"Stop that now, or by Ares, I'll make you stop!"

I widen my smile. "A threat? Too bad it's empty. I can take you single-handed. Didn't you see what I did to your friends in the park? How many were they? Ten? Twelve?" I feel my voice threatening to break, but my words come out clearly.

The guard's face grows crimson. "I'll teach you!" he shouts. He takes the cell key out of a pocket and comes in.

Before I can do anything, he punches me in the face so hard, I'm thrown back against the back wall and slide down to the ground. Black spots dance in front of my eyes.

He grabs me by the neck and lifts me, strangling me. I try to grab his hands so I can pull them away and kick him, without success. I can feel my brain about to black out and become frantic.

The guard's shout almost deafens me. I hit the wall a second time, headfirst, and fall to the floor.

Warm liquid trickles down my neck. At least I can breathe again and the black dots disappear.

The guard tries to grab me once more. I roll under the bench and see my chance. As he's still hunched over the bench, trying to get me, I crawl out as fast as I can and tackle him from behind. He roars in pain. As he turns around, I grab his sword and point it at him. The blade is too blunt to be dangerous. It doesn't need to be, as the weapon is supposed to electrocute the enemy.

The guard freezes.

I will the sword to throw a bolt, but nothing happens.

The guard looks at the sword, then back at me, and smiles.

He lifts both fists, ready to crush my head between them.

I hear a crackle. The guard stops his movements, staring at me, shocked.

I don't move.

He falls on the bench, his shirt burnt where the sword was touching him, the skin beneath blackened.

***

I carefully open the door at the end of the corridor and take a peek into the next room. It's empty, save for a table and a chair in the middle. I relax a little. I'm not sure that the uniform I've stolen from the guard would trick anyone from that close.

Lying against the wall are a spear and a backpack I immediately recognize as mine. They probably kept them here, ready for the interrogator from Parthenos. I take them and move on. The spear is easier to manipulate in close spaces, though, so I keep it in my right hand.

Behind another door, a staircase leads to the upper levels. No footsteps, no voices. I rush up the stairs and into a long hallway with closed doors on each side.

I walk as fast as I can without breaking into a run and risking running into a guard. The hallway turns left, and I reach the end of it and another closed door. As I reach for the handle, it moves, and someone opens the door from the other side.

An astonished guard faces me. Before he can recover, I hit him as hard as I can with my sword on the head. There's no crackle this time, but the force of the blow knocks him down. As he falls to the ground, he reveals a stunned Malia, who was following him.

"Malia!" I hug her briefly. "Come on, we have to leave!"

She recovers quickly and takes the lead. "How did you escape?"

I tell her about the fight. "I told you to leave. Why are you here?"

"I came back to try to get you out."

I smile. "And how did you plan to do that?"

She unsheathes a short blade from under her belt. "You're not the only one with a weapon."

I don't tell her that, with such a small blade, she would have had problems taking down the guards. I bet she had something else in mind to trick them...

We enter a wide room with large windows letting the sunshine in. I stare at them.

"It's daylight!"

"Yes," she answers tartly.

"I thought it was night. Where are all the guards?"

"The procession has started. Even guards have to attend if they're not on duty. That's why I chose to come here now."

***

We exit the building and emerge into empty streets. We run toward the nearest gate, which is, alas, guarded by two guards in front of the gate and two others on the tower.

"Shit," I mumble.

Malia takes a look at me. She smooths my uniform, and pulls on the jacket, hiding the burnt spot on the shirt. "You can be mistaken for a guard, and I for a student. I'll need some wheat for the end of the procession."

I don't have a better plan.

As we arrive at the gate, the two guards stop us.

"Where are you going? Why aren't you at the procession?"

"The High Priest sends us to get some wheat. This stupid student forgot to get some!" I snarl in an attempt to sound more truthful.

Malia puts on her best ashamed look.

The guards don't move.

"Let us through. We don't have much time to get that wheat!"

They move to the side, and we walk through the gate.

We're almost through it when a guard calls after us.

"Hey! An inquisitor should arrive soon. If he finds you out of the city, you'll be in a lot more trouble."

I wave my hand to thank him, and we walk on.

We take a path through the fields, so as not to be suspicious and to hide from the guards among the crops.

"Look!" Malia points farther down the road we've just left.

I see a dust cloud in the distance. We lie low to hide. Soon after, we see a dozen light cavalrymen surrounding a mounted man in white clothes.

"The High Inquisitor," she tells me. "They'll soon know you've escaped. We have to hurry."

As we run farther and farther from the city, the well-tended fields make way for dry flatland covered with short, brown grass and very few skinny trees. If warriors come after us, we won't be able to hide here.

And we both know they'll come.

CHAPTER SEVEN

A group of hoplites is chasing us. If only we could reach the small hills in front of us... Night is falling. We'd have a chance to hide and lose them.

We spotted them not long after we left the fields of Kurea behind us. We tried to hide as best we could, but they didn't take long to notice us. They've been after us for hours. I'm not sure we can escape them much longer. The only good thing is that they are hoplites and not cavalrymen. At least we can run as fast as they can.

Not quite as fast. They've been shortening the distance between us steadily. Malia and I don't have their training.

The ground gradually rises, slowing us down. I hear something whistle behind us. I just have time to push Malia aside before a spear flies past us.

Running is useless. We turn around to face our attackers.

I give Malia my sword and point my spear at them. However hard I try, I can't get it to shoot a bolt, though. Even if I could, there are too many soldiers forming a line in front of us.

I whisper to Malia, "I'll try to hold them back. Get ready to run."

Before she can retort, heavy, rhythmic thuds resound behind us. I turn around and duck, just in time to escape a giant animal jumping over us. It runs toward the hoplites, its auburn pelt shining like fire in the late afternoon light.

It rams through the group of warriors. Several stay down, unmoving, while the others shout and try to regroup.

The beast turns around, a bloody arm in its jaws.

Despite the ghastly sight, I can't help but find the lion majestic. The hoplites are shouting and running, and in the middle of this mayhem, it stands proudly, taller than the warriors, unmoved by the mayhem it caused, like a golden statue. Only its mane moves, brushed by a light breeze.

It throws the arm aside and runs toward a small group of hoplites.

Some throw their spears at it, but they just rebound and fall to the ground. Seeing that, the others try to shoot at it. Several warriors close to the beast fall, hit by the poorly aimed bolts. The beast is hit too, its fur blackened. It keeps fighting as if it doesn't feel anything.

Malia pulls me away from the scene. She leads us up the small hill while I keep looking back at the lion. It's so magnificent, running, jumping, fighting fiercely. I can't take my eyes away despite the danger of being its next prey.

A few hoplites have managed to form a small battalion and face the beast, swords in hands.

I stop.

"Prome, come on!"

Malia pulls me harder, but I can't turn my gaze away. I know it will kill us if it gets a chance, but I wish for the lion to win anyway. Malia forces me to crouch behind a rock, but I keep staring at the fight.

The lion's fur is almost completely blackened now, but it still fights, killing hoplite after hoplite until only one remains.

The warrior knows he has no chance, but he stands proudly nonetheless, sword held high in front of him, waiting for the final attack.

The lion circles him, staring at him fixedly. It walks on three legs, one of its front paws bending at an awkward angle. It stops, and both fighters gauge each other.

The lion roars; takes two strides, and jumps, mouth open, ready to tear off the soldier's head.

The soldier shouts and runs toward the beast.

From where I stand, the clash is eerily silent. They collide and fall to the ground.

Nothing.

For several seconds, nothing moves. They both lie on the ground.

The soldier stirs, then, very slowly, stands. His right arm hangs limply at his side, covered with blood.

The lion doesn't move. Not even its burnt mane. Something's coming out of its mouth. The hilt of a sword.

A sudden, irrepressible rage fills my whole body, pumping wave after wave of hatred for the soldier through my veins.

I run toward the soldier, shouting, and throw my spear at him. It flies straight through the air toward the unmoving soldier and catches him square in the chest.

When I reach him, he's lying dead on the ground. I pull out the spear and stab him again and again. Each stab, each shout, is my vengeance for Archelia, for everything I've lost, for the fear that's been with me all those days. And it's for the deaths of my parents. It's for the constant oppression, for all the Technologists they killed.

When all my rage is gone and my arms are tired of stabbing, I stop. The body is torn beyond recognition.

I look at the dead lion.

"Prome?" The voice is soft, as if afraid of me.

I turn and look at Malia. She's standing a few paces away.

Tears blur my vision. She takes a step, then another, and hugs me.

✳✳✳

Dusk is falling. We have to find a place for the night. The battle scene is far behind us, but it's still present in my mind. I walk in silence.

Malia eventually finds a cave, hidden in an outcropping of rocks. She lights a fire with a little wood she finds on the ground outside. The cave is deep, but neither of us feels like inspecting it. The day has taken its toll. Both my body and mind are exhausted.

We settle down to sleep.

"Prome, what happened?"

I open my eyes and look at the dark ceiling. "I don't know. I think I snapped."

Silence.

I know Malia's waiting for me to speak but doesn't want to urge me.

"It's because of your mom, but it's not just that. They destroyed our lives. They always destroy everything."

She doesn't ask who. She knows I don't mean the warriors but the Gods. Instead, she says, "It's your parents too, isn't it?"

When I was seven, my mom got sick. Real sick. The doctor came, but he needed some plants for a potion. That day, all the city gates were closed. The guards were looking for Technologists and didn't want them to escape. They didn't reopen the gates until it was too late.

It was the first time I shouted at my dad. The first of many.

He just accepted that we were not allowed to go out. He said it was the Gods' will, and we couldn't do anything.

I felt useless. I just held my mother's hand. I didn't know any other way out at that time. I tried to force the gates. The first time, the guards sent me back home. After the fourth try, they thought only a good beating could stop me.

When the burial was over, I stopped talking to my father anymore. I only shouted at him when he tried to speak with me. I came back home as little as I could. I became self-sufficient.

Three years later, I discovered the draining pipe. If I'd known about it before, I could have saved my mother. I got so angry that when I came back home, I had the worst argument with my father.

The next day, he vanished. I've never seen him since.

I blamed the guards, my father, and myself for my mother's death. But above all, I blamed the Gods.

As I grew up, I blamed myself for my father's disappearance.

A noise shakes me out of my memories. It comes from the dark depths of the cave.

I take the sword—it's easier to use in this narrow space—and prepare myself for a fight.

The noise reverberates once more against the walls of the cave. The loud rumble recedes, and a new sound takes its place. The soft thuds of a large animal, walking toward us.

I hear Malia shift behind me. We're both too tired to give much of a fight, but I'll do all I can to protect her.

As the beast comes closer, the reverberation lessens and the ominous noises merge into a high-pitched roar and light steps.

An animal appears in the flickering light of our fire. It's an auburn cat, the size of a large dog, head low in a hunting stance. It roars, but without the reverberation, it comes out as a big mew.

It's the lion's cub. I just know it, and I can't help feeling sympathetic for the poor orphan.

I slowly lower my sword. It could attack me and injure me seriously, but I don't want to fight it. Its father saved us.

"Malia, give me some dried meat," I say softly.

"What? Are you crazy? What are you trying to do? We have to kill it before it kills us!"

I see her walk forward, spear in hand. "Malia! No!" I grab the spear and throw it behind us.

The cub is surprised by my sudden move and roars defiantly.

"Shh. It's okay. I won't hurt you." I fumble around with my free hand until I get a grip on the bag. I take a piece of dried meat from it and show it to the cub. "Are you hungry? Here, look." I take a bite and throw the rest to the cub.

It stares at the meat before sniffing and then swallowing it in one gulp.

I put my sword down and take another piece of meat.

Piece after piece, we get closer to each other, until it finally agrees to eat from my hand.

I carefully lift my hand and put it on its head. It doesn't react until I start scratching it. It mews softly and moves its head around so that I'm scratching its jaws. I give it a few more pieces of meat.

Soon, it's lying on its back, and I'm scratching its belly.

"Malia, come and scratch it too."

"No. I don't think it's a good idea."

I'm surprised by the hostility in her voice. She glares at the cub and keeps her distance.

"It's okay. It won't hurt you."

"I said no."

As I walk to the fire to lie down, the cub follows me. It keeps staring cautiously at Malia, staying as far away from her as it can. He's not the one who looks hostile, though...

***

I wake up warm and rested, my arm around some furry cushion. I open my eyes and see the sleeping cub. As I move to stand, it opens its eyes and yawns.

Malia's at the entrance of the cave, warming up in the sun.

"We have to move. They'll come after us."

She doesn't answer, as if I hadn't said anything.

After a few seconds, she turns to me and shoots a wary glance at the cub. "What are we going to do?" she asks me.

"Find your mother and free her."

"But how? No human can enter Parthenos. The Gods don't want us to succeed."

Seeing her defeated before we even get there angers me. "Stop it right now! You heard what your mother said. Don't trust the Gods. We go to Parthenos. Once in the suburbs, we will find a way in. Now, pack up. We're leaving!" I get the bag and walk out, followed by the cub.

***

After a few miles, he's still walking at my side, careful to keep me between Malia and him.

"Are you going to keep it?" It's Malia's first sentence since we left.

"It doesn't seem to want to leave. I guess I'll have to name him. What do you think of Nemeos?"

She snorts.

"What? He's a Nemean lion, after all." I kneel and pat the cub. "What do you think of your new name, Nemeos?"

He licks my hands. I take it as a yes.

"See? He likes it."

"Very imaginative. How are you going to feed it? You already gave it more meat than we can afford yesterday."

I haven't thought about that. I hate it when she's right. But I'm not ready to give up. "We'll see. I'll share my ration."

She rolls her eyes.

***

Walking through the hills is easy. They are low, with gentle slopes. They also conceal us from any following warriors if we stay at the bottom of the shallow valleys. From time to time, I run up to higher ground to check for signs of approaching soldiers. For now, it seems we've lost them.

At noon, I share my meat with Nemeos. He swallows his share and keeps staring at mine.

"Sorry, Nemeos, that's all I can give you."

The afternoon is just as uneventful as the morning. Suddenly, Nemeos sniffs the air and takes off at full speed.

I run after him, calling, but he's much too fast for me. I soon lose sight of him and give up.

Malia catches up with me and stares at him until he vanishes from sight. "It... He's a beast, he's not meant to be tamed. Don't worry, he will do well."

I feel blue the rest of the day, although I try not to show it.

That night, we don't find a cave to sleep in. I suspect Malia didn't put much effort into the search. I'm sure of it when she only pulls out dried fruit for the meal. She probably doesn't want me to think about Nemeos. I know she means well.

We're about to lie down when something shuffling in the nearby dry grass alerts us. Nemeos comes out of the grass, a large rabbit in his mouth. He puts it down at my feet and rubs himself against my legs.

"Nemeos!" I scratch his head. He lies down and exposes a well-rounded belly for me to scratch. I laugh and look at Malia. "Looks like food won't be a problem after all…"

CHAPTER EIGHT

The next morning, I see in the distance a cloud of dust caused by galloping horsemen. They're not coming our way. We don't get any other sign of warriors that day, nor the next. We still should avoid roads, but for now, we don't have to fear our pursuers anymore.

The vegetation is getting greener, and we often cross small streams. With fresh water and the meat that Nemeos keeps bringing us, we're having a pleasant journey. Neither of us talks about what awaits us. We cherish the respite.

The land around us changes almost imperceptibly. The hills grow higher, the slopes steeper, until they become mountains. The ground gets more treacherous, and we stick to the bottom of the valley.

The peaceful walk is over. Stones slide under our feet; rocks that we have to climb block our path.

The pain in my thigh comes back as a bearable but constant throbbing, despite our frequent stops to rest.

On the other hand, Nemeos is having the time of his life. He jumps easily on the rocks we struggle to climb, and taunts us from above. He also discovers the echo, and spends almost an hour roaring continuously. I don't want to spoil his fun, but I'm just as glad as Malia when his voice suddenly breaks.

The afternoon drags on and on. The sun must still be high in the sky, but the mountains surrounding us hide it. In their shadow, the air is cool.

After a short climb, the valley widens in front of us. In the middle of it, a small lake glistens in the sun. We walk around it. Once on the other side, we look up the valley.

"We could stop here for today, warm up in the last rays of the sun, and prepare a camp for tonight..."

Malia slumps on the ground. I didn't expect her to take on my proposition so heartily.

Nemeos walks away. When he comes back, I'm surprised to see between his jaws, not a rabbit or some other small game, but a large trout.

There's not much to burn around us, but we manage to make a small fire that lasts just long enough to cook the fish.

***

As the night settles, the temperature drops drastically. It's not freezing, but it can't be far from it. I'm lying against Nemeos to keep me warm. At first, Malia refuses to get closer to him. I can hear her teeth clatter. Eventually, I hear her moving closer to us.

I'm drowsing more than sleeping when I hear a noise coming from the lake. I take my spear—*my spear*. Funny how I've gotten used to it. I walk quietly toward the water.

The full moon illuminates the mountains, but the surface of the lake remains pitch black. On the shore, a dark shape is bent over the water. As I approach, the shape straightens. The dim light reflects on the long, light-brown hair flowing down the back of a woman.

She turns around and takes a step back, frightened by my sudden appearance.

"Don't be afraid, I won't hurt you."

"Are you a soldier?" Her voice is soft and melodious despite the notes of fear and tiredness.

Her dress is ragged. She looks like she's been wandering for days. I put my spear down. "No, I'm just a wanderer. Are you hurt? Did a monster attack you?"

She takes a tentative step toward me. I can see her better. She looks barely older than me and has the most beautiful face I've ever seen. Her perfect, pale skin is almost glowing. Her lips are thin, and her eyes... Her frightened but magnificent eyes...

I feel the urge to protect her. My feet move on their own, bringing me closer to the distressed beauty.

A loud roar surprises me. I turn around and see Nemeos, snarling, fur shivering along his back, ready to jump.

"Nemeos? No!"

Too late. He lurches toward the woman. I turn around to warn her, but she has disappeared. Where she was, there now stands a very large dog. It stands taller than me, all muscle. Its white fangs glisten in the moonlight. Its bark echoes through the night.

It jumps aside and bites Nemeos, but its fangs can't pierce the lion's skin. Both animals are now clawing and biting, but with his impenetrable hide, Nemeos has the upper hand, despite his smaller size. Step after step, the dog is pushed back into the shallow water, and splashes mix with roars and barks.

Nemeos pounces on the dog when it doesn't escape quickly enough, and catches its hind leg between his powerful jaws, causing a yelp of pain. The dog gives a powerful kick, sending Nemeos into the lake.

Nemeos comes back to fight, but the weight of the water in his fur slows him down. The dog parries each of his attacks.

It's just a question of time before the dog finds a way to hurt Nemeos. I pick up my spear and run toward the lake. If Nemeos can emerge from the water and if I can use the spear...

"Nemeos, come here!"

He manages to run out of the lake and stands at my side. Seeing us both, the dog snarls angrily. The fur on its back stands straight up.

I lower the tip of the spear into the water and mentally order the weapon to shoot a bolt.

To my surprise, I see the spearhead emit a bright white light that spreads to the surface of the lake. For a fraction of a second, the whole lake shines.

The dog yelps and falls down into the water. When it floats back to the surface of the black water among dead fishes, it isn't the lifeless body of a dog, but that of a blonde woman.

Nemeos carefully steps into the water. It sniffs the dog and comes back to me.

"Is it dead?"

I jump in surprise. I hadn't noticed Malia but realize the fight must have been very noisy. "I think so. Do you know what it was? First, it was a woman, then a dog."

She looks at the body. "Look at her legs. One is made of metal. I think it's bronze. The other looks like a mule's leg. It was an empousa."

I've never heard that name before. "It was a monster?"

She sighs. "Yes, it was a monster."

I feel relieved I didn't kill a woman.

"You managed to shoot a bolt?"

"Yes, I think I've found the trick. I just have to do it as if I am the one throwing the bolt, instead of trying to make the spear do it." I point the spear at a distant rock. A bolt hits it while a loud crack echoes around us. The rock explodes as soon as the bolt strikes. "Yep, I got the gist."

She hugs me, whether from relief or joy I can't tell. When she breaks the embrace, she smiles at me and brings her lips to mine.

I turn my head away.

Malia frowns. "What's going on, Prome?"

Here I am, the traitorous Prome again, surrounded by my lies. Either I tell her the truth and lose her trust, or play my role, the one she wants me to play even if she doesn't know it's just a façade.

"I can't." I look away from her. "I wish I could, but I can't. I have to stay focused on saving your mother. And this..." I hesitate, unable to find another half-truth. All that come to me are plain lies, and I don't want to add others to the one I'm already living.

Malia comes to my rescue. "I understand, Prome."

I look at her face, and see all the pain I'm inflicting on her before she turns away. I feel like crying and shouting. I hate myself. But that hate is something I have to endure.

For her sake.

***

We don't sleep at all the rest of the night. Nemeos is too wet to keep us warm, and the fire is long dead. As soon as the sky brightens enough for us to see the ground, we decide to move.

By the time the sun is up, we've already warmed up. The grass has given way to rocks and pebbles, with a few green leaves protruding between them here and there.

After a few more hours, the valley narrows. The slopes on each side of us become high cliffs. It's not long before we reach a dead end. The valley stops here.

We both look up the cliff. "There's no way we can climb all the way without falling," I say. "We have to go back."

It's almost noon when the cliffs shift back to rocky slopes.

We take a quick, silent lunch. Walking back to the lake doesn't appeal to me. We fought an empousa and killed it, but who knows what else could be lurking there, waiting for revenge?

I won't go back there. I look at the steep slopes. Even from here, the rocks look unstable and treacherous, but I'm sure we can do it. "We have to climb here. Which side do you prefer? Right or left?"

Malia looks at me, then at the slopes dubiously.

I glance up at the sun above us. "We have to go west to reach Parthenos. Let's climb the left side. Let me go first."

I begin climbing the slope. After three steps, a rock rolls under my foot. I manage not to fall, but Malia has to jump to the side not to get hit.

"Sorry about that. We can do this, but we'll have to climb side by side, so we don't throw rocks at each other like this."

***

The climb is excruciatingly slow and tiring. For every three steps we take uphill, we roll down one. We have to use our hands as much as our feet to make progress.

The sun hits us pretty hard, and the heat is reflected by the stones. We're drenched in sweat.

I look up and down the slope. Most of the afternoon is already gone, and we're not even halfway up. If we can't make it to the top before nightfall, we'll have to go back down to the bottom of the valley to find a place to sleep, and start again or find another way tomorrow. The thought is disheartening.

I look around and spot Nemeos, high above us. He doesn't seem to have too much trouble climbing the slope. I know that he's an animal with four big paws, but he never sends any rocks rolling down on us. Is he especially gifted, or is it something else?

There's an easy way to tell.

"Nemeos, come here!" I shout.

"What are you doing? Don't call him; tell him not to move. He could bury us under an avalanche of rocks!"

"No, look." I point at him. "He never loosens any of the rocks."

We watch him, almost in awe, as he comes down the slope, following his own path. He stops at our level, on our left, but doesn't come closer.

I try to call him again.

He puts a paw in front of him, but he releases a rock that stumbles down the mountainside. Nemeos gives a small growl, and steps back.

"I think he found a safe path. Come on, let's follow him."

Going straight up the slope is hard enough. Going to the side is even worse. We keep sliding down, going up, sliding again. At last, we reach him, completely out of breath. We rest a couple of minutes.

"Okay, buddy, can you show us the way?"

Nemeos roars softly and brushes his head against me.

I scratch him. "Nemeos, show us the way up." I point up the slope.

He looks up, takes a step, and then looks back at me.

"Yes, Nemeos. Go!"

He seems to understand and placidly walks up the slope.

I follow him. I can see no difference from the rest of the slope, but the result is there. I still send a few pebbles rolling down, but I can walk much more easily.

"Come, Malia, he'll guide us to the top."

Our climb is much easier, and the sun's still quite high when we reach the top.

From our vantage point, we can see most of the valley we came from, including the lake. On the other side of the mountain, at the bottom of another steep and rocky slope, is another valley leading toward the west.

"At least going down should be easier than going up..." I take a step. As soon as I put my foot down, the rocks slide and I slide with them, barely managing to stay up.

It gives me an idea. I lock my two feet together and jump down. As soon as I land and begin sliding, I jump again to the left, then to the right. Zigzagging like this, I don't get hit by the rocks I've just loosened. I stop after one of these slides and look up. I'm amazed at how far a few jumps brought me.

"Malia," I shout at her, "go a little to the side and do the same as me. It's easy!"

Even from down here, I can see her dubious frown.

She jumps, but doesn't jump again fast enough, and falls back. She slides down for several seconds before she manages to stop and stand again.

"Keep jumping, don't stop," I shout.

She jumps again. This time, she immediately jumps again. She joins me in moments, smiling. "Hey, that's fun! I bet I can reach the valley before you!" She immediately starts jumping again.

"Be careful!" I don't think she hears me over the noise of sliding rocks and her laughter.

I start jumping again. Soon, I'm laughing as much as she is. The tension that had settled between us vanishes, even if it's just for a moment, and I feel almost normal again.

The slope that would have taken us hours to climb only takes us a few minutes to go down. But, jumping like this, we can barely stand when we reach the bottom of the valley. We both sit down, exhausted but laughing like crazy.

CHAPTER NINE

After the rocky slopes, the bottom of the valley feels as easy to walk on as a road. It takes us two days to leave the mountains behind us and reach the green hills that have been taunting us from afar. Now Malia sleeps against Nemeos's warm fur too. And during the day, Nemeos doesn't avoid being too close to her anymore. I guess Malia's feelings toward him have softened, owing to the fight with the empousa and the climb.

The green hills aren't as green as they looked from higher up the valley. They are mostly covered with waist-high, brownish-green grass. The leaves are hard and sharp. After I receive a few cuts trying to push them away with my hands, I resort to wide swipes of my sword and stomping on them. When my arm's tired, Malia takes the sword and the lead. Nemeos stays behind us and doesn't wander.

"I hope we leave this scrubland behind real soon. Nemeos can't hunt in it, and our rations are getting low. We're also running out of water. If we don't cross a stream tomorrow, it will become our top priority."

"Speaking of priorities, what do you think the Gaia Protocol is?"

It's the first time Malia has talked about what happened in Kurea. It makes me feel awkward. I shrug. "I don't know. Veron didn't know either."

Malia stops and turns to me. "I've been thinking about it since we left Kurea. It was hidden behind a secured door, in a hidden underground room. And if history is true, Kurea was built over the ruins of an ancient city. Which means the rooms were solid enough to resist the wrath of the Gods. It can't be a coincidence. I'm sure the men purposefully hid it from the Gods. It has to be something very important."

"How important? Do you think it could be the reason why the Gods came back?"

"I don't know. But if it isn't, it has to be related." She turns around and opens a path again.

"How do you know it's not something else?"

"I've thought about that too. Both times you used your amulet on a box, soldiers arrived minutes later." She resumes her fight against the grass without speaking.

"And?" I ask, curious to know where her thoughts are leading her.

"And I don't know. It can't be a coincidence."

"Could the boxes be a trap to catch the Technologists?"

"It's possible, but I doubt it. They would have been put somewhere easy to find for the Technologists, and they would have been easy to set off, not with your amulet..." She pauses, thinking. "No, I think they're keys to something else. Something the Gods are looking for."

"The Gaia Protocol," I answer.

"Yes."

"The other box didn't display anything. It just beeped. But now the guards have Veron's box, they have probably destroyed it."

"There might be others..."

"What's Gaia, anyway?" The name rings a bell, but I can't remember what it refers to.

"You really should pay more attention during history classes!" She doesn't stop swinging the sword. "She's the first Goddess. The mother of all Gods. She is also the Earth, from which every plant grows and every animal feeds."

"Oh." I vaguely remember something about that. "But she didn't come back with the other Gods. So, is the Gaia Protocol meant to call her back to give birth to more Gods?"

Her answer is immediate. "No. The men from the Last Era didn't believe that the Gods were real. Not in a physical way. And not until the Gods came back."

I snort in surprise. "What did they expect them to be? Ghosts?"

She doesn't answer, lost in her thoughts.

✳✳✳

We've slept well. We had everything we needed to make ourselves soft mattresses. We started the day in a good mood, optimistic that we'd find water or see the end of those plants soon.

The day is now dragging on, and we're not optimistic anymore. Long hours of making a path, sword in hand, sun burning overhead, and no change at all in our surroundings—just the same grass in all directions—took care of that. We have no more water, and our food supply is getting low rapidly, now that Nemeos can't hunt his own meals.

I see a little mount up ahead. I head toward it, hoping to see something. Anything that isn't grass.

The mount is farther away than I thought. The sun's already sinking when we finally reach it. It's not very high, but we have a good view of our surroundings. The land is desperately flat, stubbornly covered with grass. The only change is the mountains we've just crossed behind us.

Without a word, we share the last remnants of our food. I give the last small pieces of meat to Nemeos, while Malia and I share a few dried fruits. After this frugal meal, we lie down for the night, on empty stomachs and in low moods.

***

A low growl wakes me up. Nemeos is pacing nervously. I wake up Malia and signal to her to keep quiet. I lift my head a little way above the top of the grass. The sun has just set, and the land isn't completely dark yet.

At the bottom of the mount, a patch of grass is shifting. There is no wind. At best, it's just an animal approaching cautiously. When it's halfway up the slope, I get a quick peek at it. At first, I think it's a lion, but there's a second head jutting out of the middle of its back. A goat head.

We're being hunted by a chimera.

Fleeing through that knife-sharp grass would be impossible. I flatten as much of the vegetation around us as I can, to create a wide, grass-free circle. We'll fight better with more space to see the chimera coming, and to be able to move around.

When I've done enough, the three of us stand in the middle of the improvised fighting arena.

There isn't a sound. Not even the soft noise of the moving grass. Seconds become minutes and nothing changes. The chimera should already be here. All my senses are strained. All my muscles are tensed.

Nothing.

I look at Malia. She's just as strained as I am, spear in hand.

Nemeos is still growling.

I think I hear something on my right, but after a few seconds, nothing moves anymore. The wait is killing me.

It comes from behind us. Nemeos is the first to react.

As I turn around, I see the chimera running toward us and Nemeos jumping to stop it. The chimera tries to impale Nemeos on its goat's horns, but the horns just slide on the thick skin.

Nothing can pierce a Nemean lion's hide, but Nemeos is thrown to the ground. He recovers quickly and faces the monster again.

The chimera stops and growls at Nemeos. The two of them lurch at each other.

Malia and I retreat to the limit of the flattened grass.

"Shoot it!" she shouts at me.

"I can't. I may hit Nemeos..." I watch the fight powerlessly.

They kick and bite. Bleats and roars erupt in the otherwise silent evening.

Again, Nemeos is smaller but faster than his opponent, and seems to have the upper hand. He manages to jump on the chimera's back and bite the goat head. A last, desperate bleat rises in the air.

The goat head now hangs limply to the side, blood flowing from its severed neck. Its death infuriates the chimera. It roars deafeningly. It jumps and claws more fiercely than before. Blood sprays everywhere from the goat's head.

The chimera fights like a demon, as if the loss of one of its heads has given it extra strength. It parries each of Nemeos's attacks.

The chimera rams into Nemeos and sends him to the ground on his back. The monster jumps on him and tries to bite his neck to kill him. Nemeos attempts to fight back, but the monster's too heavy.

I throw my spear and hit the chimera in the ribs. The monster roars and kicks Nemeos away before turning to me. With the spear still planted in its side, it launches at me.

I'm thrown to the ground, and the chimera lands heavily on my chest, knocking the air out of my lungs. It's about to gore me with its claws when it's thrown away with a loud thud.

Nemeos's roar fills the air.

I breathe again, and Malia helps me to my feet. Other than a scratch on my left arm, I'm uninjured.

Nemeos shields us from the chimera. I walk up to him and look at the monster. It's lying on its flank and doesn't move. The tip of the spear is protruding from its back. When Nemeos threw it away, it landed on the hilt of the spear, which was pushed all the way through.

I kneel and hug Nemeos, soon joined by Malia.

✳✳✳

After last night's attack, I'm looking back at the mountains, considering our survival chances if we go back to find another way through.

Malia grabs my arm. "Prome! Look, over there!"

Something's coming toward us. Fast. At first, it looks like a fish jumping fluidly out of the sea of grass. As it comes closer, I recognize it as a hind, jumping gracefully, leap after leap, above the grass. The sight is breathtaking. Its antlers and hooves are shining in the morning light. I pick up my spear, ready to throw it, when the hind comes close enough.

"Don't!" Malia puts her hand on the spear. "It's the Ceryneian hind. Don't you see its golden antlers and bronze hooves?"

"So what? As long as it's edible..."

"It's not dangerous for us, and much too fast for you to kill anyway. Look. What is it doing?"

The hind has stopped at the bottom of the hill, too far away for me to throw my spear or shoot a bolt. It gazes at us peacefully. It walks leisurely away, stops, and stares at us again.

"I think it wants us to follow..."

I look at Malia doubtfully.

"Look," she insists.

Indeed, the hind takes a few steps, then looks back at us. It does it a few times.

"I'm too tired to think. And without food or water, we won't last long anyway. You want to follow it?"

She nods.

We pick up our gear and walk down the hill.

The hind walks lazily in front of us, at a safe distance. It opens a path through the grass that we can follow without having to use the spear. When we stop to rest, it waits for us.

By midmorning, the sun's baking hot. My mouth is completely dry. I throw a quick glance behind me and see that Malia and Nemeos are just as parched as I am. I drag my feet more than I walk. I don't think we'll be able to go on much longer.

Suddenly, the hind stops and turns its head right and left. I do the same but see nothing at all. When I look back, the hind is jumping away in huge bounds, abandoning us where we are. I try to shout but barely get a croak out. We walk to the end of the trail. I look at Malia. Seems like the hind didn't want to help us, after all.

Discouraged, I fall on my knees and then sit on the ground. Malia sits down too.

Something's moving under me. I move to the side and look down. Just where I was sitting, the earth is damp. I use the tip of my spear to poke a small hole, then stare in wonder as it gradually fills with water.

I put my mouth to it and drink. The water is cool, flowing through my body like a rejuvenating wave.

"Malia, here! Water!"

After a few minutes of drinking and resting, we all feel better. We're still hungry, but we're ready to move again.

I glance around and see the hind waiting for us a short distance away. We then resume our walk.

***

"Do you think it will find us some food too? Or maybe give us one of its legs to eat?" Walking in the hind's path is easy, but my stomach is growling noisily.

Malia doesn't answer but puts on her thinking frown.

"Hey, that was a joke, Malia! I wouldn't say no to something to eat, though..."

"Did you notice how all the beasts are helping us?"

"What?" That doesn't make any sense. "They attacked us! Nemeos is the only one helping us. And maybe that hind too. But the harpy and the others weren't very friendly."

"No, I mean the beasts, not the monsters."

"I don't usually discriminate between them. They're all the Gods' pawns, waiting to kill us."

Malia sighs. "No, Prome. Beasts are normal animals with some special abilities or traits given them by the Gods. Monsters are different. They don't look like normal animals."

"As I said. They're all the Gods' pawns, waiting to kill us."

Malia stares at me, then speaks again with the voice of a mother talking to her child. "Nemeos is a lion. With impenetrable skin, but a lion nonetheless. The boar was just a boar. A huge one, but a boar nonetheless. The hind is a hind. They are beasts. On the other hand, a monster like the chimera is a mix of several animals: the body of a lion, a goat's head and a snake's tail. And, until a few days back, monsters only came out at night. Get it?"

"Ohh, okay. I never thought about it that way. But it doesn't change a thing. The lion and the boar attacked me, and the lion attacked us."

"I don't think so. You told me the boar pushed you aside—violently," she adds when I lift a brow, "then attacked the guard. The lion jumped over us and attacked the soldiers. The hind led us to water and is making us a path. Nemeos is... Well, he's Nemeos. He's even attacked monsters."

"So you think that the beasts have let down the Gods and are helping us while the monsters are trying to kill us."

"I don't think it's *us*. I think it's *you*. It started before I came along. And Nemeos came to you, not to me."

"Is it because of the amulet?" I look at it.

"I don't think so either. Remember when we were young, and we saw a boar in the forest?"

I try to remember. "No. Did it attack us?"

"No, it didn't. It should have, but it didn't. I think the beasts have always protected you."

The thought is so silly I can't help laughing.

"I mean it, Prome. You never met any beasts when you went to the old ruins or walked through the forest."

"I'm lucky, that's all." I wink.

She groans. "The beasts, the weapons... Give me your amulet."

I do as commanded.

"Now shoot something."

"But there's nothing to shoot."

"Then shoot in the air."

I direct my spear toward the clouds. A bolt flies into the sky and vanishes.

"It's not the amulet. It's you. I don't know how, but you can do more than a human should be able to."

CHAPTER TEN

We haven't talked since I shot that bolt, but my mind is reeling. It doesn't make sense. I *am* human, although there is also truth in what Malia told me. I can shoot weapons. Only heavenly soldiers can do that. Normal humans can't. And if she's right about the beasts too... But why would the beasts turn against the soldiers and the monsters?

I can't be related to a God. Gods don't have human children. Not anymore. Not since humanity fell into disgrace. Which leaves me only one possibility. I'm a beast. A human beast. I don't even want to think about being a monster. Being a beast is already dreadful enough.

I think Malia's come to the same conclusion. I feel her gaze on my back, and when I look at her, I sometimes catch her looking quickly away.

It's crazy. I can't be a beast! I don't want *to be a beast!*

With that worry on top of my lies, I feel like I'm about to explode into dust.

The hind suddenly turns around and bounces away. I run toward the end of the track, spear at the ready. Maybe it's leading me to some water or some food?

Instead of the end of the track, I reach a road. I had been too preoccupied to notice the long, straight cut in the sea of grass.

Malia smiles at finally being out of the grass. But the happiest of us is Nemeos. He roars loudly, then runs up and down the road and around us. I have to call him several times before he calms down.

"Which way now?"

"There." I point toward the west. "It should lead us directly to Parthenos. We can't be far away. With a little luck, we'll reach the suburbs before night."

The suburbs are the only part of the city where humans are allowed. In the heart of the city itself, only the Gods are allowed.

We walk quickly; the road is so easy to walk on... But the thought of a good meal this evening and a safe place to sleep is what really causes our fast pace.

***

Kurea is the Northern Diamond, but its splendor pales compared to Parthenos.

The city is built on a small mountain that looks like one giant pillar. At the bottom, surrounding the high cliff of the mountain, is the human city, the suburbs: a mayhem of houses of different sizes and colors, among which even the streets seem to have problems finding their way. The cliff is topped by a pure white line. Nothing more can be seen from the acropolis. No surrounding mountain is as high as that one, so that even from their tops, nothing but the white ring crowning the mountain can be seen.

The city remains eternally hidden from mortal eyes.

Between the humans' and the Gods' city is only the vertical cliff. One thin, white stairway crisscrosses the cliff and is the only way to the top of the mountain.

Entering the suburbs will be easy. It is the only city without any kind of protection. I guess that being so close; the Gods don't need beasts or monsters to herd the population.

"So what's your plan now?"

Malia's question takes me by surprise. I hadn't thought about it. "First, find somewhere to eat and rest."

"Okay, but Nemeos will have to stay away from the city."

"Oh." I look down at Nemeos. "Right. He'll be fine. He'll find enough game and water."

"And after that?"

"We'll see if we can find some info about your mother, where she's imprisoned. Our best chance is to find a Technologist. If they like to use religion to hide, there's no better place than here."

✳✳✳

We enter the suburbs, mixing with the population without trouble. The spear and sword are hidden outside the city, near a twisted tree, and for the first time in days, Nemeos isn't walking at my side. I feel vulnerable without the weapons, but I can cope with it. Our best weapon at the moment is stealth.

Nemeos gives me more to think about. I miss him, but at the same time, I'm surprised to feel relieved. I shouldn't be. He's helped us so much. But here, I'm not a monster or whatever. I'm just a regular boy walking among regular people, just like a few days ago, when life was normal and easy.

We have a couple of hours left before nightfall. We stroll aimlessly in the streets, looking for any sign that could lead us to a Technologist. Night claims us without our anything and forces us to seek shelter.

There are dozens of inns spread throughout the city. A lot of people come here in the hope of seeing a God. Tourism is thriving. Finding good accommodation is more difficult, but we don't care. We can't afford much, and a meal and a bed are all we want. Tonight, no monster will attack us.

***

We're standing in the middle of the crowd, facing the stairs that ascend to the acropolis. The first wide steps lead to the face of the cliff. From there, a magisterial stairway is carved into the stone and covered with white marble.

Our hopes of climbing them are crushed by iron gates and the presence of a whole legion guarding them.

We move away reluctantly.

"I've had enough for today." Malia slumps onto a bench.

I sit at her side and lean back, looking at the reddening sky. "We've barely searched a third of the city. We'll keep looking tomorrow. I didn't expect to find anything easily." I had hoped to, though. We've been walking the whole day, from temple to temple, examining each and every one we passed, every building where students are housed. No fish, nothing. "I've seen another temple that we've missed. It's on our way back to the inn."

Malia sighs. "The last one of the day."

"Yeah!"

***

The temple is just a small, decrepit shrine dedicated to Artemis. It was probably one of those old churches the Gods claimed when they came back. It has no columns on the outside, the façade is gray, and through the open door, the inside looks dark.

The buildings around are all plain houses, some with shop fronts opening onto the street.

"There's nothing to be found here. Let's go."

Malia's walking away, but I can't take my gaze off the entrance of the temple.

"Are you coming?"

I don't answer. I don't know why, but this temple looks so inviting. Something almost physical pulls me toward it.

I turn to Malia. "I just want to have a look inside. I won't be long." I stride off.

Malia doesn't follow me.

It takes my eyes a few seconds to adjust to the darkness inside. I gaze around. The ground is covered with hay and dung. The few benches left are broken or toppled over. Everything appears old and battered. Even the animal sculptures covering the walls have lost a leg or their head with time, the missing parts lying on the ground in pieces.

I approach the altar.

Above it, a statue, one of the very few still intact, represents Artemis with her bow, a hind at her side.

I've never seen Artemis, but the hind I immediately recognize as the one that showed us the way. The remnants of gold paint on its horns and hooves are unmistakable.

The Goddess is wearing a short dress, showing her long legs. I look up at her face and a ray of the setting sun touches it through a broken window. Her face is turned away from me, neither friendly nor hostile, looking to the side as if she didn't care about the humans who had once prayed in front of her.

The sculptor carved it with such skill, it feels alive. I can almost see Artemis's head turn, refusing to see me, rejecting me, while the hind gazes at me accusingly.

I can't help but feel ashamed at the rest of the church; how everyone abandoned it to be destroyed by time.

I take out a coin and put it at Artemis's feet. I haven't prayed for years, but I can't help whispering a prayer for forgiveness.

I walk out of the shrine, and Malia leads us back to the inn for the night.

***

"Prome, look!"

Malia points at a carving on the temple's door. I see it. It's small, but it's a fish; two fishes, actually, supporting the shield of arms above the entrance. It took us two days to find it, but there it is.

My heart races in anticipation, but I have doubts nonetheless. "We can't barge in and ask for a Technologist. We're not even sure there's one here. How are we going to proceed?"

Malia doesn't have time to answer my question. The door opens and a tall, fat man appears in front of us. He's red and sweaty, his head looking like a big, red ball. His eyes widen when he sees us, swiftly followed by a smile.

"Oh, visitors! Please, come in! Come in! I was about to close early, but Apollo forbid. I'll never prevent such enlightened young people from giving their souls the unique sustenance the pieces of art I've spent my life collecting can procure."

I look at Malia, alarmed, but she looks just as dumbfounded as I am. Before we can react, the man pushes us inside.

"My name's Ethiam, at your service." He bows. "Yes, I know. Such a dreadfully common name. It's a burden I have to endure. I've spent my life making up for this mistake of my parents, Hades protect their souls. I've dedicated my whole existence to Apollo and the splendors He gave us."

His whole life... He looks barely older than thirty. As he drones on and on about his name, I look around at the so-called splendors.

Tables fill almost all the space, leaving narrow ways between them. I wonder how Ethiam can fit between them. They are covered with artfully displayed pieces of what I can only call junk. I see the broken finger of a statue near a necklace with most of its rhinestones and glass beads missing.

A little farther, in front of a tree branch with brown, dried leaves on it, I recognize something. It's a broken pipe like the one I had when I was young. When my mom gave it to me, I spent days blowing in it, emitting ear-piercing notes, until Malia threatened to choke me with it if I didn't stop.

"Oh!"

I jump at the sound. Ethiam's just behind me.

"I see you've already recognized my most treasured possessions. This is a part of a broken flute Pan discarded."

I choke back a laugh, and hopefully manage to make it sound like a light cough.

"Did it fall from the cliff?" Malia manages to sound serious.

"Oh no, no, no, my dear. It came from the other side of the continent. It almost cost me my life to get it!"

"Did you travel a lot?"

Ethiam got even redder. "Well, not exactly, but the voyager who sold it to me assured me that the monster guarding it was deadly."

My cough is louder and less convincing than the last one. Ethiam doesn't seem to notice. On the contrary, he turns to me.

"Are you sick? You should maybe take a few steps back, then. This branch comes from a tree of the garden of the Hesperides. It's so powerful, most people feel weak near it. Of course, with the years, I've grown accustomed to its effects, but I fear you're not immunized, as I am."

I look at Malia. She is clearly refraining from saying something. I look at the dusty branch. It probably comes from a nearby tree, and someone sold it to Ethiam for a large sum of money...

"I've heard rumors of a piece of art..." Malia looks hesitant, but I can tell by the glint in her eyes that it's just a show.

"Tell me, my dear. If it's a masterpiece, I probably have it here."

I almost choke on another laugh, and Malia looks crossly at me before making her downtrodden-kitty-eyes at Ethiam. Poor guy. He won't even know what hit him...

"I've heard... It's... Oh, it might sound stupid, I know. It's just some kind of metal box, with no opening. Rectangular. Not even very big. About that size." With her hands, she mimics the shape of Ekon's box.

"I'm sorry, my dear, but I don't have anything of that kind. I've never even heard of it. And if I don't have one, it's not worth collecting. Now, I can show you the real helmet of Athena. She had to get another one when this one was seriously dented during the war against the Titans..."

As he turns away, I look at Malia. She just shrugs. He's probably no Technologist, but I want to try something just to make sure.

I take out my amulet. "Excuse me, sir—"

"Call me Ethiam, please," he says, smiling.

"I've bought this from a boy in the street. He said it comes from Zeus's belt itself. As you're an expert—"

"Not just any expert. *The* Expert."

"Of course, si... Ethiam. As you're the best, can you tell me if it's true?"

Ethiam barely looks at my amulet for a few seconds. "Sorry, boy, but you've been tricked. This is just a piece of junk."

✳✳✳

As we finally walk out, an hour later, we're both worn out. Ethiam wouldn't let us go.

"He's definitely not a Technologist, or he would have reacted at the sight of my amulet."

"We'll have to start looking again tomorrow."

We go back to our inn, battered by another fruitless day, and dreading the next one.

CHAPTER ELEVEN

Another two days have passed, just as fruitless. We've searched all the places in the city where we think a Technologist can hide, to no avail. I'm running out of ideas, and Malia's getting nervous. We're no closer to finding her mother than when we arrived.

Sitting on a bench, facing the cliff and its unreachable stairs, we eat a piece of bread sullenly.

I look up at the cliff, and the most desperate plan comes to my mind.

"You'll never be able to climb that cliff, Prome."

"And you'll never be able to walk past the guards unnoticed," I retort.

We both laugh humorlessly. We know each other too well. Under other circumstances, this would have triggered a friendly fight to try to immobilize one another.

Not today. Not in this God-damned city.

I shift my gaze from the fateful stairs, and look at the crowded street. Not far from us, someone is moving away, slipping clumsily through the crowd. All I can see is a shock of black, curly hair. It looks familiar, and even though I don't recognize it, for the first time today, I feel happy.

I stand and follow him. "Malia, come."

"Where are you going?"

"Look, over there."

She doesn't recognize the guy either—I think it's a guy, but I can't really be sure without seeing his face. He's carrying a bulging satchel at his side.

As he turns around to look at something, the face I see makes my heart skip a beat. He's unmistakably the nameless boy who couldn't dress properly for the ceremony in Kurea. I feel a smile spread on my lips, until Malia walks in front of me to get to him.

Reality kicks me back to Earth mercilessly. I vowed to help Malia. I can't let him distract me. I've already failed Malia's friendship, although she doesn't know it yet. I'll stay at her side. I'll be the perfect, lying, betraying, stabbing-in-the-heart friend. I'll hide the beast in me and keep smiling.

A sudden thought occurs to me. If I'm a monster, I'm just a pawn in the Gods' game; a pawn they can manipulate at their whims and fancies. What if they sent him for me to fall in love with? Meeting him once might be possible. But meeting him twice, in two places so far away from each other, cannot be a coincidence. Could he be here because of us? He was in Kurea before the guards barged in, and now he's here. If he was spying on Veron and us, he wouldn't have done otherwise.

I don't share my doubts with Malia. Not yet. I just grab her hand to stop her and tell her we should be careful. For now, we're content to follow him through several streets. I remember the streets from our earlier stroll, and my doubts about the boy strengthen.

"Malia, I think I know where he's heading."

And, sure enough, after a few turns, we arrive at the square in front of Poseidon's temple. The boy enters it.

"Come on, Prome, we have to follow him inside."

We climb a few stairs, then walk between the gigantic columns and through the equally impressive wooden door.

Inside, a resplendent statue of Poseidon riding a chariot pulled by four horses with fish tails instead of legs looks down at us. The skin of the horses is made of green marble, their scales of electrum. Poseidon himself is made of ivory covered with gold and precious gems.

Some priests are presenting offerings to the God, while a crowd of believers pray.

I can't see the valedictorian anywhere.

Malia leads me around the crowd, toward the side of the temple. A wide door leads to another temple. The guy is there, talking with a priest, in front of the statue of Amphitrite. At the foot of the statue is a small pool.

We hide behind a column. Alas, from this distance, I can't hear anything. After a few seconds, they both leave through a small side door.

We walk to the statue and the pool, among a much thinner crowd than in Poseidon's temple.

We both look up at the statue. This one isn't made of ivory but of white marble, and although it is adorned with gold and gems, these are much less present than on Poseidon. I guess that the Gods are misogynistic. Poseidon's wife can't have such a glorious statue as Poseidon himself.

I drop my gaze and look at the pool. It is shallow, filled with pure water. Some believers have thrown coins in it, and some of the colorful fishes play with them.

I gasp. "Malia, look! Could it be...?"

She looks down at the pool. I see her eyes widen, and she suddenly sprints off toward the side door. She opens it, and we both rush through.

The narrow corridor runs along the wall separating the two temples, toward their rear. The only dim light comes through a ceiling so high it's almost invisible.

There's a sharp turn in the corridor, and I almost bump into Malia, who's stopped. In front of us is a door, slightly ajar.

The room on the other side of the door is wide, with bright light coming in through large windows. A statue of Amphitrite stands proudly against a wall, incense burning at its feet. The rest of the furniture consists of a few chairs and a low table.

The room has two other closed doors, but two voices come from the stairs leading to the upper level.

We cross the room and climb the stairs as silently as we can. At the top, we hide in an alcove.

"...told me to bring you this." The voice is young but strained. "He said it's important but dangerous."

A much older and calmer voice answers. "I want to know exactly what happened. But first, show it to me!" Silence, then, "I imagined it to be bigger."

I move to take a cautious peek, but Malia has the same idea and we bump into each other. We almost fall down, right in front of the valedictorian and an older man wearing the white gown of a high priest.

"Who are...? *Guards...*"

The boy unceremoniously puts a hand on the old man's mouth to silence him. "No, sir, don't call the guards. They are the ones who came to see Veron." He takes his hand away when the man calms down. The boy looks horror-struck by his action, but the priest ignores him.

"Tell me who you are and what you want, before I call the guards!"

I look at him. He's holding Veron's box. If he isn't a Technologist, he'll have us arrested and killed anyway. I decide to take the chance and tell him about our journey. I only keep two things out of my narration. The first is that I can control the spear. The second secret is Nemeos. If we're killed, at least he won't be hunted down.

When I'm finished, the man stares at us silently. After what feels like an eternity, he lifts the box in front of me. "Prove it!"

"I beg your pardon, sir," Malia bows curtly, "but I don't think that would be wise. Twice Prome used his amulet on a cube, and twice the heavenly warriors arrived shortly afterward."

"Hmmm... Show me that amulet of yours!"

I usually rebel when someone snaps orders at me like this, but I need him to believe us. He looks at it, then tries to grab it. I move it out of his reach before he can close his fingers on it.

"Give it to me!"

"No! I'll keep it."

"Fine. I'll call the guards!"

"Nice bluff!" We all look at Malia. "But if you are who I think you are, calling the guards on us will be just as bad for you as it will be for us. Now, tell us who you are and why we should trust you."

If looks could kill, Malia and I would die on the spot.

"Garbos, give me that letter!"

Garbos. So that's his name. Learning something about the boy I can't love is so sweetly painful.

Garbos takes a battered letter out of his pocket and hands it to the priest, who opens it and reads it silently. When he's finished, he just walks away to a seat at a nearby table. We follow warily.

"My name is Beris. As you've probably noticed, I'm Amphitrite's and Poseidon's High Priest. And yes, I am also a Technologist."

Although I'm relieved, I'm also surprised. He probably notices my reaction as he continues.

"A few decades ago, Technologists were on the verge of extinction. The legions tracked us down and found us too easily. We decided to use the adage, 'Keep your friends close, but your enemies closer.' We began hiding among them. It took us many years, but we succeeded. Our cover identities leave us much less time for our research than we'd like, but they have other benefits."

"Do you trust us now?"

"Yes."

"Why?"

He shows us the letter.

Highly revered friend,

The preparations for Demeter's festival are over. Everything would have been perfect without two thieves, or, as the guards think, two Technologists, who have stolen something hidden in our basement.

I will bother you with this trifle no longer.

More important is that Garbos has finished his studies. Despite his clumsiness, he's a good student and has learned a lot, though he still has even more to learn.

I send him to you with a gift for Amphitrite in the hope that he learns more about Triton and Benthesikyme, her children, to whom, I have no doubt, he'll be closer at your side.

May Hermes protect him during his journey, and Poseidon's blessings be on you.

Veron

"He got away by putting the blame on us!" I shout, before realizing it was the best solution. We were already fleeing from the heavenly warriors, and this way he managed to keep his cover. "I guess it's okay," I concede.

"Veron told you we'd come," Malia says, staring at the priest.

Beris smiles for the first time. "And by comparing you to Triton and Benthesikyme, two of Poseidon's and Amphitrite's children, he lets me know you are most important and I must protect you."

Triton I know, but Bentixime, or whatever he said, I've never heard about. All that Godly mess is lost on me. I just pretend to understand. It's easier, and if I'm lucky, Malia won't lecture me about skipping school...

I just ignore all this and go to the most important point. "Will you help us?"

Malia and I look at him silently as he ponders his answer, elbows on the table, head on his fists, staring at Veron's box. Near us, Garbos keeps fidgeting uneasily.

Beris suddenly stands up. "Come with me."

He leads us to a small room with a bed. "This bedroom is meant for my aide. Garbos has his own room, but you two will have to share this one. It's not meant to accommodate two people, but you'll be safe here. Don't come out, though. Garbos will bring you some food. Come, Garbos."

He's about to exit, but he still hasn't answered my question. "Will you help us?"

He stares at me. "I don't know, yet."

✳✳✳

I can't sleep. The questions reeling through my mind would keep Hypnos awake. "Malia, do you trust them?"

"I don't know."

"Me neither. Beris didn't call the guards, but that's all he did—or did not—do. I'll give him until this evening to decide if he's on our side. After that, we leave. Until then, we'll stay on our guard."

"And Garbos?"

I know that tone. It's the same one she uses when she sees an injured cat or a famished dog she wants me to carry home.

"Malia! He's not a lost puppy," I say warily. "We can't trust him yet. For all we know, he could have brought the box to trap us."

"But there's the letter. Beris would have told us if it were a fake."

"Malia, we don't even know if Veron's still alive. All we have is Garbos's word for it. For now, all we can do is wait. But shh. I hear footsteps."

Someone walks past the door. Once the footsteps have disappeared, we don't resume our conversation. Malia falls asleep, but I'm thinking about Garbos. How is it possible to love and hate the same person at the same time? I can't help loving him. I like his voice, and even his clumsiness is nice. And I feel happier for no other reason than being around him. But at the same time, I can't help but distrust him. He is the trap the Gods set up for me.

CHAPTER TWELVE

"I hope there's enough for both of you! I couldn't take more without being noticed." Garbos puts a large tray on the bed. So many pastries are piled on it, I wonder how this klutz managed to bring them all back without losing half of them on the way.

"There's enough to feed ten of us!"

"Thank you, Garbos," Malia says softly while looking at me crossly.

We both eat more than we've eaten for days, but even so, more than half of the pastries remain. Even though he's already had breakfast, Garbos has no problem eating more.

He's smiling and friendly. I'm sure I'd enjoy his company, but I can't let my guard down. I have to remind myself that I can't trust him.

"Is Beris here?"

Garbos swallows a mouthful of pastry and nearly chokes. "No, he's working. Being the High Priest of Amphitrite and Poseidon isn't a sinecure. He'll be back this evening."

"Come on, Malia. I don't want to spend the day here. I'm going out."

"What?" Garbos drops the pastry he's eating. "No, you can't! The High Priest told me you had to stay hidden here!"

"Sorry, Garbos, but I won't take orders from him."

As we reach the door of the hall leading to the temple, a puffing Garbos comes running after us. "Wait for me! If you don't want to stay, at least I have to stay with you!"

I shrug. "Feel welcome." If need be, I'm sure we'll be able to lose him easily.

***

"...and the stairs have been carved by Hephaestus himself. They are made of a single piece of marble, from bottom to top!"

Since we left the temple, Garbos has become our personal tourist guide. He keeps pointing at everything, telling us how this or that was created, or about an event that occurred long ago. He never stops babbling, even if we don't say a word.

Malia seems interested, though. "How do you know all this? Have you visited this place often?"

Garbos looks at Malia, surprised, then at the ground. I see his face turn red. "No, it's the first time. But I've heard and read quite a lot about it. Veron always says I remember everything, but can't do anything."

I can't help thinking Veron got that damn right, even if it sounds a bit harsh on Garbos.

The two of them begin a long conversation about architecture and history. I don't care about that, so I just keep walking, looking around. The guy's nice, but seeing the two of them chatting and smiling like old friends is really getting on my nerves. Looking at a house, Malia says something I don't get, and Garbos laughs. For no reason, I feel angry at Malia.

I point to a bakery. "Hey, Garbos, walking like this really made me hungry. There's a bakery just over there, but I think I've seen a priest walk in. would you mind going in for me and getting me a little something to eat?"

Malia looks at me with a creased brow, but Garbos smiles like I've just given him a gift. "Of course! I'll be right back!"

I feel a pang of guilt as he runs off, but as soon as he enters the shop, I take Malia's hand and hurry away.

"Why did you do that? He's so nice!"

"Told you. We can't trust him!"

I don't have to look at her to know that she's rolling her eyes. "Boys!"

After a few minutes of running and turning through busy streets and narrow alleys, I'm sure we're definitely Garbos-free. I stop, and Malia immediately shakes off my hand.

"What's going on?" she asks me sternly.

"I wanted to talk freely. I don't trust Beris, and I don't trust Garbos anymore."

"But they helped us!"

"No, they didn't. Beris didn't call the guards on us, but it doesn't mean he helped us. I'm not sure we should go back."

"What?" Malia paces around, closing and opening her hands as if she were trying to strangle someone. Possibly me. She stops and glares at me. "You'll listen to me, Prome. We've already spent days here, and the only thing we've found are Beris and Garbos. You don't trust them? Okay. But if we don't go back, tell me what we're going to do, because I

won't resume a blind search for I don't know what. What's your plan?"
A tear is gleaming in the corner of her eye.

"I... Uh..." I don't have a plan. We can't climb the cliff, and there's no
way we can pass the guards to use the stairs either. Even if we did, I don't
know what we'd do once we were up there. She's right; we can't keep
roaming aimlessly in the city. Her mother is somewhere around here,
but we'll never find her that way.

Reluctant as I am to acknowledge it, she's right. "You know what
we're risking, if they betray us? They won't let us live."

She smiles faintly. "Yeah, I know. But I want to find my mum, and
they're the only chance we have. I promise you that at the first hint of
treachery, we'll flee."

We meander through the streets, but it isn't a merry walk. We're too
aware of the sword of Damocles hanging above our heads. I'm still not
convinced we should go back to see Beris. If he had wanted to help us,
he could have done so yesterday...

The crowds filling the streets are just as boisterous as ever. Everyone
talks and shouts in the merchant's street.

"Hey! You, over there!" The shout, louder than the others, makes me
look back.

Escorted by four mounted soldiers and riding a black horse, a man
dressed in white is coming toward us. I've only seen him once, from afar,
but there's no way I can mistake the High Inquisitor pointing at us.

As he looks at my face I see his eyes widen in recognition. "Guards!
Catch those two!"

I look at Malia. She has recognized him too. "Run!"

The crowd slows us down, but I can hear that the horses have even
more problems finding their way through it, their neighs mixing with
the shouts of frightened people.

I lead us to the most crowded streets I can see. But now, the people,
warned by the noise, are making way for the horsemen. They are gaining
on us.

I look around for a way to escape and see a very narrow gap between
two houses. It's barely wide enough for a man, definitely not for a horse.

"Malia! Over there!"

The horses are catching up. They're almost on us. Malia runs into the
gap. As I follow her, I look back and see two guards jump down from
their saddles a few strides behind us.

"Faster, Malia!"

A loud crash drowns out her name. I don't look back, but hear angry shouts from the guards and someone apologizing.

We've almost reached the other side of the gap when I hear running feet behind us again. Just as we emerge into an empty square and turn left, a bolt flies by, fired by one of the guards.

There's a large, broken door to our right, close enough to hide in before the warriors arrive. I take Malia's hand, and we rush through it.

Without knowing, I've brought us to the former Artemis temple. We crouch down in a corner, hidden behind a pile of broken benches.

We hear running feet and shouts outside, then nothing. They can't have given up so easily. The silence is unnerving. We don't have a single clue about what's happening outside.

Slow footsteps near the entrance. We both lie lower, holding our breath. The guard stops in the entrance, blocking the light coming through the door. All I can hear is the fast beat of my heart, so loud I'm afraid the warrior may hear it.

Pabam...

The warrior moves slightly. From the other side of the nave, a dozen scared birds take off in a fury of beating wings. Both Malia and I crouch lower.

After a minute of complete silence, I hear the soldier walk away and shout something at the other soldiers outside.

We wait for half an hour, not moving, scared that he may come back. When nothing happens, we relax and sit up.

"We're lucky he didn't come in." I really can't believe our luck.

"He wouldn't have," she answers flatly.

I look at her, surprised. "Why?"

"This is still a holy place, even if no one prays here anymore. Entering it with a weapon is forbidden, even for a Heavenly Warrior."

It sounds rather stupid. "Do you mean we were safe the whole time?"

Malia laughs softly. "Of course not, you idiot. They would have called reinforcements and bare-handed fighters to get us!"

I look at her and suddenly burst out laughing, releasing the stress. She laughs with me.

It takes me a few minutes to stop. Every time we look at each other, we laugh harder.

Eventually we calm down, and I remember the voice I heard during our escape. "Malia, when the warriors were about to catch up with us, there was a crash and someone spoke. I think it was Garbos. How did he find us, and why did he help us?"

"I don't know how. Maybe sheer luck. And, maybe, he really wants to help."

I ponder her answer for a while. It's another coincidence I don't trust. "It certainly is a possibility. But things have just gotten more dangerous for us and everyone who tries to help us. We have to find your mom fast. We're going back to Beris..."

Silence hangs heavily between us.

"Let's look on the bright side. With the High Inquisitor after us, if Beris isn't on our side, this will be sorted out very soon..."

Chapter Thirteen

"It was foolish of you to go out. You put us all in danger!" Beris's tantrum has been going on and on.

Malia's looking down. She's always been the one who obeys the rules. I'm the one who breaks them, repeatedly and unrepentantly. And this admonition is stretching my control over my boiling temper to dangerously thin extremities.

"Shut up!"

Beris stops ranting, mouth hanging open. I bet he's never been addressed this way.

I speak again before he can recover. "Yes, we went out. And yes, we almost got caught. But did you really expect us to stay here when you didn't want to talk to us for the whole day? When we don't even know if you'll help us or if you'll send guards to arrest us? Garbos is the only one who did anything to help us! By the way, thanks, Garbos, for slowing down the guards," I say more gently.

Garbos mumbles, "You're welcome," and looks away.

Beris glares at me, red-faced and jaws locked. He unclenches his fists and then puts his hands on the table. "I was away the whole day, indeed. If I don't want to be found, I have to play my part, as a High Priest. Besides, I've been looking for information."

His voice is strained by the effort to stay calm. I don't care. He'll have to talk now. "What kind of info?" I don't make any effort to keep the antagonism out of my question, my eyes locked with his.

Beris's nostrils flare. He clenches his fists again, but he doesn't shout at me. "First, about Veron and what happened to him. If you're interested, he's well, though I expect him to be kept under close watch for a while. He also lost most of his irreplaceable material. Second—" he shifts his glance and looks at Malia "—about your mother, as Garbos told me she's the reason you're here."

Malia's questions burst out like a flock of frightened birds. "Do you know where she is? Is she okay? Can you take us to her? Is she—?"

Beris interrupts her with a hand gesture. "I'm afraid I didn't find out much."

Malia's face loses its composure, and my heart sinks.

"But I did learn something, though," he continues. "Or didn't learn, as it would be more correct to say. She was indeed escorted here by guards, but right after that, she vanished. I couldn't find out anything more. It was as if she had never put a foot in the city."

"Isn't she in jail?" I don't dare ask the other, more obvious question.

"No. She's never been there. And they didn't kill her either," he says in reply to what I didn't ask. "All traces of her vanish just where she entered the city."

"What does it mean?"

Beris sighs. "She's not the first one to disappear like this. Over the centuries, many have vanished. Always important Technologists. No one ever discovered anything about their fate."

Silence. Malia's shoulders shake with silent sobs. My throat is obstructed by a painful lump.

"As I told you, only the most important of us disappear like this. Others are either jailed or executed. She's probably been taken elsewhere to be questioned."

"Where?" Malia and I ask at the same time.

"I don't know."

This won't deter me from trying to find the place. I won't let Malia down.

"Haven't you found any hint? Any rumor?"

"No. But your mother's disappearance, and the High Inquisitor looking for you... He never intervenes himself. There has to be something. A link, a detail I'm missing."

I remember what Veron said about Malia's mother. "Could the Gods have taken her to work on the Gaia Protocol?"

Beris looks at me, then resumes his thinking. "No. It's a Last Era thing. The Gods would destroy it, not have some Technologist work on it. And they've probably already destroyed it during the Purification."

"But if it's a weapon...? What if the box can help us recreate it?"

Malia's the one to answer me this time. "If it's a weapon, why didn't the men use it to fight the Gods when they came back, then?"

"I don't know. Maybe they didn't have time to build it? If we can find out how to use it, we could get rid of the Gods and free your mother!"

"Prome, you're dreaming. No human weapon could ever hurt a God. The men of the Last Era had the most terrible and powerful weapons, and none helped them."

I can almost hear my bubble of hope pop.

"You're right, Malia," Beris says. "It's probably not a weapon. But Prome has a point. If the Gods reacted so promptly, it's definitely something they don't want us to have. Something that could cause them problems."

Hope is here again. "Do you hear, Malia? If we find whatever it is, I bet the Gods will be ready to bargain with us. We can have them free your mother!"

"No!"

I turn my head, surprised by Beris's shout.

"If you find it, you can't give it to the Gods. It's something that belongs to humanity alone. It might even be what all Technologists have been looking for all these centuries."

"For now, we just have to find it. We'll decide what we do with it after that. But if we can use it to free my mother, we'll do it."

When Beris doesn't say anything, Malia adds, "Remember that you'll never find it without us and Prome's amulet anyway."

I can't help smiling. She's all sweet on the outside, but she certainly can bite when she feels like it. Beris doesn't look too happy but finally agrees to our terms.

Now that I have a goal, I have a plan. "For now, we need to know more about that protocol. We need to use the box again, but we'll have to do it somewhere far enough from everywhere to have enough time to get useful information before any warriors arrive."

"I can help you with that." Beris goes away. We hear some shuffling down the hall. He comes back with a roll of paper that he unrolls on the table in front of us. "I used to have a laboratory that would be suitable. It is empty now, so there won't be any damage if the warriors find it. There."

I can see his finger pointing at a place with nothing around it. No city, no village, not even a road. But that's all my poor map-reading skills can tell me. "How far is it from the nearest city?"

"Two full days with horses if you know the way and ride fast. Even if they run their horses to death, the phalanxes will still need at least a full day. You can have a few more hours if you use the box only after noon, as they'll have to stop for the night."

I look at Malia. "We'll have only twenty-four hours to find how the box works and get the information we need."

"We'll do it!" She turns to Beris. "We'll leave tomorrow morning."

"You don't have to. You can stay here a few more days to prepare and—"

"No. With the Inquisitor after us, we're not safe in the city anymore, and we're endangering you. We'll leave tomorrow morning."

Beris doesn't look too pleased. "You won't change your mind?"

We both say, "No," at the same time.

"Then, all I can do is give you the map to get there and have two horses waiting for you on the outskirts tomorrow morning."

"Three."

We all look at Garbos, whose face becomes bright red.

"Three horses, please, sir. With your authorization, I'd like to go with them."

"No, you're not," I snap. "I'm going with Malia alone. It doesn't concern you!"

"But I could be of some help to work on the box." He looks at Malia.

She looks back at me and lifts her brow questioningly. She's already on his side.

"No! Three people will attract more attention than two, and we need to leave the city unseen."

Garbos doesn't answer that one. But Beris does. "You'll take the road to Nerea. I can write him an official letter sending him there for me. It will be the perfect cover. You'll be his escort. Even if guards stop you, they won't bother you as long as they don't recognize you."

Garbos flashes a wide smile. Malia's smiling too. I'm outnumbered. I can't counter that.

"Fine," I grumble. I can't object anymore, but I really don't think bringing a spy with us is a good thing. "If we're leaving through the west road at first light tomorrow morning, I'll leave this evening and join you there in the morning. We left something just outside the city, near the east road, when we arrived, and I need to recover it."

Garbos and Beris look curious but say nothing. Malia only nods.

✳✳✳

I'm packing some spare clothes and some food when Beris enters the room. "Be careful. I don't know what you're fetching, but it had better be important. Even if there are no city gates, someone leaving the city during the night will attract attention. The kind you'd better avert."

I don't even look at him as I close my bag. "I know." What's bothering me is not the attention I may get, but Nemeos. Will he have waited for me?

As I'm about to open the door to leave, I turn around. Thinking of Nemeos reminds me of a question I've asked myself, and which Beris might be able to answer. "Are there human beasts?"

Beris looks surprised but answers anyway. "No. Only monsters can assume a human form. Not beasts."

His answer relieves me, even if it creates even more questions.

"At least, I've never heard about such a beast before, but I'm not an expert."

Shit. A simple no was too good to hope for. That possibility remains. There's another question I need to ask. "Could a human-looking monster forget its true nature and think it's human, live in a city, and grow like a human?"

If he lifted his brows at my first question, he now furrows them. "Is there anything you haven't told me, Prome?"

I still don't trust him enough to tell him about my fears. "No. We met an empousa on our way here, and I almost fell for her trick. We still have a long path to take, and I'd rather know the Gods' dirtiest tricks." I open the door and exit.

✳✳✳

Leaving the city unseen is easy enough. There are dark, narrow streets everywhere. Walking on the road, I stand out. A dark shape in the night. I hope no one is looking carefully.

After a few minutes, I start running. My heart is beating furiously, my innards are twisted, and I don't know if I feel like crying or laughing. My anxiety about Nemeos is too much.

After an hour of running and walking, I look around. In the dark, I don't recognize anything. I don't know if I've gone too far or not.

"Nemeos!" I whisper loudly.

Nothing. I feel the knots in my belly.

"Nemeos!" This time I shout. I turn around, looking for a movement, for any sign that could tell me he's coming.

Nothing.

"Nemeos! Nemeos!" I shout and look all around, but I can't see anything through the tears.

Bam!

Something hits me in the back and sends me to the ground. I try to stand to fight, but a weight on my back pins me down. I hear something sniffing, then feel a warm, wet tongue lick my head, and the weight lifts off me.

I turn around and hug Nemeos. "You're here!" I realize the irony. I can't trust anyone, except Malia, and I have to lie to her. And I'm doomed to hate the one I love. The only one I can be myself with is Nemeos.

As I finally stand up, I look at him. The darkness might trick my eyes, but he looks taller than I remember. I push the thought aside. For now, I have things to do.

"Nemeos, can you lead me to the weapons?"

He looks at me and tilts his head to the side, as if asking me what I mean.

"Nemeos, take me to my spear." I gesture, mimicking something long.

He doesn't move. That would have been too easy. I'll have to try to find them myself. I look around, but it's too dark to see much. I'll never find them. I can't wait for the first morning light. I would only endanger Malia and Garbos if I forced them to wait for me.

"Okay, let's go!"

I start walking, but Nemeos trots the other way, away from the city.

"No, Nemeos, we're going to the city. I have to find my weapons first."

He ignores me and keeps trotting away. I have no other choice than to follow him.

After a couple of minutes of walking, he stops and lies down at the foot of a tree.

"Great! Now you want to sleep. No, Nemeos, we have to go!"

I try to push him, make him walk away, but he won't move. At long last, I sit on the ground, my back to the tree. It's quite uncomfortable, though. The tree isn't straight...

I shoot up and look at it. Its dark shape twists in every direction.

"Nemeos, you're a genius!"

I push away some rocks and branches at Nemeos's side and find the weapons. He's probably settled here this whole time to keep them safe.

Now's the time for us to go to our meeting point.

CHAPTER FOURTEEN

I don't sleep much, but when the first hint of daylight appears in the eastern sky, I'm wide awake, standing near the road at our meeting point.

A man appears with three horses at the same time Garbos and Malia arrive. Without a word, he gives them to us and then leaves.

As I climb on my horse, I hear a small laugh.

"You know, Prome, you won't need your walking staff."

I glance at my disguised spear and answer Garbos without even looking at him. "We'll see. But for now I'm keeping it."

"Where's Nemeos?" Malia asks.

"He's waiting a little farther down the road, safely out of sight of the city."

"Who's Nemeos?" Garbos inquires.

It's my time to chortle. "You'll see in a minute."

A few minutes later, Nemeos joins us. The darkness of the night is already dissipating. The horses neigh nervously, and Garbos sees him coming toward us. "Oh my God, a lion! It's going to attack us! Kill it!"

I burst out laughing. "This, Garbos, is Nemeos." I jump down and pat Nemeos on the head. "And by the way, he's not just a lion."

Still wide-eyed, Garbos stutters. "It's... It's...it's a..."

"Yes," I finish for him, "he's a Nemean lion. We've adopted each other. Nemeos, this is Garbos. He'll be with us for a while."

As we start moving again, I can see Garbos keeping a fearful eye on Nemeos. And when he looks at me, doubt and fear are mixed in his eyes.

"Don't worry, he won't attack you. He only attacks monsters."

Garbos laughs nervously.

"Seriously, he does."

Malia changes the subject. "Why did you decide to come with us?" she asks Garbos.

"Through my Technologist training, I've learned that there is another truth than the one in the Book of the Gods. This is my chance to be a real

Technologist, and not just some kind of sleeping agent awaiting orders that may never come. You know, to do something really important..."

"Sorry to interrupt," I say, "but now that we can see better, we'll have to ride faster if we want to be there tomorrow."

Malia and Garbos just nod.

***

The road gets busier in the late morning, but no one stops us, though Nemeos has to leave the road and follow us from afar, where no one can see him. In the midafternoon, we leave the road and ride through green plains.

When the night finally comes and forces us to stop, I fall from my horse more than I climb down. I tie my horse to a small tree and lie on the soft grass, unable to move anymore. My whole body's aching. The pain causes me to discover muscles I didn't even know I had.

Malia and Garbos aren't in a much better state. Even Nemeos looks tired. If a monster comes tonight, we're done for. But even that thought can't prevent me from falling asleep.

***

When I open my eyes, I see a clear blue sky.

"Shit!" Malia and Garbos are still sleeping. I shake them. "Come on, move! The day has already begun!" I throw them a few pieces of bread and meat. "Eat this and we'll go."

Malia looks at the sun, already high above the horizon. "Prome, I don't think we have to hurry that much anymore. We won't make it today."

I look at her. "That's precisely why we can't lose another minute. We'll have to ride faster today!" I hear some shuffling behind me.

"Malia's right." Garbos is looking at a map. "It's already midmorning. According to the High Priest's information, we're still a full day's ride away, and we won't be riding on a road anymore. We'll be slower. Trying to cover the distance in one day may be too much for the horses. And for us."

I'm about to retort when I get the feeling I'm being observed. Before I can turn around, Malia puts her hands on my shoulders.

"He's right. We'd better slow down a bit. We'll get to the lab by tomorrow noon."

Nemeos roars softly.

"See? Even Nemeos agrees."

I sigh. "Okay, but no slacking off either. I know we weren't attacked last night, but I don't like this area much."

When I finally turn around, I see nothing, but the sensation of being observed is still here, and doesn't leave me. No one else appears to feel it. Even Nemeos is acting normally, wandering off and coming back later. Maybe it's just my imagination.

***

By the end of the day, I'm even more tired than yesterday. There's no place to settle down that offers us any protection. We just stop near a few trees. As I come down from my horse, my knees give way under me and I collapse.

"Prome! Are you okay?" Malia asks.

"Yeah, just a bit tired from the ride. I'm not used to it. I'll have to learn how to walk again," I say, standing up.

Nemeos comes to me. He sniffs my left arm and growls.

I jerk back in surprise and look at my arm. The scratch from the fight is bleeding slightly. "Don't worry, Nemeos, I just scraped off the crust when I fell. It will stop bleeding in a second." A new crust is already forming, gray with the dust and dirt of the day. "I hope there's water to wash ourselves at the lab."

Nemeos immediately runs off to hunt.

The feeling of being observed is still bothering me. I don't want to light a fire, but when Nemeos comes back, he brings us a rabbit. We dig a small pit to make a fire and cook it.

"We'll have to keep a watch tonight. We were lucky last night, but tonight could be different." I don't want to unsettle them with my fears. It would either upset them or make them laugh at me. "I'll take the first watch. Malia, you can take the second and Garbos the third."

During the meal, none of us dares talk about what will happen tomorrow, though it probably weighs as much on their minds as on mine. What if the box doesn't work? Will we be able to use it? Will we find anything?

The conversation dies out quickly, and the others settle down for the night. Malia lies down close to Nemeos and me, whereas Garbos chooses a spot at a safe distance from my lion.

As the shadows grow and the night falls, the feeling gets stronger. Tonight, clouds obscure the sky. The night is pitch-black. If something is watching us, I won't be able to see it before it's on us. I'd feel better with Nemeos keeping watch with me, but he needs to sleep too. I hope he or the horses will sense if something gets too close.

Darkness got eyes, goes the saying, *and eyes got claws.*

I can't see anything, and all I can hear is the soft rustling of the wind on the grass. I turn to the left, alerted by something, but I can't say what. I feel—no, I know—I'm being watched.

Behind me!

As fast as I turn around, my spear is pointing at nothingness. No sound, no glowing eyes... I sense that my observer has moved. Swiftly, soundlessly.

I look at Nemeos, who opens an eye and then goes back to sleep. How can he smell and hear nothing?

I must be paranoid. To calm myself, I walk around the camp in a wide circle.

⁕⁕⁕

My shift's about to end. I can barely keep my eyes open or think straight. Despite my fears, nothing has happened. But nothing's changed either. I'll tell Malia to be careful when I wake her up in a few minutes.

Something furtive moves in my peripheral vision, and I hear a muffled snap.

Without thinking, I twist, and a bolt shoots out of my spear. For a fraction of a second, it's like daylight. The plain is just its usual empty self. Darkness comes back and the rolling thunder dissipates into the distance.

"What happened?"

I stay rooted to the ground, staring at the darkness.

"Prome? Did you see something?"

I shake myself out of this torpor and look at Malia. "I thought I saw something, but it was just my imagination."

"Did the bolt strike nearby? It sounded awfully close. Do you think it will rain?"

We both turn to Garbos. It's too dark for him to see the point of my spear and the burnt fabric around it.

"Yeah, it may rain…"

"It's my turn to keep watch, Prome," Malia says. "Go to sleep."

"I will, but stay alert. I didn't see anything, but I did hear something."

"Go to sleep! You're getting paranoid. I'll be careful."

"Being paranoid doesn't mean there's nothing out there waiting to kill us…"

Before going to sleep, I take out a shirt, walk some distance from Garbos to tear it apart and wrap it around my spear.

"Why didn't you tell him?" Malia whispers.

"I'm not ready to tell him. Yet. Did you notice how he looks at me since I showed him Nemeos?"

She shakes her head. "Garbos looks at Nemeos. No wonder. While we were in the city, Nemeos got bigger. And with the mane that's beginning to grow, he looks even more intimidating."

"Garbos is wary. He keeps an eye on me as much as he does on Nemeos. I don't think he ever trusted us, but now he doesn't even pretend anymore…"

"You're right… You are paranoid."

"It's a miracle he didn't recognize the spear for what it is, but from now on, I'll keep it with me at all times. And I'll use it if need be."

I purposefully walk back to our camp and lie down against Nemeos.

Maybe Malia's right. Maybe it's just my imagination. But I still have that nagging feeling. I strain my ears, waiting for any suspicious sound.

Nemeos shifts and puts a heavy paw on me. His soft fur and his warmth are already so familiar…

I blink, but my eyes don't open again.

* * *

"Prome? Malia?"

I open my eyes. It's still dark, but the sky announces the coming dawn. The realization that I fell asleep wakes me up more effectively than Garbos's voice.

I can't believe I did that. Nothing happened, but I fell asleep! Anything could have attacked us. I'm so angry at myself.

And despite the rest, I'm still tired.

"We're lucky: it didn't rain."

Garbos's reminder of what happened last night really gets on my nerves. I throw a look at him that makes him recoil. Malia knows to leave me alone when I'm in such a foul mood.

We take off as the first sunray hits the ground. Malia and Garbos's chatter is more than I can bear. I gallop a little to ride silently in front, Nemeos at my side.

As I look at him, I realize that I don't feel watched anymore. At last, a piece of good news. I smile and look in front of me. The day may still end better than it began.

***

There's something strange in the distance. A line, as if the world ended. Malia and Garbos are still chatting happily. I feel like shouting at Malia to stop it, not to trust him. At the same time, I'm jealous of her, talking with him, riding at his side.

"Nemeos, feel like a little run?" I kick my horse, and we shoot forward. At least I have a good excuse to get away from them.

Getting closer, I realize the line isn't the end of the world after all. I stop when I reach it.

A perfect line splits the land in two. On my side: bright green grass. On the other side: black rocks and dirt, with a few green leaves growing here and there. I look right and left but can't see any end to the line.

"It's the limit of the Dead Steppes." Garbos looks stern, staring at the black land in front of us. "During the Purification, men used such horrible weapons that the Gods had to burn some entire countries to clean the evil unleashed by humankind. To remind us of what we did, and the extent of their powers, the Gods decided that those places would forever stay like this. Are you sure you want to go there?"

"Yes," I answer glumly and start off.

"Beris told me the laboratory is in the middle of the Dead Steppes," I hear Garbos say, before he follows me.

Malia joins us, but all chitchat has stopped.

Before an hour has passed, the landscape starts to get to me. If we didn't have to go to that lab, I would turn around and run back as fast as I can. Even feeling watched is better than this barren plain. I begin looking around for a small hill, indicated on the maps, that will tell me we're almost there.

In these gloomy surroundings, time stretches endlessly. The unchanging landscape makes me feel like we're not moving at all. It weighs on my nerves too. Malia and Garbos are still riding side by side. All I can do not to explode is to stay away from them.

One hour after noon, we reach the base of the hill.

It's black, like everything else, but it's not smooth and round like any other hill I've ever seen. It looks almost geometrical, like a crumbled pyramid. Maybe that was what the Gods wanted to destroy...

I look at the map and point at one side of the hill. "The entrance should be over there."

As we ride around a corner and along another side, we see a hole in the hill. It's roughly rectangular, and leads slightly down. At the end of the short slope, I can see a door.

CHAPTER FIFTEEN

"It must have been a building, long ago. Some Technologists probably came back here after it was destroyed and cleared that entrance. They had to do it in a lot of places." Garbos is nervous and obviously finds being a guide reassuring. I shut out his constant babble and move.

What I thought was a door is just an old plank. I push it aside and step into a dark room. I don't know when Beris came here last, but whatever used to be in that room is long gone.

Pieces of broken furniture litter the ground. Other than that, there is no sign that man or animal has set foot in here for a long time.

"The lab's destroyed..."

"No. That's just a setup to deter warriors from searching too much. Look." Garbos walks to a clutter of broken furniture piled against a wall. He puts his arm through a hole, waits a few seconds, then takes it out and does it again in another hole, and another, and another...

"It should be here somewhere," he mumbles unhappily.

I turn to Malia and whisper, "Has he gone nuts?"

Malia elbows me in the ribs and watches Garbos.

Several minutes pass without any change. Garbos is now grumbling and puffing. Even in the poor light, I can see his face is crimson.

I feel pity. "Ahem. Maybe I read the map wrong. There's probably another entrance nearby."

"No!" Garbos almost shouts. "I know it's here somewhere..."

There's a click. Garbos turns to us, smiling from ear to ear. "See I told you!"

"I still don't see anything..."

Garbos puts his hands on the wall and pushes. Part of the wall rotates to reveal a hallway beyond.

Okay. Maybe I should give the guy more credit.

The hallway is wide enough for two people to walk side by side, but unlike any other Technologists' place I've seen, the lights are very dim, some flickering.

"Why is there no more light?"

"Beris told us, the night you went to get Nemeos, that according to the records of those who came here before him, the lights have been dwindling for years. That's also part of the reason he abandoned the place. We can only hope the box will work anyway."

"It had better. Now, let's see what this lab looks like."

***

At the end of the hallway, we open another door and go down a metallic, spiraling staircase that plunges into the depths of the earth. The farther we go, the less I like the place. There's absolutely no life here. No rats, not even a fly or a spider running up a wall. Even the air smells different. Cold, dry. Stale...

Dead.

Now I understand why Nemeos refused to follow us. The sound of each and every step we take reverberates around us, shouting at us that we don't belong here.

At last, we reach the final step. A short hall and a door later, we reach what used to be the laboratory.

It looks like Veron's lab, though much bigger. All the shelves are empty. A few heavy concrete tables still have some metallic debris scattered on them. Three other doors lead out of the room.

"So, here we are. Should we begin?"

Garbos nods to me and begin to unpack the box.

"Wait!" Malia stops us. "It's still early. We should explore the place, see if we can find some water. I'd like to clean off the dirt from the journey..."

The first door opens on a closet full of tools and junk. The second one leads to an empty closet.

The last one leads to a long hallway. On each side, there are doors with a glass panel. Behind them, all the rooms look the same. Plain white, with empty tables. One door has no glass. Malia opens it.

"It's here!"

Inside is a locker room with a sink, toilets, and shower.

***

When we finally reach the exit of the building, Nemeos jumps around me happily.

"Here, Nemeos, drink." I put down the bucket, made of a flashy pink material I've never seen before, and he immediately starts drinking.

"Why did you want me to bring back the box?" Garbos sits down on the ground.

"There's something I want to try. From down there, we'll never see if someone's coming. If the box works here, it will be easier for us to flee. Down there, we'll be trapped. But first, let's eat."

At that word, two heads turn up to me, and I burst out laughing. He may not like Nemeos, but at this moment, they both wear the same hungry expression.

***

We're sitting on the ground around the box. Nemeos seemed, at first, mildly interested by the box but soon retreated into a corner to take a nap. He's the only one not stressed by the situation.

I have the amulet in my hand. "If I do it, the countdown starts. We'll have at most twenty-four hours to find what we need. There will be no turning back."

They both nod to me.

I put the amulet on the box.

Nothing happens. No sound, no light, nothing.

I let out a disgruntled humph. "We'll have to go down into the lab." I stand. "Let's go. Garbos, pick up the box. Malia, erase our traces. Nemeos, stay here and keep watch. Roar if someone's coming. We'll leave the doors open so we can hear you."

"Do you think he understood you?" Malia looks dubious, but Nemeos immediately stands and walks away.

"I'm sure he did. I have the feeling he understands even more than I think he does."

***

"Where should we put it?"

"On a table," I answer. "In Veron's lab, that's where it was."

I push the mess off one of the tables, and Garbos puts the box on it.

"Ready?"

They both nod.

I approach the amulet. This time, the box reacts, but all that happens is a feeble, low-pitched beep that vanishes quickly, as if the box was too tired to beep properly.

"What was that? Why didn't it work?"

Garbos answers me. "Maybe it's the same problem as with the lights. There may not be enough energy to make it work..."

"Can you repair it?"

"No. We've lost that knowledge. I don't even know how they produce the electricity or transfer it without cables."

"What's electricity?" I ask.

"It's what creates the light. A technology the Gods destroyed," Garbos answers.

"Prome, we could try in the other rooms."

Malia's suggestion is our best course of action. But, after having tried in all the rooms, we're back in the laboratory, feeling down.

I turn the amulet in my hand. There has to be a way. The box in our village and the one in Kurea both worked. If the men of the Last Era managed to build boxes that resisted the Gods' wrath, they certainly made sure we could use them, like in Veron's secret room...

I jump up. "Malia! Garbos! There has to be another secret room! Every lab we've seen so far had one! Help me find it."

"What should we be looking for?" Garbos asks.

"I don't know. Anything. A small, metallic plate on the wall, anything that could work with my amulet." I describe the metal piece from Veron's laboratory to Garbos. I can't do more. It could even look completely different. But there *has to be* a secret door! "We have to hurry. The box didn't work, but it still did something. Let's assume that the countdown has begun."

The search begins in the lab, frantic, unnerving. The longer it takes, the less time we have to get info from the box.

I brush the walls with my amulet, while the others touch and look everywhere. From time to time, Garbos or Malia call me to look at something: a switch, a knob, a change of color. I use the amulet on it, but to no avail. It takes us over an hour to search the room, without success. But I won't give up.

"Let's search the other rooms too."

✳✳✳

It's late afternoon when we go back outside, downtrodden. Even I have lost my optimism, though I'm pretty sure I'm right about the secret door.

As the sun goes down, the temperature drops. We light a small fire so we can prepare food and warm ourselves. Garbos keeps glancing at the hallway leading to the lab.

"No, Garbos. I don't think that's the door we're looking for. In Kurea, the secret door could only be opened with my amulet."

"But the one in our village was simply hidden behind shelves."

I think about it. "Yes. But what is a laboratory doing in such a small village? I bet it was created after the Purification, maybe to save things from a destroyed lab? Or one that was about to be discovered? I don't know. But it was definitely different from the other labs. Have you seen other labs, Garbos? What did they look like?"

"Hmm?" He's still looking at the hallway. "Sorry. No, I've never seen any others. But Veron told me those he saw all pretty much looked the same." He shivers.

I'm feeling the cold too. "We'll sleep inside the laboratory. We'll be warmer there."

✳✳✳

After another search of the lab, we settle down for the night. It will be strange to sleep with those lights on, and even stranger to sleep without Nemeos. He agreed to come with us along the hallway, but not down the stairs.

I lie down near Malia and try to close my eyes. Garbos keeps shifting.

"Garbos, can you stop making so much noise, please?"

"Sorry. It's the lights." He stands and goes a little farther, hiding under the table. After a few seconds, he says, "Prome?"

"Yeeees?" I say, irritated by this new disturbance.

"You said we were looking for some metal plate in a wall, about as big as my hand?"

"Yes."

"Could it be not on a wall?"

"I guess so, why?"

"I think I've found it..."

I run on all fours toward him. "Where?"

He points at the underside of the table. A piece of metal is attached to it. I take out my amulet and touch the metal with it. I hear something shift, and Malia shouts, "Over there!"

Like upstairs, part of a wall has opened. From the opening, white light pours blindingly into the lab. The room is pretty much the same as the one in Kurea: bookshelves around the wall, plain metallic tables, and a black box, identical to the one we brought. I put ours near it.

"What do we do now?" Garbos asks.

I shrug. "Try them. That's why we came here."

I put my amulet on our box. It emits a beep. Almost at the same time, the other box emits the same beep. After a few seconds, the words *GAIA PROTOCOL* appear above each of them, floating in the air.

"Oh!" Garbos exclaims. "It's a computer!"

"A what?"

"A computer. Never mind. I've read about them in books. This one looks different, but I should be able to work it out." And with this, Garbos puts his fingers on the table and moves them around.

"Can we help you?"

"Yes. Let me concentrate. I've read a few books on computers, but it's the first time I've actually used one. And it's not the same as in the books. I need to find how it works."

He moves his fingers some more, and the words disappear, replaced by small pictures.

"What are those?" I point at one, and the picture starts blinking. Garbos grabs my hand and moves it away from the small picture.

"I think it's called an icon. Now don't disturb me, please. You can look on the bookshelves to see if you can find anything helpful about those icons, how to operate this computer, or the Gaia Protocol."

Malia and I immediately begin searching through the shelves. We take a book, look quickly through it, and dump it unceremoniously on the ground before taking another one. At first, I can hear muffled sounds of outrage from Garbos, but he soon becomes too absorbed by his task.

None of the books make any sense to me. Some talk about the stars, some about particles. Most have lots of complicated mathematical formulas, some of which are so long I wonder if anyone ever understood them, including the writer.

It takes us a while, but we find nothing. We sit by Garbos's side and look at what he's doing.

Pictures, or icons as he calls them, flicker, and sometimes change. From time to time, a few words appear, but nothing much happens apart from that. It's a boring process.

CHAPTER SIXTEEN

I wake up with a start. I fell asleep at the table. Near me, Malia and Garbos are sleeping too. In front of us, some icons are still floating in the air.

Fear gnaws at my insides. "Malia! Garbos! Wake up!" I shake them up. "Garbos, did you find something?"

A puffy-eyed Garbos answers me. "No, not yet."

"Keep searching. I'll run upstairs to see what time it is. Malia, come with me and take my bag."

As we reach the exit, I see daylight on the outside. Nemeos comes to me happily.

"Sorry, pal, but there's no time to play right now."

The sun shines high. It's midmorning already. We have two to three hours left to find any information. I go to the horses and ready them for a rushed departure. I take my spear and give the sword to Malia. The spear feels heavier than it used to.

"Nemeos, stay here and watch out for anyone. Malia, come with me. We'll see if we can help Garbos."

In the lab, Garbos is at work again. Malia sits in front of the second box and begins moving her fingers like Garbos does. I notice letters have appeared on the table, in front of the cube. "Maybe I can help you. How does it work?"

Garbos explains it to her quickly, and she immediately begins working too. I can see that the icons and words in front of Garbos change much more quickly than those in front of Malia.

I take some food from a bag and give it to them. I don't know when we'll next be able to eat something. Especially if we have pursuers.

Time passes. I'm nervous. To calm myself down, I keep checking on Nemeos and the horses outside every few minutes.

"I've got something, but I can't understand it." We both look at Garbos. "The document is supposed to explain what the Gaia Protocol is about, but words like *super strings* or *twelve-dimensional space* keep popping up. I understand that they built something to create something, but I don't know how."

"Very helpful," I say sarcastically, making him blush. "Keep looking, we need something useful."

"Garbos? What about this? They're talking about a facility..."

Garbos looks at Malia's display and pushes her aside. "That's it. It's where they built the protocol. That's where we have to go!" He moves his fingers some more. "There's an address, but it won't help us..." He resumes his search, Malia and me hunched over him.

After a few minutes, a large picture appears. To one side is a wide lake. Its banks are green, but a little farther away, the land is all reddish-brown sand and rocks. In the middle of the picture is some kind of village made of shiny, square, white houses. One is almost completely made of glass.

"That's all I can find. That's where the Gaia facility is."

Malia shakes her head. "We can't find it like this. The land has changed so much, the desert could have disappeared and the lake too."

"Maybe if I..." Garbos moves his hand around and the picture changes. It is now a view of the village alone.

"These houses are certainly destroyed. We need something else that we could recognize." He moves the picture to the side.

"Here!"

At the end of the lake is a dam, its curved, smooth wall obstructing a red canyon.

"It's a canyon," Malia says. "But it could be any canyon. I've never seen a dam like this. It certainly doesn't exist anymore. Even if it did, I don't know where."

"You're right, Malia, but look here, above the canyon." Garbos points at the screen.

"It's a bridge." It's my turn to be unimpressed.

"Not just a bridge. Look."

High white pillars stand proudly at each end of the bridge. Between them, a plethora of cables go down to the suspended road at various angles.

Still not impressed. "It's a nice bridge..."

Garbos sighs. "Now imagine it with the towers less white, and partly broken, most of the cables missing, and some replaced by ropes attached to planks instead of a sturdy road..."

Malia is wide-eyed. "It's the bridge near the agoge!"

"What's...?"

"The military camp where all warriors are trained," she answers before I can finish my question.

"Then, that's where we're going. Now move. We have to leave. We'll discuss what to do on our way."

"Wait. There's something else that I want to look at." Garbos goes back to his box.

"We don't have time, Garbos."

"It could be important. It's some kind of diary."

"Come, Garbos!" I take one of the boxes, and both displays disappear.

As we exit the room, I use my amulet to close the wall again. I put the box on the table and leave.

"Wait! We can't leave it here!"

I turn to Garbos. "We have to. We can't take it where we're going. I hope that if they find that one, they won't try to look for the other one, in case we have to come back. Now come on!"

We run upstairs to the first room. "Close that door," I order Garbos. I'm sure they'll eventually find the secret door. But it will delay them and give us more of a head start.

A loud roar comes from the outside. Nemeos is pacing nervously, keeping his eyes on a fixed point of the horizon.

I can see a little dust cloud. "They're coming! We have to go!"

We all climb on our horses and ride not in the opposite direction, but west toward the agoge.

As we lose sight of the destroyed building, I can see our pursuers haven't sighted us. The dust cloud, a little bigger, is still aiming at the laboratory.

＊

A couple of hours later, we reach the end of the Dead Steppes. We stop for a few minutes for the horses to eat some grass. I appreciate the break too. Even after the short ride, I feel drained. I try to hop down from my horse, but my tired legs give up and I fall.

Nemeos is the first at my side. He sniffs my left arm and growls.

"Shh, Nemeos. I'm just tired."

That doesn't stop the growling.

"Prome, are you all right?" Malia sounds concerned.

"Yeah, just dead-tired."

"Why is Nemeos reacting like this?"

"Your guess is as good as mine."

"What happened to your arm?"

I look at it. A stain has appeared on the fabric of my shirt. Malia rolls up my sleeve before I can react and gasps.

"What...?"

A big, greenish-white lump has formed where the chimera scratched me.

"Don't move. I have to drain the wound and treat you."

"We don't have time. We have to move." I try to stand, but she pushes me back.

"Don't move, I said." She takes out a knife and pierces my skin.

I don't feel any pain, but the flood of pus coming out of the wound, and its awful smell, is enough to make me feel sick.

"I have to clean and close the wound."

"We don't have time for this right now. Just clean it and put a bandage around it. You can tend to it properly when we stop for the night."

She reluctantly does as instructed. We're soon riding again.

By the time the sun goes down, I'm so exhausted that Garbos and Malia have to help me stay on my horse. I feel cold, then hot the next moment, before turning cold again.

They help me down, and I lie on the grass, unable to move. Malia immediately takes her knife and some vials out of her bag, and rolls my sleeve up again.

I hear Garbos moving around. I turn my head and see him kneeling on the ground in front of a pile of dry twigs.

"Don't make a fire! They could see it!"

"But I thought..."

"No! No fire."

"Yes, light one," Malia counters, "but dig a hole first to hide it in. I'll need it to heat my blade."

That doesn't sound good for me. But for now, I don't feel a thing. She's pierced the skin again and more pus comes out of the wound.

"It's not a nice wound, Prome. You should have shown it to me sooner."

"I didn't know it was more than a scratch. I don't feel anything."

She puts the blade of her knife in the small fire Garbos lit. After a few minutes, she takes it out. "I'm sorry, Prome, I'll have to hurt you."

"Go on." I grit my teeth.

At first, I don't feel anything. I hear the sizzle of the flesh and the smell of burnt meat fills my nostrils. Suddenly, a white-hot pain shoots through my arm. I shout and everything turns black.

✻✻✻

When I wake up, the sky is paling.

"Hey. How are you feeling?" Garbos is standing near me.

"Fine. Where's Malia?"

He points toward the horses. "She watched over you most of the night. You were delirious. I finally convinced her to go to sleep over there so that she didn't hear you speak."

I look at my arm. It's wrapped in a bandage. I can smell the medicine she put on the skin through it.

I stand up and then walk over to her. "Malia."

She opens her eyes. "Morning. How are you feeling?"

"Good. Thanks. But wake up. It's almost dawn. We have to leave."

"Okay, but let me get a look at your wound first."

She unwraps the bandage carefully. The wound is an unpleasant mix of red and black, but at least there's no pus.

"Good. But I want to check something first. Nemeos! Come here!"

"Why are you calling him?"

"He growled at you. I think it was because of the wound. I want to see if he still smells something."

Nemeos approaches my arm hesitantly. He sniffs and immediately emits a low growl.

"We'll have to see over time, but there's the possibility that the infection's already in your blood."

I snort humorlessly. "The monsters don't even have to attack; they just have to wait..."

"Maybe that's what they're doing?"

We both turn to Garbos.

"I mean, it's a wound caused by a monster. It's possible it was poisonous. If Nemeos can smell it, maybe the monsters can too. That could be the reason we haven't been attacked since we left Parthenos. They're waiting for you to die..."

"Garbos, shut up!" Malia snaps.

I put my hand on hers. "Actually, he might be right. We haven't been attacked since the chimera scratched me. And if he's right, it means I'll need more than your ointments to heal. Don't!" I stop her before she speaks. "But it also means we won't be attacked during the nights. No need to keep a watch. We just have to reach the agoge before I die. They'll certainly have a doctor there."

I can see the outrage on Malia's crimson face. Garbos doesn't show any emotion.

"You know I'm right, Malia. And anyway, there's nothing we can do about it. Now let's get ready. We still have to decide what we'll do next..."

***

Malia and Garbos vetoed me when I asked that we ride as fast as we could, in case we were being pursued. I could see that Malia is torn between getting me to the agoge's doctor as soon as possible and risking tiring me too much.

We keep a steady pace, fast enough not to be caught, but at the first sign of tiredness from me, we stop for a few minutes.

"How will we get into the camp?"

I smile at Garbos. His innocent questions are refreshing. Could he have poisoned me? "You know, there's only one way to get in, and it's pretty obvious..."

He gapes. "You don't mean..."

"Yes, I mean it. Malia and I will have to enroll."

"What will I do?"

"You'll have to ride back to Parthenos. I don't mean to insult you, but I doubt you could survive the training."

"There's no way I'll leave you. I'll come too. I know I can do it."

The tremor in his voice tells me otherwise.

"Of course you'll come."

I frown at Malia. "Why do you say that?"

"Because if it was me, I wouldn't want to be left out either."

I don't like that. If I had it my way, I'd go alone.

CHAPTER SEVENTEEN

The days are blurring into each other. Every morning and evening, Malia looks at my wound. It now looks clean, but every time Nemeos sniffs it, he growls. Even without his confirmation, I know that the poison is spreading. I'm now constantly tired, even when I wake up. I'm losing track of time; falling asleep on my horse. Yesterday, I fell asleep and slipped off my saddle. Well, I think it was yesterday, but for all I know, it could have been a week ago or this morning. My eyes ache, and I have to keep them closed most of the time to reduce the pain. I'm also getting delirious. I think I hear sounds or see things that can't be real.

Things are getting worse. A moment ago, I was on my horse under the sun. Someone was with me, I think. A second later, it's already night and Malia's forcing me to eat and drink. Even my eyes are going awry. Everything's blurred, the colors too bright or too dark, the forms shapeless. I only recognize Malia because her face is so close to mine.

"Malia, I..."

"Shh. It's okay, Prome. We're almost there. The doctor will heal you. Eat. You have to."

I struggle to open my mouth and swallow what she puts in it.

***

"We have to hurry. How far is it?"

"Four days at least. He won't make it."

"He will! He has to!"

I don't know if my eyes are open or not. I hear the voices, but I don't know to whom they belong. Maybe they're not even real. I understand the words, but the sentences don't make any sense. *Who's making what?* I try to speak, but no sound comes out.

***

"Hold on, Prome. Don't let me down!"

Sounds distorted. What's Prome? Why wake up? So tired. Sleep...

***

Pain! Pain everywhere. Want to shout. Can't.

***

"I've done all I can. He probably won't survive. If he does, he'll be a tough warrior... if he survives the training."

***

I force my eyes open. I feel tired like I've never been before. An old man with white hair approaches me.

"There you are! I didn't think you'd come back. Drink this."

He lifts my head and puts a bowl to my lips. The liquid in it tastes wonderful, sweet and refreshing.

When I'm finished, I already feel a bit better. I look around. I'm in a wide room with rows of simple beds. Several are occupied by heavily bandaged boys and girls.

"Where am I?"

"You're in the infirmary of the agoge. When you arrived nine days ago, you were almost dead. The chimera's poison had spread through your whole body. It's a small miracle you survived."

"And my friends?"

He smiles. "They're already training. There's no slacking here. Sleep. Now that you've woken up, your training will begin in a week." He turns away and walks to attend to someone else.

I really don't feel like I'll be able to train in a week. I lie back down and fall asleep almost immediately.

***

When I wake up again, I feel much more energetic. I try to stand, but I have to hold on to something. I manage to take a few steps, to have a look out of the window. From the position of the sun, it's already late afternoon.

In front of me, a multitude of tents is neatly aligned. Boys and girls in full armor run or walk between them.

"Already up?"

I turn around and almost fall. I catch myself on a bedpost.

The doctor's staring at me. "I expected to find you asleep until the evening, at least, certainly not up and walking."

"I wouldn't call that walking..." I take my hand off the bed but immediately begin wobbling.

"You shouldn't even be able to stand. Back to your bed. Don't overexert yourself for the first day."

I take a last look through the window before walking away.

"You won't see your friends. This is the training camp. Your friends are with the new recruits. You'll all have to earn the right to train."

Back in my bed, I try to formulate a plan. If only I knew the design of the camp, I could slip out of the infirmary and try to find the lab. My first mission: discover the layout of the place.

***

This morning is perfect for a first round of reconnaissance. I'm feeling better. I stand up to test my strength. No problem there. I'm still walking shakily, though. As I reach the end of the row of beds, my knees buckle and I have to grab the frame of a bed so as not to fall.

"Hoy, there! Not so fast. You're not ready for a marathon yet." The doctor comes to me. "If you want to walk, you'll need these." He gives me two crutches. "Seeing how fast you recover, I thought you might need them today. I just thought they wouldn't be used before noon..."

With their help, I can walk much more easily. "Can I go and see my friends?"

"Hmmm." He stares at me. "I guess it couldn't hurt. Archos!"

Barely two seconds after the shout, a boy in his late teens rushes in. He is a head taller than me, has blond hair and twice as many muscles.

"Our new recruit here wants to see his friends. Can you take him to the new recruits' training ground?"

"Hi, I'm Prome."

Archos ignores my hand and turns around. "Follow me."

Okay. So he's not very talkative...

Once outside, Archos stays at my side. The only words he says are "right" or "left." He keeps his hand on his spear, and I have the feeling it's not meant to protect me but to kill me if I try something stupid.

The infirmary is a low gray building in the middle of tents, rows and rows of them. Archos leads me through them to a wooden fence. He signals to the two guards who open the doors to let us through.

On the other side, the sight is a shock. It is not a military camp but a refugee camp. The tents are made of whatever material must have been lying around. Most shelters can't even be called tents. There's no order, no street. It doesn't deter Archos, who simply walks through this shanty town in a straight line, trampling on everything in his path and even destroying some basic constructions with his spear if they stand in his way.

In the middle of these tents, there is a wide, flat sand circle. I can see people hand-fighting. As we come closer, I single out a girl with short light-brown hair from behind. She's fighting with a boy twice her size. It takes her a couple of seconds to send him sprawling to the ground. As she moves to another adversary, she sees me. A smile spreads across her face.

Malia!

She doesn't come to me but keeps fighting opponent after opponent.

I look around and soon find Garbos. He's thinner than I remember him. Unlike Malia, he's eating the dirt as often as not, which is already quite a feat. I wouldn't have bet a dime on him against an angry toddler. Again, I feel both joyful to see him and malevolently satisfied to see him being mistreated.

After a while, training swords are brought in. All recruits stop fighting. I hope Malia will have some time to talk to me. I want to ask her about Nemeos. But, a few seconds later, they're all called to stand in a line and repeat the same moves with their swords over and over again.

My chaperone's growing impatient, and we soon leave. On our way back, I try to see how the camp is organized, and where the Last Era building could be, but I can't see much, mostly tents and high fences.

✳✳✳

Back in my bed, I'm completely exhausted by my little stroll. Some assistant comes in and makes me drink another glass of the sweet liquid.

I wake up in the late afternoon, quite refreshed. I take a small walk around the room without my crutches. None of the windows offers a useful view. The layout of the camp still remains hidden to me.

As I'm staring out of a window, the doctor startles me with a "Hello." I turn around, wondering how he can move so quickly and so silently.

He's standing straight, hands behind his back, smiling. "I see you've recovered. Well, at this rate, I expect you'll be able to start your training tomorrow. This will be your last night here." He turns around and leaves without another word.

Shit. If I want to go exploring, it's tonight or never. Once I've joined the recruits, the camp's fence will seal me out. I take a good look around. Of all the beds, barely a dozen are in use.

I walk around the room again, looking at the other patients. All look very severely injured. I wonder where they put those with lesser wounds. Anyway, I doubt they would notice if I skipped out.

Finding a way out is more difficult. The windows don't open, and there are only two doors out of this room. One to the showers and toilets, and the one I went through with Archos. At least, it makes my choice simple.

***

The night is dark. Through the windows, I can barely make out the tents. It will be easier for me to hide. Earlier, I poured the sleeping draught into a glass I hid in my bed. The doctor didn't notice. He made his last round a while ago, and the room is soundless except for the laborious breathing of one of my roommates.

I tiptoe to the exit. I open the door silently and step out. A soft *whoosh* and the feel of cold metal under my chin stop me.

"Where are you going?" The voice is full of anger.

My heart beats furiously "I... I just needed some fresh air. I can't stand hospitals."

"No one's allowed outside during curfew."

"Sorry, I just arrived. I don't know the rules yet."

"You're the newbie?"

"Yes."

The sharp steel moves away. "Go back to your bed. If you try to come out again, I won't hesitate to use my blade."

I close the door and do as instructed. No unguided tour for me tonight. I drink my medicine and go back to sleep.

***

"You're ready to join the new recruits. Get ready; Archos will take you there."

"Thank you, Doctor."

"Don't thank me. I didn't do it for you. I was just curious to know how long I could prevent you from dying. Against all odds, you didn't."

As usual, he turns around and leaves me. He was looking so serious. I'm quite sure he wasn't joking. How can a doctor be so cold-blooded? I'm already beginning to dislike this camp.

"Follow me!"

I don't have anything to pack. Malia probably kept my bag.

Archos takes me to the same gates in the wooden fence. This time, he doesn't pass through them, though. "Go!" he simply orders me.

As I pick my way through the shelters, I hear the doors close behind me.

CHAPTER EIGHTEEN

When I reach the training ground, the discordant sound of a cracked bell fills the air. Immediately, dozens of kids rush in and form straight lines. The youngest are barely in their teens. The oldest are about my age. I notice Malia and Garbos, and take a place between them in the front row.

"Hi, Malia," I whisper.

"Shh." She doesn't even look at me.

A man in shining armor walks to the center of the training ground and stops, facing us. He must be about thirty years old, but the numerous scars on his face make it difficult to judge. It looks like every inch of his exposed skin is scarred. His stare travels up and down the rows and comes to rest on me.

"You!" he barks. "You're new." He comes to me and inspects me from head to toe. "So, you're the new recruit who survived a meeting with a chimera."

The words ring like an insult, but I hear whispers of awe coming from some kids behind me.

"You were lucky to escape and to survive its poison. But luck won't help you here. The test will take place in a week. You've already lost too many days of training. Let's see what you're worth." He takes a few steps back. "Taeros!"

From the left of the row, a dark-skinned boy comes to stand at my side. He's a head taller than I am and built like an athlete.

"Don't go easy on him. If he's here, he has to be able to fight. Everyone step back! Now, you two! Fight!"

Before I can react, Taeros punches me in the face and sends me crashing to the ground. I roll to the side to escape a kick and then stand up. He's already on me, trying to punch me.

All I can do is move around to avoid his fists. He's too fast and hits me in the ribs. I manage not to fall and take a couple of steps back. I already know I don't stand a chance in a regular fight against him.

As he throws his next punch, I duck and try to knock him over with a swipe of my right leg.

Again, he reacts promptly and jumps to avoid me. A grin spreads on his face, and he assaults me with his legs as well as his fists. I can't avoid being hit. I try to protect myself with my arms, but after a few blows, I'm sprawled on the ground again.

"Stop!"

Our instructor glares at me as I stagger to my feet. "Not much of a fighter. The doc wasted his time saving you. Everyone! In position! Repeat yesterday's stances!"

I take my place near Malia again as everyone spreads out on the training ground. At the instructor's shout, everyone moves as a single man into an attacking stance with a loud "Ha!" I mimic them, silently, so as not to get noticed anymore. Another "Ha!", another stance. I look at Malia to copy her movements. After a dozen stances, mixing attack and defense, they repeat themselves. I learn the stances easily and soon move in step with everyone.

I feel like we've gone through the routine a million times when our instructor stops us.

"Now, groups of two. Repeat all the routines."

Garbos turns to Malia.

"Sorry, Garbos. I'll train with Prome today. I'll show him the routines."

We face each other and repeat the routine, but I start with an attack while she begins with a parry. When I do it to her satisfaction, she teaches me other routines. There are so many I'm soon mixing them all together. I often adopt a wrong stance and get punched or punch Malia. I try to soften my attacks.

Something hits me hard in the face and sends me to the ground. Malia is lying near me. As I try to understand what just happened, a voice booms above us.

"You're not here to play. If you're afraid to take a blow, leave. If you want to stay, fight!" The instructor kicks the ground, sending a shower of sand over us.

Malia's jaw is bright red, already swelling. Judging by the pain, I must look just as bad.

"Fight!" The angry bark is enough to make us start immediately.

Malia's moves are now much faster and more powerful. Each mistake I make calls for an immediate and painful sanction. She even throws me to the ground every now and then. I have to really concentrate to remember the routines.

By noon, I feel like Malia's beaten the crap out of me, but I make very few mistakes. From what I've seen, Garbos is doing much better than me. I feel a pang of resentment.

We only get a very short respite, barely long enough to get a bowl of gruel and eat it.

"Where's Nemeos?" I whisper.

"We did the same as last time," Malia tells me.

There's no time to speak. At least, I know Nemeos is safe, keeping an eye on our weapons and the box.

A warrior comes and throws training weapons on the ground; short swords, long swords, and spears. Another one brings wooden shields.

"Take a weapon and a shield! I want to see what you can do with them!"

I take a shield and a spear, and get a familiar feeling, though the training spear's weight is different. Most of my comrades try to grab a sword.

"Taeros! Want a go with your friend?"

Everyone takes a step back. Taeros comes to me, a long sword in his hand and a mischievous smile on his face.

This time, I know he won't go soft on me. As he takes a step, I crouch and swing my spear in a wide arc. I hit his legs with enough force to swipe them from under him.

He jumps up again, and I poke him in the belly. I swing my spear, trying to hit him on the side of the head, but he jumps back, out of reach.

We circle each other. His face is distorted by hatred. For now, I'm able to keep him at bay. That's my only advantage. If he manages to come close, he'll have the upper hand with his sword.

Suddenly, I see him drop to the ground. Before I can react, he's crouched in front of me. He grabs both my legs in a strong hold and pushes me back with his head.

I can't do anything to break my fall. I'm lying on the ground, and he's towering over me. His sword comes down on me. I lift my spear in front of me in a desperate attempt to block it. Both weapons collide. To my relief, the hilt of my spear doesn't break.

Taeros pushes down with all his might. I won't hold out for long. I kick him with my legs as hard as I can. A howl of pain rewards me. I roll away and stand. I throw my spear as fast as I can, turning in a circle to give it momentum.

The noise as it hits his head is enough to make me wonder if I've just killed him. He's thrown to the ground. He lies there, unmoving. A trickle of blood stains the ground.

I'm too stunned to react. I didn't mean to kill him, I... I feel like throwing up.

"You two! Take Taeros away! He'll be out for a while."

A sigh of relief escapes me. *He's not dead!*

Two young boys take the unconscious Taeros by the wrists and pull him to the side of the training ground.

"Our newbie is full of surprises! The spear seems to fit him. For the rest of you, the choice of your weapon is still to be decided. During the next two days, you will train with spear, sword, and bow. At the end of that period, you'll have to choose the weapon you want to be trained with."

✳✳✳

The rest of the day is just as backbreaking as the morning. We keep repeating sword-fighting moves. I've seldom used the sword, and I feel awkward with one in my hand. When the one-on-one training begins, I feel completely unprepared. Alas, our instructor dispatches us around the ground, and I can't train with Malia.

My partner is a young girl, two heads shorter than me, with short brown hair. She looks barely older than twelve. But, unlike me, she knows all the stances, moves fast, and isn't afraid to hit. Hard. A few minutes later, she's already hit me a dozen times.

I glance around and see that Malia and Garbos aren't doing much better than me. Garbos even manages to let his partner disarm him. His sword goes flying in a wide arc and lands at our instructor's feet. Garbos retrieves it with a crimson face.

The training only stops when the sun disappears over the horizon. I feel like every part of me has tasted the blade. I hurt everywhere and am dead-tired.

Malia and Garbos take me to our sleeping place—a patch of dry mud with our bags and blankets.

I drop on mine. Garbos and Malia walk away. Jealousy, love, and hatred all come back to me as I watch them, walking side by side like old friends. They come back a few minutes later with bowls of food.

I don't even care what it tastes like. I gulp it down and fall asleep as soon as my head touches the ground.

***

"Your hand-fighting training is now over. When you come back after lunch, we'll train with swords."

"I can't believe it's already over," I tell Malia and Garbos a few minutes later, my mouth full of food. "Are we supposed to be able to fight already?" I still haven't mastered all the moves, and Malia hit me more than once during the training.

"You missed several days of training, but you're right. We're not ready yet."

"That's not the point." We both look at Garbos. "Being ready or not, I mean. The training for newbies isn't meant to be complete. It's just there to teach us the basics. The tests will show what we can do with that. Only the best ones will pass; those with natural skills."

It's the first time I've heard about tests. "What happens if we pass?"

"We become trainees."

I frown. "Aren't we supposed to be trainees already?"

"No. Until we pass the first test, we're nothing."

"And those who fail?"

Garbos looks down silently. Malia answers me in his stead. "They're killed."

"What? Why?"

"I guess they think even a poorly trained civilian is too much of a threat."

I can't believe it. "That's..." I can't find a word for it. "Can't they just run away before failing?"

"You missed the welcoming speech. Anyone who's discovered to be missing will be used as prey and hunted down..."

"The Gods' rule," Garbos finishes.

"And if we pass—"

"*Once* we pass," I correct Malia.

"Once we pass, we become trainees. We'll move inside the agoge and begin the real training."

"When is the test?"

"They didn't tell us."

For a fleeting moment, I play with the idea of Garbos failing. But failing concerns all of us. That's not a risk I'm ready to take. "Is there another way in?"

They shake their heads.

I didn't really believe there would be. I've already seen too much of the agoge for that. And even if there were one, there are too many guards around to enable me to prowl and find another box in another secret room.

***

The sword training lasts three long and excruciatingly painful days. Every evening, once the training ends, I grab something to eat, too tired to talk, and fall asleep straight after. Malia and Garbos are hardier than I am and stay up longer.

I've improved, much, even besting Malia, but compared to Taeros, I'm still a beginner.

I have no doubt Malia can pass the test, but Garbos is quite a problem. There's no doubt he is the worst of us. I saw how he did today. He made a few great moves that made me unwontedly proud of him. But for each such move, he blundered ten times. Malia's help doesn't seem to be enough. And, honestly, I wonder if his failure at the test would be so bad. If he's spying on us, as I suspect, we'd be rid of him. Though I don't want to admit how much I'd miss him if he were gone.

The fourth day brings a change. No more swords for us, as we move to archery. This time, Malia's showing unexpected skills. I guess her training to become a priestess comes into account here. I'm not as good as her at controlling my breath and staying calm. She hits the target every time. On my first try, the string slips from my fingers and releases the arrow before I can even aim. The arrow lands a few paces in front of me. I hear a few laughs around me, and I can't blame them. I'm lucky not to have shot myself.

By the end of the first day, Garbos is better than me, but barely. Half of his arrows hit the mark, though none close to the center. The others fly by haphazardly. It looks like Malia has her weapon. She's the best, and will definitely pass the test. As for Garbos and me, we only have the spear left. I have an advantage that should take me through the test, but I can't picture Garbos with a spear in hand.

***

"Malia, did you notice Garbos looks dead-tired?" For our first spear-training day, I managed to pair up with Malia. As long as we make enough of a fighting show and only whisper, we can talk.

"No wonder. He barely sleeps."

I've been too tired to notice anything. "Why?"

"I don't know. He wakes up during the night and walks away. That's why he's up before us every morning. He wouldn't tell me why, though."

We stop talking as our instructor walks by.

"Don't you think he could be—?"

"No!" Malia's voice is a bit too loud. I look around to look if anyone's watching us, but we've been lucky.

"No," she says more quietly. "If you're about to say he's reporting to someone, stop right now. He could have died several times. And without him, I wouldn't have been able to bring you here. He's not a spy. He saved your life!"

Our conversation is ended by a change of partner. Despite what Malia's just told me, I can't disregard the possibility that Garbos is up to something. Waking up during the night when the nights are already too short... And we don't know him. I'll have to keep an eye on him tonight and discover what's going on.

CHAPTER NINETEEN

Malia's mad at me. She saw me watching Garbos during our training. She doesn't say anything, but I know her face too well and her disapproval is written all over it. For once, I appreciate not training with her and being too tired at night to talk.

I haven't found anything yet, though. During the day, Garbos acts perfectly normal, clearly giving everything he has. It's obvious that the spear isn't for him either. As much as a part of me would like to be friends with him, I keep telling myself he's a spy and he'll soon be dead.

Last night, I wasn't able to stay awake to follow Garbos, and tonight is perhaps my last chance to discover what he's up to. I don't feel as sleepy, though. Maybe the effects of the medicine are finally wearing off. I lie down, pretending to sleep. Time passes, and Garbos doesn't move. Eventually, sleep claims me.

***

I wake up alert. It's still night, and around me, everyone's sleeping. I hear the faint shuffle of fabric. I roll over, and sure enough, Garbos is missing. I stand up as noiselessly as I can and follow the sound. Strangely, it doesn't lead me toward the center of the camp or the agoge, but away from everything, toward a large bush. The noise stops for a few seconds, then starts again...

I stealthily approach the bush and look around, careful not to let Garbos spot me.

He's moving his arms and legs deliberately, breathing in rhythm, sometimes freezing in the middle of his strange dance. I really can't make any sense of it. If the dance is a message, why is he doing it where he can't be seen from the agoge or the camp?

I wait a little, trying to understand, waiting to see if someone comes, but nothing changes. His ever-so-slow dance keeps going, uninterrupted.

After a while, I have to admit that no one is coming. I walk back to my bed wondering what his dance means. He may not report to someone, but it still doesn't mean he's not a traitor.

***

"Remember that today you will fight for your life! There will be no mercy for those who fail. You will choose your weapon. You won't have a second choice. By now, you should know where your strength is."

The instructor pauses, glaring at us. He doesn't look at anyone in particular, but I can feel his eyes piercing me to my shaking soul. They carry a threat the words didn't have and make me doubt my choice. Is there even a good choice? Shouldn't we try to run away? I can feel the unease growing around me.

He steps aside, revealing rows of swords, spears, and bows. A low gasp escapes from our group. Even from here, we can see that the weapons are not the training ones, which are designed to inflict minimal harm.

"Choose! Now!"

We all pick one, surreptitiously checking it. They definitely are real—and deadly.

"You will each be pitted against a trainee. If you win, you pass the test. If the trainee wins, he keeps fighting."

Then the only way for a trainee to win is to beat the last of us.

Everybody's too stunned to react, except for Taeros. "Sir, will the trainees be able to fully use their weapons?"

The instructor glares at him, but Taeros doesn't shrink back. I have to admit the guy has guts. And his question is a good one. We can't use the powers contained in our weapons; at least, I'm not supposed to be able to. But trainees can, and if they can use those powers during the fight, it will be severely lopsided.

The instructor smirks. "Yes, they will. You'll fight the worst trainees, those who haven't proven their strength. Those who can't control a weapon properly. For them, as for you, it's either win or die."

Silence ensues.

"Clear the ground. Swords, stay. You'll fight first."

As I take up a place just outside the training ground, Malia joins me. I'm surprised to see Garbos with her, carrying a bow too. Following yesterday's spear-training session, I really didn't expect him to choose one, but a bow? At least with a spear, he would have had a chance to hit his opponent... The spy will die today.

Malia must have read my thoughts again. She elbows me in the ribs and glares at me, until I look back at the trainees-to-be readying themselves.

"Do you think the trainees will kill us? How can we stand a chance against them?" Argos sounds almost scared, and I understand why.

"No, the instructor told us they can't use their weapons."

The second question is answered just as soon. The instructor calls forth the first fight. I don't know the trainee, but the newbie is a thin boy, looking barely older than twelve. I've trained with him once, and he wasn't much of an opponent. Indeed, the fight is over just as soon as it starts. The boy makes a messy attack, the trainee parries, and in a swift movement beats the sword out of his hand and hits him with the flat of his sword behind the head, knocking him out.

The newbie is pulled by a leg out of the ring, and another one is called to take his place.

"He never was a good fighter. I wonder why he came here. He would have lost against a puppet. Look, this one stands a much better chance—"

I don't have time to finish my sentence before the fight is already over and the next one starts. I don't even try to reassure Malia—or myself—anymore and look aghast at the fight.

Two more newbies lose, but with much more of a fight. I haven't trained with them, but I remember seeing Malia doing it. They were good. The first fought well, and exposed the trainee's weaknesses. I could point out a few in the way he moved, or how he protected his lower body. But the newbie either didn't see them or couldn't exploit them. The second one did. He had the upper hand when we saw the trainee's sword emit a faint light as he parried desperately and grazed the newbie's arm. It was probably not much, but it was enough to stun the newbie for a few seconds, long enough to win the fight.

They wouldn't kill us, but being able to use their weapon's power even poorly really made a difference. Although I can use it, I won't be able to. It would raise too many questions, and they'd probably ask them in a very unpleasant way.

The next to fight is Taeros. He enters the ring grinning. The fight starts, and Taeros immediately takes advantage of his opponent's weaknesses. The trainee is hard-pressed and can barely fend off Taeros's blows.

"Why doesn't he use his weapon?"

I look at Garbos, then back at the fight, and it dawns on me. "I think he does."

"What? But why is Taeros still fighting?"

"Look how Taeros fights. The trainee never gets to touch him. Taeros uses his sword as a shield too. It looks like his sword absorbs the other sword's power." I had never thought a weapon could do that, but looking at the fight, it's obvious. How Taeros discovered it is a mystery, though. Maybe just luck during the fight...

For the next couple of minutes, Taeros strikes blow after vicious blow, drawing blood from his opponent, but never disarming him. I can't help thinking that he's just playing, enjoying the pain he inflicts. When he tires of it, he easily parries his opponent's attack and deals him such a hard blow to the head that I'm certain he killed the trainee.

He doesn't so much as glance at his victim and leaves the ring. He walks away, not pretending to be interested in the other fights.

As they pull the trainee to the side, I hear him groan. Somehow, I'm both relieved that he's alive and anxious about what they'll do to him now. I'm not very optimistic.

***

As much as I dislike Taeros, he has a positive effect on us all. He showed us we can win. Trainees can be beaten. After him, many newbies lost, but about as many won.

When the last sword test finishes, it's already well past noon. Archery follows without a pause for lunch, to our disgruntlement. The instructor probably sees it as a reminder that, during a fight, we don't have time for such trivia as food. We see it as another advantage for the trainees, who clearly aren't starved, some even bringing food to eat while they wait for their turn.

The archery test doesn't take place on the training ground but a short walk from it, where a special shooting range has been prepared. Ten targets are hanging from a structure quite a distance from the archer's position. The archers must shoot all of them. But if I've learned anything, it's that it can't be that simple.

"Malia, look. The structure isn't stable. It will probably move."

"Yes, I've seen this. What's bothering me is on the other side of the targets. What's that supposed to mean?"

I watch where she points and see another stand. "Oh shit!"

"What? What's that?" Garbos sounds tense.

"It means that a trainee will stand on the other side of the targets. Malia, you know what it means?"

For the first time, she really looks scared. "The two stands are almost within shooting distance of each other..."

"Yes. The winner will be either the first to hit all targets or the last one able to shoot. You'll have to shoot the targets when they're between the two of you. If you miss, your arrow may hit or at least distract the trainee..." I don't dare say that the easiest way to win would be to aim directly at the trainee...

"If I..." Her voice breaks up.

"You won't hit them. Even if you did, it probably won't be serious. Not from so far away. But keep an eye on incoming arrows. You'll probably have to move around a bit to escape some."

"You over there! You're first!" The instructor points at Malia. She walks to the stand.

"Oh, no, Malia, take a step back!" I murmur.

"Why?"

I had forgotten that Garbos is still here. "Look at the stand. It offers no protection."

"Of course not," he replies, "it's just there to prevent the shooter from walking closer to the target."

"And from moving to the side too. If she takes a step back, she'll lose a little distance to the targets, but she'll be able to move better to evade the arrows of her opponent."

"But she can't do that!"

"Why?"

"That would be against the rules."

I look at him. "There's just one rule: win. Okay, you're not allowed to walk closer to the targets, but have you ever been told you couldn't walk farther from them?"

He thinks a few seconds. "No. I don't think so, no."

"There you are. The downside is that she'll have to come back to the stand to get more arrows..."

Malia and the trainee are ready to start. She's facing a boy, maybe fourteen, with black hair. From where I stand, I can see he's tall and muscular. He won't have a problem shooting an arrow at Malia. He looks confident.

"Shoot!"

Immediately, the structure with the targets begins shaking madly, the targets jumping everywhere.

The trainee shoots his first arrow and hits a target. Malia shoots a second later and hits another one.

"She shouldn't aim at the targets!"

I'm surprised at Garbos's comment. "That's what she's supposed to hit!"

"Yes, but the targets are moving too much. If you look, though, they all cross the line of fire between Malia and the trainee. If she repeatedly tries to shoot him, she's bound to hit the targets and, as you said, distract him if she misses."

The trainee has already shot three arrows and hit as many targets. Malia's only shot two and missed with one.

The trainee's next arrow flies past the targets, right at Malia. At the last second, she tries to move to the side, but bumps against the stand. Luckily, the arrow misses her. I can see she's taken the hint, though. She takes a step back, out of the stand, and keeps walking left and right. She knows that if the trainee can use his arrows properly, if he hits her once, she's as good as dead.

Malia shoots her arrows faster now. She must have come to the same conclusion as Garbos. The result isn't that good, though. Her first arrow hits a target she has already hit. The second misses altogether. The trainee holds his shot to look at the arrow coming. It hits the ground before reaching him, and he resumes his shooting. She keeps on shooting, but when she misses, her arrows all fall too short to bother the trainee, who doesn't even take notice of them anymore.

"They both have hit half the targets each. Now it's up to her speed in shooting the arrows, reflexes in evading those of her opponent, and luck in hitting the targets..."

Count on Garbos to point the obvious.

"Look, the trainee has changed tactics."

I look at him and the change is quite visible. He still shoots at the same fast pace, but he's given up trying to aim at the last targets. He tries to hit Malia instead.

CHAPTER TWENTY

"Hitting the opponent is easier than hitting the last targets." I grit my teeth. I'm still not used to seeing Malia with a weapon. To me, she's still the studious little girl learning to become a priestess. Seeing someone shoot at her... it's unbearable.

Malia spends more time evading arrows than shooting them. And when she does, they don't hit anything. She doesn't get hit, but there are too many near misses. I doubt she can keep on going like this much longer.

The trainee knows she can't hit him and drives her to the far side, making it almost impossible for her to hit the targets, and impossible to get new arrows.

She shoots another arrow at the targets, but from that angle, it rebounds on them. I see her pick up her last arrow. She shoots at the trainee, but it falls short. I can almost hear him laugh at her.

She tries to run to the stand, but he cuts off her path. She plunges to the ground to evade the arrow. This time the trainee takes his time to aim. He's smiling, and my blood is boiling. I'm about to run to her when he launches his arrow. It flies straight toward Malia, lying on the ground. The trainee doesn't even load another arrow.

At the last moment, Malia rolls onto her side and the arrow hits the ground a few paces behind where she had been. In a swift move, she picks it up, stands, and shoots. The trainee doesn't react, sure that it will fall short. But this time, the arrow flies faster than any other she's shot so far.

He realizes his mistake too late. The stand prevents him from moving to the side, and the arrow hits him in his right shoulder.

I hear a cry and see him drop his bow.

Shouts of victory erupt around me, but my heart is still beating too furiously to join in. I realize I've been holding my breath and exhale.

As the trainee is led away, Malia walks back to me. She doesn't smile, doesn't cheer, doesn't display any emotion. I know how she feels.

Hurting someone intentionally is against everything she believes in.

I wish I could hug her, that we could both cry for her torn soul, but such a display of emotion is impossible.

"You don't have to watch the other fights. Go get something to eat."

She shakes her head stubbornly. "No. I want to be with you and Garbos when it's your turn."

Things don't get better. The next newbie, another girl of about Malia's age with black hair, stays in the stand and is hit by the trainee's first arrow. The trainee makes a show of shooting six other arrows in every possible direction. They veer in the air, homing in on their target, and all hit her square in the chest. The fight is over in a matter of seconds.

Our side becomes silent as we all realize the disadvantage we're at. I doubt this will be the last death of the day.

The next fighters have understood the lesson. None stay in the stand. There are many injuries but only one death. The trainees now stop shooting after the first incapacitating hit. Out of all the newbies fighting, only a few win. Two manage to injure their opponent, and five hit all the targets.

One of the newbies hits the trainee and thinks he has won. As he turns away, certain of his win, the trainee manages to shoot another arrow and hits him in the back.

When Garbos's turn comes, Malia whispers encouragement to him. He walks assuredly, but I can see the bow trembling in his hand.

He walks to the stand but doesn't even pretend to take his place in it. He just stays one step behind it, free to move around but close enough to take arrows. He stays as still as a statue, eyes closed.

As soon as the fight begins, the trainee shoots at him. But the change in Garbos is so great, I wonder if it's still him. The fat, clumsy boy I knew has disappeared. For the first time, I notice the clothes hanging loosely around him. I wonder how much weight he's lost since we left Parthenos. But the greatest change is his attitude. He had always been timid, trying to hide as if afraid to be where he was, but now... he's moving around like the most experienced dancer I've ever seen. His feet barely touch the ground while he describes small circles, undisturbed by the trainee's arrows that fly by without touching him. For a moment, impious as I am, I really think that he's been blessed by the Gods.

He lifts his bow and, still dancing, starts shooting. His dexterity is impressive. From the moment he picks up an arrow until he releases it, all his moves are in such perfect synchronicity and harmony that it looks like the arrow itself is a part of him.

The first arrow flies and hits a target. Three steps of his dance and the second one is already taking flight and hitting another target.

The trainee increases his speed, still aiming at Garbos, but Garbos only accelerates the rhythm of his dance. He keeps shooting, and all his arrows are true to their aim. A minute later, the fight is already over. He shot eleven arrows and missed only one, never touching the same target twice.

Cheers fill the air as he comes back to us.

"How did you do that?" I still can't believe what I've just seen.

He blushes and throws a look around, but the other newbies are already paying attention to the next fight. "I've been practicing at night. I read an old book long ago about archery and training stances."

I'm more than a little impressed. "But the way you moved around..."

His face turns crimson. "That comes from another book... Dances that I've been practicing for years. I didn't expect to ever use them. Especially not in a situation like this. I'm very lucky it worked."

Malia and I can't help laughing. "I wouldn't have thought a book could teach so much."

Garbos looks almost pained. "They really can teach lots of things!"

Malia elbows me. "I think you owe him an apology."

Garbos looks at us, flummoxed. I grumble. I still haven't abandoned all my doubts about him, but he certainly just proved me wrong about his little escapades.

"He thought you woke up at night and went off to betray us."

"No! I..." I can feel my face getting warm.

"Yes, you did."

"Okay, I did. Sorry, Garbos."

His face breaks into a wide smile. "Did you really think I could be a spy?" He says this as if he were pleased, and I'm embarrassed to answer.

"Well, yes. I'm really sorry!"

"Are you crazy? It's so cool! No one ever thought I could be more than an attendant. Did you really? I mean... Woooow! I've read so many books about spies..."

He rants on about books and people I've never heard of before, but he's so happy that I don't have the heart to stop him.

***

When the last archery fight is over, the sun is close to the horizon. Our instructor doesn't stop the tests, though. He leads us back to the training ring and, without further ado, calls forth the first newbie with a spear and the opposing trainee.

After a couple of fights, night falls. But even night doesn't stop the test. The moon offers just enough light to see the opponent.

I'm paying more attention to those fights. After all, I might be fighting next. Knowing what a spear is capable of, I'm not surprised when a trainee, a squat dark-skinned girl shoots a bolt. Obviously, she can't use it to its full potential, and her poor aim misses the boy facing her. But the light has blinded him, and she uses the advantage to step around him and sweep him off his feet. A second later, with the point of her spear on his neck, she's declared the winner.

Being temporarily blinded is not an option. We study the trainees who use the spear to create light. They don't close their eyes early enough to be a warning, but I soon notice something else.

"They all have to concentrate to shoot a bolt," I whisper.

Malia looks at me, hopeful. "This will give you a warning to close your eyes."

"That's not much, but it's a beginning. I wonder if they have to do it because they're trainees, or if it's always the case. I've never noticed it before."

"I hope it's always the case," Malia says somberly. "If not, your opponent may not have that problem. We'd better find their other Achilles' heels."

But the next fights don't bring anything new.

There are fewer newbies with a spear than bow or sword, but there are still many fights, until I'm the last one waiting.

The instructor signals for me to come into the ring. I'm waiting for my opponent to do the same, but instead of one trainee, I see two of them, one with a spear and the second with a sword.

"A special test for Miracle Boy. You've survived worse. This should be easy for you. Fight!"

I don't have time to recover from the surprise before the spearman freezes. I only have time to close my eyes and point my spear at him, hoping for it to neutralize the bolt. I expected the same feeble crackle the other trainees had produced, but a thunderous crack deafens me. I open my eyes and see my two opponents exchanging glances, not believing that I'm still standing, unhurt.

Never before has a trainee shot a bolt so early in the fight, and never such a big one. Not only do I have two opponents, they're much better fighters than the others, and they intend to kill me as soon as possible without giving me the slightest chance. I don't know how Garbos managed that trick, but I'm going to kill him.

Okay, forget fairness. Now my small advantage is gone. They know I can counter their bolts. I bet next time the swordsman will create a diversion.

They split and move along the edge of the ring, to get on each side of me. They both come to me at the same time. I manage to fend off the spear and kick back the swordsman, but that was more luck than skill. They repeat their attacks. I jump, roll, and run to get out of their way, trying to find an opening that doesn't exist.

Again, they change tactics and take turns to test me. While I'm fighting the swordsman, I keep an eye on the other trainee for any sign that he's about to shoot another bolt.

With this method, they're wearing me out quickly. If I don't end this soon, I won't be able to resist much longer.

As I'm fighting the spearman, he suddenly looks over my right shoulder. In a desperate move, I turn around, and throw my spear. I hear a loud gasp as the attack of the swordsman is stopped by my spear skewering him in the guts.

Weaponless, I run to him to retrieve my spear.

Now that he's alone, the spearman is less keen to attack me, but I haven't eaten or drunk the whole day, and the first part of the fight has worn me out. I decide to do the unexpected. Instead of my spear, I pick up the sword and run to him. I hope it can resist a bolt. Sure enough, I've crossed only half the distance when he freezes. I hold the sword in front of me, close my eyes, and keep running.

A loud bang erupts again. I open my eyes, still running. I'm almost on him. He reacts too late and misses the chance to impale me on his spear. I have now reduced the distance enough to engage him in close combat. I strike him left and right, as hard as I can. He tries to parry with the hilt of his spear, but its size hinders his reactions. He takes a step back, but I won't let him get away. I keep dealing blows, looking at the fear filling his eyes.

I feint an attack to the right. He moves his spear to stop the blow, giving me the opening I need. I change direction, shift my feet, and hit him on the side of the head with the hilt of my sword.

He falls to the ground on all fours, stunned. I kick him in the face as hard as I can to finish him.

In the pale light of the moon, I see the blood oozing from his nose. I look around at the other trainee. Someone's already pulling him out of the ring.

The instructor is staring at me fixedly. I can't break down. I stare back, then stick the blade of the sword into the ground, and retrieve my spear. I walk back to Malia and Garbos.

"The tests are over. Go to sleep. You'll get your new assignments tomorrow morning."

On our way to our sleeping place, we all were silent. I've killed monsters before, but it's the first time I've killed a human being. I feel like throwing up.

Chapter Twenty-One

I wake up early after a restless night. In my dream, I replayed my fight, killing the trainee with my spear. But when I went to retrieve it, it was Malia lying on the ground, holding the spear sticking out of her belly, breathing raggedly.

Walking and breathing the chill morning air doesn't rid me of the nausea. Killing someone has changed me. I don't know how much yet, but something in me has snapped. I can feel it. It won't mend. I'll have to live with it.

The dream has strengthened my fears for Malia. If anything happens to her, I'll never forgive myself. I found that stupid amulet and caused all this. Now the innocent, joyful girl I used to know is gone. I watched her when I woke up from my nightmare. She was moving in her sleep, shaking. Her face is thinner than I remember, sterner. I crushed her whole life.

I don't know what will happen, but I vow to protect her and make her happy again, give her back the good life I stole from her.

I walk back, determined to do whatever it takes to find the box. And fast.

Garbos and Malia are already up and waiting for me with a piece of bread. I try not to punch Garbos. His archery skills, my two opponents. This time my doubts are gone. I won't let the Gods manipulate me. However much it will hurt me, I have to get rid of him, and it shreds my heart. I'll pretend to trust him until I find an opening.

"Today, we get into the agoge. The longer we stay, the more dangerous for us it will become. I want both of you to stay inconspicuous. This evening, I'll try to discover where the Last Era buildings are. Tomorrow, I'll find a way to get in. I want us out of here before a week is gone."

Garbos and Malia look at each other, smiling, the way two parents do when their three-year-old child announces proudly he'll become a God when he's older.

"What?" I snap.

Garbos looks at me. "You can't be serious?"

"He means that just finding the buildings will take more time than a day," Malia says diplomatically before I can make an angry retort. "The agoge is the size of a small town."

"Okay, then it will take me two or three days, but it doesn't change a thing."

"Do you really expect us to do nothing? We'll help as much as we can."

My temper rises. "No! You keep a low profile. That's not negotiable."

She shakes her head in exasperation, then breathes deeply to calm down. "Prome, you can't do it alone. Either we do it together or we don't do it at all. Besides, you'll need us once inside the building. You don't know what you'll find, and you can't use the box. Only Garbos and I can."

She has a point, but after my dream, I won't give up. "Then, Garbos will come with me. But you stay here." If I have to put a sword on his throat to make him cooperate, so be it.

She rolls her eyes. "We'll see," she says, then turns to Garbos. "First, we'll want a map of the area. Same again?"

Garbos nods. "We'll have the map soon enough."

For the first time, I realize that they must have done quite a lot and taken risks while I was being treated for the chimera's poison. I feel left out.

Malia looks at me. She knows me well enough not to misread my face. "We'll explain it to you this evening. Now we have to hurry."

✻✻✻

We're not the last newbies to reach the training ground, but our instructor is already there, facing us. Behind him is the cruelest sight I've ever seen. Hung by their hands from high poles, about twenty corpses are displayed in a neat row. Some have the innumerable bloody marks of arrows that have killed them. Others are half-charred, as if thunder had hit them. Others are missing limbs. Many have more than one kind of injury.

"Those failed the test and thought they could run away." The instructor doesn't need to shoot. His words pierce the ghastly silence. "Let this be a lesson for all of you. There is no failing, and there is no escaping! Those who failed yesterday and stayed will at least have an honorable death. Now, let's see who passed." He nods to several trainees carrying baskets.

The trainees walk to each newbie, and hand them something small. As one of them gets to us I can see small pebbles, black or white. Malia and Garbos both get a black one. My heart sinks. I expect to get one too, but the trainee passes me by, without giving me anything.

"Now, to my right, those with a white pebble. To my left, those with a black one."

Garbos and Malia look at me hesitantly. I nod to them in encouragement, and they walk away. Having nothing, I decide to stay where I am.

Soon, everyone is staring me. On the faces surrounding Malia, the biggest group, I can see doubt, fear, and bafflement as they surreptitiously peek at their stones and at their neighbors'. Very few look calm. Taeros is one of them, and for once, I'm relieved to see him. I'm certain now that the black stone means they passed.

I look at the other group and immediately spot a kid, maybe three years younger than me, smiling faintly, relieved. I soon spot others. I'm appalled. How can they not understand? They should look at each other. Of course, there are injured boys and girls in Malia's group. But in the white group, most of them are injured, some badly enough to need help to stand.

There's a girl. She looks around twelve, with lovely red curls. She's not injured. She could still learn a trade, marry a nice boy, and have babies. Live a long and happy life.

I recognize one of the boys. He fought with a spear yesterday, and won. It had been a close call, but a win anyway. He's smiling, certain of being on the right side, and suddenly I have doubts. What if winning wasn't enough? What if Taeros was disqualified? Did Malia fail too?

I stop looking at both groups. I can't stand it. Instead, I turn my attention to the instructor.

"You with a white pebble! You're unworthy of Ares. Now, only Hades will accept you!"

I should be appalled by the death sentence, but I'm relieved Malia is safe.

Soldiers in full armor immediately surround them, to prevent any escape.

"Death will be bestowed upon you swiftly. Soldiers! Take them away."

The boy who won shouts, "No! I won! I pass!" A soldier punches him in the gut to shut him up.

Many of them cry as they're led away. I clench my fists in a desperate attempt to control my anger. How can any so-called God let this happen in his name?

"Now, Miracle Boy!"

My head snaps back, and I stare at the instructor, who's now standing just in front of me.

"You fought with a spear, but you failed!"

I'm rooted to the ground. How can he say that! "I didn't lose. I won!"

"No!" he roared. "You fought with a spear, but you lost in the fight. You won, but with a sword!"

He wants to play with words? Fine! But I'm not a little girl, and I have someone to protect.

"There's just one rule: Win! I won!" I didn't intend to shout at him, but I'm too angry to keep my voice under control.

"But you cheated!" He looks amused, taunting me. "You threw away your spear, and you stole a sword! During a fight, you—"

"*Shut up!*" My voice explodes, and he seems taken aback. From the corner of my eye, I see soldiers ready to intervene, but I don't care about them. He's the one between Malia and me. "It was a fight! I did what I had to do to win." I want to punch him in the face.

"But throwing your weapon away would have gotten you killed in a real fight!"

"*Keeping* my spear would have gotten me killed!" *How can he not know it? He's supposed to train us to fight!* "Picking up the sword surprised my opponent and gave me an advantage."

"But that's against the rules!" he barks back.

I feel my fist trembling. I'm about to lose control and assault him. "There are no rules! It's just win or die! And anything's good if it helps you win. You never said we had to fight fair. The trainees certainly didn't! And you'd have been a moron not to pick the sword in my stead!"

Before I snap completely, he turns away and walks toward the newbies. I can see Malia and Garbos, horrified by the scene. Not far, Taeros is smiling, glad to see me humiliated like this.

"Did you hear him? I'm a moron!"

His last word lingers in the air. Taeros's smile widens.

"What did I teach you about your weapon?"

"Our weapon is a part of us. We keep it or we die," all the newbies answer in perfect unison.

I look around and see four soldiers, sword in hand, surrounding me should I do anything. If I'm fast enough, I could reach the first one to my right, get his sword. The one next to him would be easy to get rid of. But the other two will have time to prepare and...

I notice that soldiers three and four are not in a position to attack. I quickly glance again at the other two. None of them is ready to attack. Something's off. My anger is changing to confusion. At the same moment, the soldiers take a step back and relax.

The instructor, who had turned his head to look at me, faces the group again.

"But he's right! In a fight, there is only one rule: Win!"

I can see Taeros's smile falter.

"And you have to take advantage of anything that can help you win! I would have done the same! And anybody who wouldn't have, wouldn't be just a moron, but *a dead moron*!" He shouts so loud, some of the newbies flinch.

He comes back to me. "What's your name?"

"Prome... sir," I add in a second thought.

He turns around. "I only learn the names of the recruits worthy enough to become great soldiers. That's the best reward you'll get from me!" He glares at me. "But I can also forget it. And if you ever call me a moron again, I'll kill you! Now, join the others!"

As I walk back toward a clearly relieved Malia, I notice Taeros, an expression of loathing on his face.

"Follow me!" The instructor leads us through the wooden gate, then through rows of tents, away from where the hospital is. After many turns, we reach an empty space as big as the marketplace at home.

I feel a pang of longing at the thought.

"You are not yet trainees. You'll have to pass another test first! This is your new training ground. Your quarters are just there." He points at a long tent on the far side of the training ground. "For the next few days, you'll be either training here or sleeping in the tent. Stray anywhere else, and you'll be killed!"

The instructor leaves, replaced by a hoplite, who explains to us what will happen from now on. The next test will take place in three days. It isn't good news. During those three days, we'll learn how to use the weapons' powers. If, by the third day, one of us can't use their weapon correctly without it, they will fail the test.

The training will take place every afternoon. If any of us thought we'd be able to sleep late, the illusion doesn't last long. Mornings will be used to strengthen our bodies: wake-up call one hour before sunrise, then two hours running, a light breakfast, and more endurance and strength training until noon. The afternoons won't be that easy either. First, we'll have combat training like we used to, then what is ironically called "power training," as if the rest of the day is just light training... And after that, we'll train to fight until nightfall.

The hoplite in charge of us during our morning sessions seems eager to begin. As soon as he's finished talking, he makes us run for an hour around the ground as a warm-up before a tiny breakfast.

By noon, he has us so exhausted we barely notice our hunger.

The power training has us all on edge. It's what the test will be about. Our instructor is back with a crate of light silver gloves. They're supposed to help the connection between us and our weapons.

Practice archery targets are installed at one end of the ground, and spearmen are to train at the other end with a dummy. Swordsmen will train in the middle. I won't be able to talk to Malia and Garbos, and with the swordsmen in between, I can barely see them.

"Put your gloves on! Feel your spears and shoot the dummy!"

When I take hold of my spear with the glove on, the feeling is so unexpected I drop it. I quickly pick it up with my bare left hand, but not without amused looks from my fellow newbies and a very annoyed one from our training hoplite. At least our instructor didn't see me. He'd probably have forgotten my name right away.

I hold it with my glove-free hand, and approach it with my other hand carefully.

As soon as the fabric touches the spear, I feel it again. It's like the spear and my hand have merged together. I can't even tell where the limit between them is. I release the spear, and the feeling disappears, only to reappears when I take hold of it again. I try to keep my hand clasped around it and move one finger after another. They comply without problem. But there's that new... *spearly* finger with them. I'm sure I can use it too, but it radiates so much strength, I'm afraid to fire it, lest I blow up the whole agoge.

"I told you to shoot!"

I snap out of my thoughts. The hoplite glares at me. I nod and point the spear at the dummy as if I were trying to shoot it. I look around and see no one getting even a tiny spark, so I feel quite safe pretending but not doing anything.

The hoplite keeps giving us orders like "picture what you want to do," "feel your spear," or "once you get a link with your spear, concentrate on it."

I wish he'd tell me how to weaken the link instead... I can't help snorting when he tells us not to try to bend the spear to our will, but to show it what it needs to do. Luckily, he misinterprets my reaction. I get another annoyed look, though.

By the end of the training, every newbie is sweating with the effort. For once, I'm glad it's so warm today: despite my lack of effort, I'm just as wet as them. Alas, most of them have managed to get at least a spark. One even shot a weak bolt that hit the target. If they all improve that fast, I'll have to find a way to bridle my spear.

And soon.

CHAPTER TWENTY-TWO

"How did you do?" I don't dare raise my voice above a whisper, though everyone around us is busy eating.

"Garbos managed to shoot a second arrow without aiming."

I look at Garbos, barely surprised. One more proof of his treachery. Malia doesn't look up from her plate, and I feel something's wrong. "What did you do?"

"Nothing."

"Malia, please! Tell me!"

"I didn't manage to do anything. I can't feel anything special about that stupid bow!" Tears are glistening at the corners of her eyes.

"It's okay, Malia. You still have two days to train. I'm sure you'll do it."

"I told her that."

Malia clenches her teeth, glaring. Garbos looks down at his empty plate and walks away.

"How did you do it? I mean, you didn't have a glove before. What did you do to use it? Can't you teach me?"

"I just... didn't think." I see puzzlement on her face and try to explain better. "When I tried to think about what I wanted it to do, it didn't work. The first times I shot a bolt, it was inadvertently. Don't try to do it. Treat it as if you're just moving your hand, or blinking." I don't know how to make it clearer. It doesn't brighten her mood. Garbos is coming back, so I decide to change the subject. "I'll wait for everyone to fall asleep and then I'll go scouting the camp."

Garbos looks up, alarmed. "Don't!"

"Why? We have to find the box!"

Malia answers me. "We've tried to step out of the training ground today, but every time, a trainee sent us back before we had taken more than a step. They really won't let us out."

"But that was during the day. Tonight will be different."

Garbos points to the right with his spoon. "See over there, in front of the tent?"

It's already too dark for me to see much. I only make out a shape. "You mean that trainee?"

"It's not a trainee but a full soldier. He hasn't moved at all since we arrived. I'm certain he's a sentry, and there are many of them around the place. I noticed others this morning on our way here. The watch is too tight for us to move around unnoticed."

I don't like that. "We'll have to find a way."

"For now, Malia and I have managed to make a rough layout of the place. At least, part of it." He draws a rough circle in the dirt. He marks what I understand to be the door, then a line turning to the left to a small square. "This is the gate we came through to get here. That's the training ground."

I draw another small square, this one to the right of the entrance. "This is the hospital."

Garbos nods and resumes his drawing. "In between, it's just trainees' tents as far as we can see." He points to a place closer to the center. "Over there, the tents look different. It must be the soldiers' quarters."

"Our guess is that the agoge is made of concentric circles. Trainees on the outside, then soldiers," Malia says, "and probably the command in the middle. No sight of a building yet. I bet they're right there." She draws a cross right in the middle of the circle.

"It makes sense. But if you're both right, it means we won't be able to even get close to it before we're soldiers..."

"I hope we'll find an opportunity before that."

"So do I. I won't rely on luck alone, though. I'll give it a try tonight." Malia's face makes me add quickly, "I'll be careful. If I see it's too dangerous, I won't come back."

***

I wake up silently, determined to go out. If anyone sees me, I'll pretend to be too upset about the training... Everyone around me is asleep. I walk to the door of the tent and take a peek outside. I immediately retreat as I hear footsteps. I listen until they go away, and then take another glimpse. The soldier's not to be seen to the left, but as I look to the right, I see a sentry not far away. I move toward one of the walls of the tent and lift it to take a peek. Two sentries are keeping watch. Garbos is right. There's no way to go anywhere.

***

The next day begins before dawn as a soldier shouts for us to be ready in two minutes on the training ground.

"Come on, Garbos, hurry up!" Malia's already dressing.

Garbos and I dress quickly. When we reach the training ground and assemble with the others, Garbos still looks half-asleep. After having run twice around the place, he's wide awake and keeping pace with Malia and me. Again, I wonder at the change in him. A few weeks ago, he would have been panting, unable to run anymore.

Today goes on much as yesterday did. The closer we get to the power training, the more nervous I am, and by Malia's expression, I'm not the only one. After lunch, we separate for the training without a word.

As I put my glove on, I see that today's soldier isn't the same as yesterday's. This one is a head taller than me, with dark skin. He looks at us all in turn. When he sees me, I think I see the beginning of a smile. I must be mistaken.

After two hours of training, most of the newbies can at least create a sparkle, and many shoot small bolts. I'm among the few who can't, afraid to lose control of the spear.

The hoplite comes to me. "Don't try to force anything. Try to see your spear as a tool: a screwdriver, for instance. You have it in your hand. But when you twist your hand, it's not your hand that acts upon the screw, it's the screwdriver. When you do it, you don't think about the screwdriver, do you? Now use the same method with your spear."

I'm completely startled by being addressed nicely. Of course, he's off the mark as far as I'm concerned, yet his explanation is closer to what I feel than yesterday hoplite's. I'll try it with Malia when I see her if she hasn't managed it yet.

"Concentrate."

I am concentrating. But I can't tell him I'm not doing it to shoot a bolt but to try to shoot a tiny one... *If only I could take off that bloody glove.*

Of course, no bolt.

"Do you see that boy over there?" He points behind me at the spearmen.

Turning around, I can't miss who he's pointing at. Taeros.

"He managed to use his weapon after a handful of minutes. He's getting better at it. I bet by the end of the day, he can do it without the glove."

Taeros needs a second of concentration to use his weapon, I notice.

But he's making a show of stunning newbie after newbie by touching them with his sword. He probably has orders just to stun them and not hit them hard, but each time one falls down, he grins. And when he thinks no one sees him, he doesn't miss a chance to hit harder or kick the poor newbie lying on the ground.

He clearly enjoys it.

It's disgusting. Oh, how I'd like to shoot a bolt at him, just to teach him a lesson!

"Now, turn around. You see the dummy? This is Taeros! *Shoot him*!"

The shout triggers my outrage before I can react. A loud crack shakes the air at the same time as a bolt hits the dummy.

I curse myself for being so stupid. Charred pieces of the dummy are scattered around.

"Wow! That certainly was a bolt!" The hoplite, along with every newbie, is looking at me. I don't look behind, but I'm pretty sure that the swordsmen and bowmen are also staring.

I try to look as surprised as they are. "How did I do that? I didn't mean to!"

"Yes, you did. We found a trigger. If you can do it again, we'll try without the glove."

I take my stance again. As nothing happens, people go back to their own training.

"Imagine this is Taeros. Shoot him again."

I'll have to do it again eventually. Why not now, while the hoplite thinks it's thanks to his advice?

I breathe deeply a couple of times to calm down. I guess shooting the same bolt would be okay, but not a more powerful one. I concentrate on my spear, as if it were one of my fingers. Just a twitch. A small twitch.

Another crack, but not as loud. My bolt hits the dummy, but this time the dummy stays up. I feel so relieved, I smile.

The hoplite misreads my smile. "Not as good as the first one, but still impressive. Now take off your glove and try again." He then moves to the other newbies.

Someone shouts behind me, and I turn around to see Taeros standing over a newbie who's lying on the ground. He's looking at me, seething.

I don't care about his stupid grin. I'm too happy to be rid of that silly glove. And now it's okay for me to relax for a while and just pretend I can't shoot without it while looking for a way to shoot smaller bolts.

As I take my spear in my now-bare hand, I can still feel its power, but not as strongly. I wonder if my control of it is better. It feels so.

I aim at the target, feigning concentration, and give the smallest twitch of my spear-finger.

Instead of a bolt and thunder, I get something looking more like a thread of sparks flying from the tip of my spear to the dummy.

Wow! I feel shivers running on my skin. *I can control the spear!* I wish I could run to Malia, but I'll have to wait for the end of the day to see her.

***

"I still can't do it!"

Malia's face is hidden in her hands, and I have a sick feeling growing in my guts. If she fails the test tomorrow, they'll—

No! I can't think about it!

"You have to!" I tell her about the screwdriver. Maybe it will help her.

"Garbos told me something like that before, but even so, I can't do it!"

Unlike her, Garbos can use his bow. His only problem is the long time he needs to concentrate to use it properly, but he should still pass the test. He's the scholarly one. If he can't teach her, how am I to help? Why isn't it the other way around? I don't care if he fails. It would even make my life easier. But Malia...

I glance at Garbos. He looks miserable and leaves us alone. I feel a pang of remorse, but I can't be friendly with him.

"Listen, Malia." I take her hands and force her to look at me. "Tomorrow, you'll do it. Don't think about succeeding or failing. Just do it as if you had done it a thousand times before, without thinking. And if you fail, we'll make a run for it. I'll have my spear. I'll blow them all out."

She smiles wanly. "I know you would, but you can't. You have to find the box!"

"But you're my priority. I don't give a damn about the stupid box! I'll get you out, and we'll find another way to get it."

"Prome..." She fondles my cheek. "They have my mother. You have to save her. Promise me that if I fail tomorrow, you'll keep on looking for her!"

It sounds ominously like a last will. A lump blocks my throat. I can't promise her that. I can't let them kill her.

"Prome, please. Promise me." A tear runs down her face.

"We'll run away tonight… We'll find her together… We'll…"

"You know it's impossible. Please, Prome, promise."

I can't. I can't stand to look at her like this, and I can't lie to her. I stand up and walk out of the tent.

Without thinking, I walk in the dwindling evening light to the only place I know and stand there, unmoving, the lump in my throat sending waves of pain through my whole body.

The dummy is as tall as me; a wooden puppet blackened by our bolts. And each black spot is a blaring insult. The whole puppet is silently taunting me.

See how you shoot me! All the efforts you make not to destroy me with one of your bolts! But mighty as you are, you're not even strong enough to help Malia! You can't even show her something as easy as hurting me! She'll die because of you!

I punch it. My fist crunches on the hard wood, but I don't register the pain.

She'll die because you're so dumb!

I punch it again.

You promised to protect her, but you never meant it!

"Shut up!" I hit it with my right fist, with my left. I kick it to make it shut up. I punch it and kick it again as hard as I can. And again. And again. I know there must be pain, but I'm too numb to feel anything. I just kick and punch my rage into the dummy.

Without realizing it, my body has slipped into its well-rehearsed routines. I punch, block an imaginary kick from the dummy, reply with a left uppercut, block again. I don't have to think; my body knows what will come next and reacts to it.

Eventually, my rage wears off. The sweat and the exhaustion soothe me. I've felt them so much these last days, they have gotten familiar. Safe.

I begin to feel the strain in my shoulders, in my thighs. I'm breathing heavily. But I feel better. I won't explode, nor will I cry. I will just stay strong. For myself, but, most of all, for Malia.

To that unmoving piece of wood, I make the promise I haven't been able to make Malia earlier. I'll save her mother.

CHAPTER TWENTY-THREE

Malia's standing silently among the other archers. She doesn't move. From where I stand, among the spearmen, she could be a statue, not even breathing. We woke up together, ran together, ate together, always side by side, not talking, barely acknowledging the other in a sort of silent truce.

Garbos is next to her. He's been trying to talk to us but has long given up. He keeps looking sideways at Malia. He looks worried for her, but I know it's just an act. He doesn't really care about us. Not that way. I'll have to get rid of him as soon as I can. If I get the chance during training, I'll shoot him with my spear or break his neck. It's his fault if Malia dies today.

Well, maybe not. There's still hope. She can still pass the test. I have to believe she can.

This time, spears go first, then swords, and bows last.

"Prome! You'll go first!" The instructor is back. At his side, I recognize the dark-skinned hoplite who trained us, and two others who must have trained the other groups.

I nod, then turn to face the dummies.

Except that they're not there. There's just a boy. I turn to the instructor. What am I supposed to shoot at? With a small jerk of his head, he tells me to look back.

There's still no dummies, only the boy. He's such a mass of filth and dried blood I can't tell the color of his skin. Only his green eyes make him look human. Barely. He stands there, looking through me as if I weren't here. He's taller than me, and bulkier. If he chose to fight me, I'm not sure I'd have the upper hand without my spear. But he doesn't fight, he doesn't react. I don't know what they did to him, but he's resigned to die.

The truth dawns on me. I don't have to look at the instructor to know what he expects from me. I can feel his eyes on my back.

In my throat, the lump that hasn't left me since yesterday evening is bigger than ever. Just breathing is painful. But there's another set of eyes on me. And I can't fail them. I've made a promise I intend to keep.

I lower my spear. I concentrate. This time I need to. I want the bolt to stun. I'm not ready to kill. Not like that. Not even someone who's already given up.

Crack!

The thunder doesn't roll in the air. It vanishes before the boy hits the ground.

I want to run to him, make sure he's still alive, tell him I'm sorry. Instead, I look at two soldiers pulling him away.

I trudge to the side of the training ground, behind the other spearmen waiting as the next one takes my place and another target is brought.

This is another boy, but much smaller. He's as bloodied and filthy as the other, but his hair still stands out. The red is so bright even the dirt clogged in it can't hide it.

The sight hits me harder than a punch in the guts. He's the boy I saw after the last test, being led away.

They didn't kill the ones who didn't pass. They're making us kill them now!

I throw up so hard, black spots dance in front of my eyes when I open them. One of the trainees turns to look at me, disgusted.

I don't know how I manage to stand through the test. Some targets—I can't bear thinking of them as people—try to run away but are pushed back by soldiers. Some are killed by bolts, but many aren't as lucky. A girl's clothes are set on fire by a messy shot. The soldiers don't even extinguish them as they take her away. Many are so badly hurt the air is filled with the smell of burnt flesh. The soldiers pull away the moaning bodies.

We discover that there won't be a pebble ceremony this time.

A boy about my age fails to shoot a bolt. Two soldiers immediately take his weapon away and place him as the next target.

It's mass murder. And I'm revolted to see some spearmen take delight it.

I stand, but I don't look anymore. I try to shut everything off. The images of boys and girls falling, of charred bodies. The sound of thunder and the cries and whimpers that follow. The smell that gets stronger and stronger.

Swordsmen replace spearmen and the sickening smell eventually drifts away, only to be substituted the metallic smell of blood. They don't just stun, they hack, they chop.

A girl, unable to use her weapon's power, throws herself on her prey, shouting. A soldier comes and stuns her. She falls on top of her victim's barely recognizable body, in a pool of gore.

And the test goes on.

Of course Taeros passes, though for once he doesn't give any wicked blows. He just touches his target lightly. He seems almost gentle. The girl stiffens and falls without a cry. I'm certain she's dead.

Another newbie, another target. Some fail, some succeed. I don't care.

Another newbie, this one with a bow. My torpor lifts off somewhat, replaced by my fear for Malia.

The target isn't like the others. Her skin is clean. It's harder to pretend this target isn't human. I hear her sobbing and I look at her more closely. She's crying, but it's not what makes my guts turn to lead.

She used to have a spear in her hand. I remember her. I've trained next to her. And today she failed the test.

The first arrow flies and hits her under the left shoulder.

Another piercing shout of agony.

The archer turns to his left to face another target. That's another punishment. If the archer fails, he'll kill two newbies instead of one.

He shoots another arrow.

Instead of flying straight, the arrow describes a curve to the right and hits the first target again. Another arrow follows and hits the heart, killing the girl almost mercifully.

And the game continues, even crueler than before.

When it's Garbos's turn, I see his hand shaking. When he agreed to become a spy, did he know he would have to kill? Has he already killed?

Despite his trembling, his first arrow hits the boy facing him between the eyes. So the spy is not heartless. He doesn't inflict useless pain. His next arrow hits the dead body sprawled on the ground, after turning in midair.

The next newbie, a girl, fails the test. She's hit both targets but kills neither of them, and their cries are maddening. She is so defeated that she doesn't react when a warrior takes her weapon and moves her to be the next target.

Another newbie comes forth without hesitation. His first arrow hits her in the belly. Her shriek makes my skin crawl. Why didn't he kill her with his first arrow?

He turns to his left, unmoved by his victim's pleas. Two seconds of concentration later, his next arrow takes flight. It curves its flight inward, but not enough, and misses the girl by some distance.

I hear concerned whispers around me. Everyone thought it was all or nothing. Now a new way of failing has been discovered.

The boy tries to run away, but some soldiers kick him to the ground, bind his hands and feet, and then drag him back.

Malia is last to go. She approaches with reluctance. The boy is crying, pleading for his life.

And I know that, even if she could use the power of the bow, Malia wouldn't be able to shoot him. Not the Malia I know. Not the one who treated me when I was hurt or sick. Not the one who wanted to become a priestess to beg the Gods to bestow their blessings upon all who suffer.

Her first arrow lands at the foot of an astounded boy. Her next one flies straight and hits the ground at the feet of her other target.

"Bring all the leftovers!"

A dozen soldiers immediately obey the instructor's order. Malia and five other boys and girls are brought in front of us.

"All of you are now trainees!" He doesn't need to speak loudly. Even the boy who failed before Malia is quiet, trembling like a leaf. "Tomorrow, you will be paired with a soldier who will become your trainer, and your nemesis. They'll be in charge of you. Step out of line and they'll punish you. Don't expect them to be softer than me! If I judge they haven't punished you enough, I'll punish them for it! They'll have one year to make a real soldier of you. At the end of the year, you will face your final test."

He pauses long enough to look at each of us.

"Now, about them!" He points at Malia and her group. "They are failures. They're useless, and they endanger us all. How do we treat failures?"

"We kill them!" comes the answer from the trainees.

"We use them to our advantage."

"Who said that?"

Everyone looks around to see where the outrageous comment came from.

From among the archers, Garbos steps forward.

"And what advantage could they be to us?"

"They can do chores, like cooking, cleaning..."

"We have slaves for that. They're much more obedient and, should they rebel, they're easier to dispose of. So what advantage could we have keeping those pariahs?"

Garbos doesn't answer. He had a good idea; it was worth a try. But all the instructor's interested in is military. To save them, they would have to be of use during a fight...

I push aside the trainee standing in front of me and step forward. "We could use them during a fight." *Think of something... Fast!*

The instructor seems amused. "And what can they do that a seasoned fighter who's spent years training can't do?"

Years training... That's it. "As you just said, a soldier takes years to train. Losing one is costly. They—" I point to the group who failed "—cost nothing. If we suspect a trap, we can just send them first. Use them as cannon fodder." To get sympathy from the other trainees, I add quickly, "Rather them than me."

"Return to your ranks, both of you!"

As I turn to obey, I glimpse a tiny nod from Garbos and he mouths a silent thank-you. I don't know what game he's playing, but if his idea works, he'll have won at least a respite for Malia.

A little speech later, the idea is adopted. Malia will do the chores in the agoge until she's needed in a fight.

***

"Trainee Prome!" The tall, dark-skinned soldier who trained me is walking to me, sword in hand. "From now on, I'm your trainer. I'll show you your new quarters. Follow me." He starts off, running.

I follow him. "My bag's in..."

"You won't need it anymore. You're a trainee now. Everything you'll need is already waiting for you."

I have nothing of importance in my bag anyway. I'm glad I took the risk of keeping my only worthy possession around my neck at all time.

We run a half circle to the opposite side of the agoge. In this part, all the soldiers are swordsmen, and it baffles me when he stops in front of a faded, red tent and enters it.

I follow him in.

The tent isn't big. Just enough to hold two sleeping mats and offer a little room to move around. At the foot of my mat is a pile of clothes.

"My name is Pyrias, but outside this tent, you call me either Sir or Trainer." He smiles, and we shake hands. "Now, put on your tunic and I'll show you around. Training will resume tomorrow morning."

As he doesn't move, I turn my back to him to undress. I try to hide my amulet.

"What's that around your neck?"

Shit!

I put on my tunic and turn around. "It's just an amulet I wear for protection."

"Well, it's not against the rules to wear one, but don't let others see it. A few years back, two trainees got in a heated argument about which God granted the best protection. The argument broke into a fight. They were both executed the next day. Remember that we're here to serve all the Gods!" In a softer tone, he adds, "But of course, favoring Ares or Nike wouldn't hurt..." He winks.

"We'll run the full circle. I'll show you the different quarters, where to eat, to wash, and the hospital, though you already know where that is." He becomes serious. "Yes, your story's already been round the whole place, but don't rejoice. You've become some kind of challenge. Many soldiers will want to confront you, to see if you can survive them. I don't expect them to try before you've had a little more training, though. You should be okay for the next month, depending on how you do during training. And believe me, you'd better be a fast learner!"

Good thing I won't be here in a month, then.

We start running again. We come across a few trainees. We're all dressed in the same tunic now, but they all have a sword at their belt. Around us, all the soldiers are swordsmen, even Pyrias.

We keep running and, suddenly, swords are all replaced by bows. The same happens again a bit later, and I'm finally surrounded by fellow spearmen.

"The trainees' quarters stop here. Now it's just soldiers' quarters."

As it turns out, the soldiers' quarters take up about half the agoge.

When we're finally back to our starting point, he runs toward the center, but stops before we can even see it. In front of us, two spearmen block the way. Behind them, the tents are an immaculate white.

"This part is only for the officers. If you trespass in this area without being called for, you'll be executed. Only the soldiers on duty there are allowed."

The design of the agoge is simple, as Malia and Garbos had suggested. The agoge is round, and the tents are packed in blocks separated by streets forming concentric circles. From the center, four avenues form a cross. The buildings we're looking for are probably right in the center. Finding a way to get there will be the next step.

Once back to our tent, I can't help asking something that's been bugging me since we began our tour. "Why am I in the swordsmen's quarter?"

He smiles. "Because I'm a swordsman and you have to stay with me."

"But I'm the only spearman here. There must be a mistake."

"No. I chose you. It's quite unusual, but not unheard of, that a trainer chooses a trainee with another kind of weapon. You're the only one for now."

I'm surprised to hear that he picked me. "Why me?"

He smiles. "I was at the first test results. I saw how you judged the swordsmen around you, ready to attack the instructor if he sentenced you to death. Then I saw your first bolt." He pauses. "And I also saw you win with a sword. It won't be easy, but I'm sure that with your spear and my skills, you can best all the other trainees."

CHAPTER TWENTY-FOUR

Pyrias wasn't lying. I don't know how I survived the last ten days.

When I woke up the next morning, I thought I had it good. I saw how many other trainers rough-handled their trainees. Pyrias didn't hit me. But when the training began, the illusion quickly vanished.

Instead of running to the training ground and around it a few times to warm up, like every other trainee did, Pyrias made me run the longest circular street twice. He then put a weight in each of my hands and made me run the full circle twice more, the second time because the first had taken too long.

After a minute breakfast, we went to the training ground. There, I was rewarded for my early run with a series of push-ups, squats, and many more exercises to "strengthen my body and improve my agility and endurance." They were so effective that by noon I had no more endurance or agility whatsoever, and I was, rightly so, certain my body would ache all over before nightfall.

The afternoon began with two hours of power training, before spear training. Pyrias went all-out on me, and each mistake I made was painfully punished. I quickly learned how not to make those mistakes twice.

Each following day has been the same since.

***

"You're really improving faster than I thought."

I don't agree with him. He still breaches my defense easily, whereas I can't find a hole in his. I don't answer but just lift a brow. We're sitting on our mats, and I'd rather fall asleep than listen to a pep talk.

"Yes, you are. Now you react faster when I find an opening. You stalled me twice. Your reflexes are better. You're also faster and stronger. Your body's adjusting."

Another lifted eyebrow.

He laughs. "It is! See? You're not asleep yet. Five days ago, you fell asleep before touching your mat."

"That was just to gain a few extra seconds of rest." I lie down. "Good night." I close my eyes, unwilling to make petty conversation.

"I know you think I'm pushing you too hard, but you don't have much time left before someone challenges you. You'll be ready..."

He means well, but the training isn't the only thing that's stressing me. These past days, I got a few glimpses of Garbos training with a dark-haired girl, but I didn't see any signs of Malia. I know she's here somewhere, but not knowing if she's all right is killing me. Especially as I'm no closer to finding the box than I was when I last saw her. The center of the agoge is a fortress inside a fortress, and I don't have a second to myself to find a way in.

I feel like I'm letting Malia down.

Again.

✳✳✳

It turns out the month Pyrias had predicted has just been shortened to a fortnight. Finding a dead snake with its head cut off in front of our tent in the morning isn't a nice surprise. Pyrias warned me of the way to challenge someone, but the discovery still freezes my blood. The hunting season is open, and I'm the main prey.

"Why are you standing... Oh." Pyrias doesn't look very surprised. "I knew it was coming, but I hoped we'd have more time. Come, we'll talk while we run."

He sets off at an easy pace. "The challenge comes from Thelya. Her trainee arrived five months ago. He's not good. He barely escaped being chosen for your first test. Thelya must be anxious for him to prove his worth, and so she's rushing things. The challenge will take place just before sunset tonight. We'll take it easy today, and I'll prepare you for it."

The training is, indeed, much lighter than in previous days, and focuses on the coming fight. My opponent is Olias, an archer. He's two years older than me, but shorter. According to Pyrias, his aim is very good, but he takes too long to shoot an arrow.

Pyrias introduces me to a girl. She's taller than me and built like an ox, with very short black hair, but has one of the prettiest smiles I've ever seen.

"Artridia, this is my trainee, Prome. He was challenged by Olias this morning. Care to help us?"

At once, she's all serious. "Your trainee's too new here. You could ask for a delay."

"It wouldn't help. Challenges would pile up. We have to take this one now."

"You know you're probably headed for the Grand Slam?"

Pyrias nods. "And I hope to stop it there. At least for now."

"What's a Grand Slam?"

Artridia turns to me. "It's when a trainee is challenged by a bowman, a swordsman, and a spearman. If you succeed at your first challenge, that is." She stares at Pyrias. "Can he do it?"

"Yes."

A wicked grin twists her mouth. "Then let's train him to kick Thelya's butt."

"Don't you mean Olias's butt?"

"Prome, a trainer and his trainee are a pair. Whatever one does affects the other. You're too new for a fully trained soldier to challenge you yet, so that is the only way for Thelya to fight you. You beat Olias, you beat her."

"And you don't want to lose to Thelya! Understood?"

Artridia's glare warns me that if I don't win, soldier or not, she'll be my next challenger.

I gulp and nod.

"Let's go!"

✳✳✳

Our training session takes place outside the agoge, allowing us to have as much free space as we need without risking injury to someone.

Fighting with an archer is both difficult and easy. Difficult, because we're allowed to use our weapon's power. Although we're forbidden to kill during a challenge, that rule is more flexible for archers. And if I get hit once, I'll be killed. Easy, because my opponent isn't a close-range fighter, and if I elude the arrows and close the distance, victory will be mine.

The first part of the training is just about dodging arrows. Despite her build, Artridia isn't to be taken lightly. She shoots arrows faster than any trainee I've seen, and they fly straight to their goal. Dodging them from the other side of the training ground is easy, but from half the distance, the arrows are too fast for me. Although Artridia uses headless arrows that won't injure me, they still hurt like hell.

After getting hit in the neck by a nasty arrow that had me struggling for air for a minute, I try a different approach. "Why don't I shoot her from here if I'm allowed to shoot?"

Pyrias laughs. "You'll need months of training before you can shoot someone at that distance, trust me. But feel free to try."

Artridia isn't much farther than the rock I shot another lifetime ago. I'm certain I can hit her. But Pyrias is right, even if not for the correct reasons. I can't do it. From that far away, I'd have to shoot a powerful bolt, and I don't know if I can make it mild enough to just stun her. And, of course, I can't show anyone that I can do these things I'm not supposed to. I don't know how Pyrias would react.

"Okay, I'll dodge in order to come closer, then."

I retrieve Artridia's arrows and start from the beginning again. She has five quivers of twenty arrows, and I have to reach her before she shoots her last one. During the challenge, after that, it's a draw, and a draw means more archers will challenge me. I have to get a clean win.

By midafternoon, I manage to close two-thirds of the distance between us, but that's not enough. My bolts are supposed to be feeble ones. Besides, I don't want to risk killing my opponent. I just want to stun.

There I go again. I jump to the right and avoid five arrows. Suddenly, the ground slips under my foot as I jump to the side to evade another arrow. The arrow flies over my head as I fall to the ground, but another one is flying straight to me. Without thinking, I shoot it. By some miracle, the bolt hits it, and the arrow explodes in the air.

"How did you do that?" Pyrias shouts, running to me.

"I shot it," I reply, still recovering from my lucky escape.

"I saw that. But how did you do it so fast?"

"What?" The question is stupid. How can I make a bolt faster or slower? And then it dawns on me. He wasn't asking about the bolt, but about me. How did I shoot so fast? I completely forgot to simulate a second of concentration. "Ehm... I don't know. I just saw the arrow, and didn't think."

He doesn't look convinced. "We'll have to see about that once you win the challenge. Now start again."

I don't like his tone, nor the way he looks at me. I put the thought aside. I'll worry about it tomorrow. For now, I have more urgent problems.

***

The training ground is empty, except for Olias and myself. Everyone is watching from the side. The sun isn't down yet, but it's low enough to make it more difficult for me to see a flying arrow. I'll have to end this fight fast. In a few more minutes, I won't see them at all.

I hear a whistle, and the first one comes toward me. From that far away, I'm able to dodge it easily and start running toward my opponent. Pyrias was right. Olias is much slower than Artridia, and his aim less accurate. He also lacks Artridia's tactics of blocking my path. After today's training, I'm relieved. I never reached Artridia once. But I'm confident I can reach Olias. I cover half the distance without even a near miss. He shoots only three more arrows before I've halved the distance again. Shooting him would be easy, but I already made a blunder today. I don't want to make another. Especially with so many witnesses.

Olias shoots another arrow. We're so close now, the arrow almost brushes my arm, but it doesn't matter anymore. I reach him before he shoots another one, unarm him with a whirl of my spear, and, with one swift kick, throw him to the ground. I pin him there with one foot, the point of my spear on his collarbone.

I hear another whistle. My first challenge is over, and I'm still alive.

***

The next morning, Pyrias is waiting for me outside the tent.

"As I feared, there's another challenge. You're on the fast track for the Grand Slam. This one is from Ishar." He doesn't look pleased.

"Is he another archer?"

"No. He uses a sword. But it doesn't fit."

"Why?"

"I understand that Thelya would push Olias to challenge you. But why Ishar? Chrestia isn't one to take such a risk. There has to be someone pulling the strings..." He stares at the dead snake in his hands.

"What does it mean?"

"I don't know." He shakes his head, perplexed. "Except that, today, I'll be training you for a challenge again."

Ishar has more training and is taller and stronger than me, but according to Pyrias, he lacks much in subtlety. He'll go for the obvious move with brute force. He also has poor control of his weapon's power.

Pyrias warns me not to take account of that point, though. Ishar has enough control to stun me.

For today's training, there's no need for Artridia's help. Pyrias changes his own style to match Ishar's.

By the end of the day, I'm pretty confident I can beat my challenger.

"You can defeat him, but remember that if you want to discourage other challengers, shooting him from afar won't be enough. You'll need a spectacular win."

With this last reminder, I take my place on the training ground, ready to fight.

As soon as I hear the whistle, I fake a second of concentration and shoot a feeble bolt. Ishar easily counters it with his sword. I don't care. It was just an act. I was expected to try it, and having produced such a poor bolt, I'm giving him a false sense of confidence.

My trick works better than I hoped. He immediately rushes to assault me. He's fast and strong. Keeping him at a safe distance and parrying the thrusts of his sword takes all my concentration, despite my training.

While I prepare to deflect a blow coming from my right, his sword deftly alters its course to hit my other side. Surprised, I barely manage to get out of its way. I feel the blade graze my arm, which immediately goes numb.

I take a few steps back and move around. I may have temporarily lost the use of my arm, but I've learned more than he intended me to. First, he can feint. He's not as dumb as everyone thinks. Not quite. Second, and more important, he keeps his weapon on at all times, probably because he can't turn it on and off fast enough, like the others do. And last, his sword is weak. Even though he touched me, he didn't stun me. He'll have to touch me several times to incapacitate me completely.

For a while, I'm content to move out of his way at a safe distance until I regain the use of my arm.

Encouraged by his first success, Ishar accelerates his attacks, putting all his strength in each blow. Holding my spear with only one hand, all I can do is retreat. Feelings gradually return to my fingers, but my arm is still useless. I can't shoot him. I don't have time to pretend to concentrate, and with one arm only to aim, he'll have no problem blocking it with his sword.

Besides, if I want to stop the challenges, I need a better win that that.

Ishar has pushed me back through half the training ground before I can move my arm again. Seeing that he's lost his advantage infuriates him. He comes at me in a full-frontal assault.

I block his sword with the hilt of my spear, but he doesn't give up and keeps pushing. We're locked in a strange embrace, glued to each other, our faces so close I can smell his breath, our weapons stuck between us.

He pushes, forcing me to take a step back. If I give up, I'm done. He has one hand on the hilt, the other on the blade to push harder. It means he's turned off his sword, otherwise he would have stunned himself.

He forces me another step back. I am no match for him. I would shoot a bolt now if I could, but it's not an option anymore. I'd shoot myself. That would be a spectacular win, but for Ishar.

I stifle a smile. I just realized how to win.

I shift my feet, but instead of moving back, I take my right hand off my spear. As Ishar is thrown off-balance by his own strength, I lower my spear, and move to his side. In one swift move, I grab his arm and twist it around, not to take Ishar into a lock, as we've learned in close combat, but to put his own sword to his neck. Our faces are inches away.

The metal touches his skin, but nothing happens.

Ishar smiles at me. "I'm not stupid enough to stun myself."

"Aren't you?" I put my hand on the hilt of the sword. The feeling is different from my spear, but not enough to stop me.

Ishar's eyes widen as I shock him. The pressure he's putting on me lessens somewhat. I take a step to the side, and he falls to the ground, unconscious.

It takes several seconds for the whistle to come. As soon as it does, a blonde girl rushes to Ishar. His trainer.

As I reach the crowd, I hear much laughter and comments about Ishar stunning himself, but also awed comments about my win.

As Pyrias walks back with me to our tent, I ask him, "Stunning him with his own sword. Did I make my win spectacular enough?"

He bursts out laughing. "I didn't see that one coming!"

I'm too pleased with myself to take notice of the edge in his laugh.

CHAPTER TWENTY-FIVE

I wake up drained, with aches all over my body. I turn and see that the other mat is empty. I get dressed, reluctant to start another day, and step out of the tent. The sun isn't up yet.

I look down. A dead snake lies on the ground, right where the other two had been. I take it and look around. Everyone's getting ready. Some trainees are emerging from their tents, many of them kicked or punched into motion by their trainers.

I see Pyrias walking briskly back to me. I show him the snake.

"Yes, I expected that much." He looks down at it. "Urgeios... So it was him behind all this. He's tricked Chrestia. And now he reveals himself before you can recover..." He takes the snake and throws it away. "We'll come to that, but first, I want to check something. Come."

He starts off running, and I follow him. When we reach the training ground, he orders me to wait for him and runs away.

A minute later, he comes back with a bow and quiver. "Come."

Once again, we run out of the agoge, but this time he leads me to where the archery's second test took place. The targets are still hanging.

He takes my spear from me, and gives me the bow and quiver instead. "Shoot a target."

I look at him, surprised. "Why? I'm not an archer, I'm—"

"Shut up and shoot a target!"

I aim and release an arrow. It misses all the hanging targets.

"Shoot another one!"

I aim again at the center one and let the arrow fly. This time, my arrow hits a target, though not the one I was aiming at.

"Now use the power to shoot the same target!"

Pyrias is stone-faced. He's never snapped orders at me this way before. There's something wrong, but I don't know what. I decide to play it safe and just pretend. My arrow misses by a long distance.

"I told you to use the power!" he barks at me.

I shoot another one that almost hits a target.

"You feel playful? Fine! So do I!" His nostrils are flaring. He walks off and stops a few paces away from me, right between the targets and me. "Shoot again! If you don't want to use the power, you'll hit me! Now shoot!"

"But... I can't... I..." I can't think of a way to talk myself out of this mess. If shooting bolts like I can is already way beyond what I should be able to do, using other weapons certainly is too. So far, I haven't seen another trainee do it.

"Shoot, or I swear to Ares I'll train you like I'm supposed to, and make you wish you had died when you arrived!" His whole face is red with anger.

I swallow hard. Nothing I could say would make him change his mind. I'm sure nothing good will come out of this, but, until now, Pyrias has always helped me.

I notch an arrow and lift my bow. For once, I really concentrate. Judging by the test the archers had, their arrows needed some distance to turn. He's too close. I feel the arrow as if it were a part of me. But as I release it, instead of a little twitch, I move it as hard as I can.

As soon as it's released, it turns to the left, gives Pyrias a wide berth, and hits the same target as the other arrow, right in the middle.

Pyrias's shoulders slump. He turns around, looks at the target, and walks back to me. "I knew it. Ishar didn't stun himself, did he?"

I look down, defeated. It's over. I won't save Malia. My best chance would be to make a run for it right now, but I can't give up. Not yet. I've made a promise.

I stare at Pyrias. "No."

"I knew it!" Pyrias shouts and turns around, hands in the air, eyes open wide and... smiling.

"How did you guess?"

"I've known something was wrong since your first test, when you picked the sword. My doubts strengthened during your training when you shot that first bolt. No trainee has ever shot one like you did. Yesterday was only a confirmation. Everyone's making fun of Ishar for stunning himself, but even he isn't that stupid. I saw your hand on his sword."

"And about the bow?"

He shrugs. "Just a hunch." He smiles.

I'm furious. "Are you crazy? You played your life on a hunch? I could have killed you!"

"But you didn't. Don't you understand? You can use all weapons!"

"Just like probably about any soldier around here! You almost made me kill you!"

He ignores my last comment. "No, not like any soldier! Like no other soldier! I've never even heard about one that could do it. You're the first ever!"

"Shit!" Suddenly, I'm not furious at him anymore. I'm furious at myself for being so dumb. "What will you do?"

"Nothing," he answers simply.

"You won't tell the instructor?"

"No. I don't know why the Gods gave you this talent, but the secret's not mine to reveal. I'll just keep training you to become the best soldier. Come on, it's time to have something to eat!" He takes the bow and quiver, runs to retrieve the arrow, and hands me my spear back.

I can't believe it. He won't say anything. I know he means it. I still have a chance to save Malia. It also means he trusts me. Another person I'll have to betray.

I follow him.

"By the way, you don't have to concentrate either, to use your spear, do you?"

I dare to give him a smile. "No. But at least when it comes to that, I'm not the only one. I've seen soldiers do it."

Pyrias shakes his head and sighs noisily. "Even weathered soldiers have to. The only difference is that we've learned how to do it while moving so that we don't have to freeze for a second and expose ourselves to the enemy." He shakes his head again and murmurs, "I can't believe it."

✳✳✳

"This time, you won't have to go for a spectacular win. Or, should I say, your spectacular win will be by shooting your opponent. The real challenge will be to create an opening. Otherwise, she'll absorb your bolt with her own spear. I know you already know that; I've seen you shield yourself like this during the test."

He's really been observing me closely for a while...

"How can I do it? I mean, create an opening?"

"Through closer-range combat. But be careful. She's good with a spear, but she's even better without it. So not too close. First chance you get, you shoot to stun her. Okay?"

I nod.

"Now, to help train you, I've asked two soldiers to fight you at the same time. This will make up for her speed and technique."

"But if she's that good, why did she challenge me?" I really don't see what she would gain from it.

Pyrias hesitates before answering. "She has... other issues."

"What issues?" Seeing his reluctance, I add, "It can't be worse than what you know about me..."

"Her issue is Urgeios. He thinks too highly of himself. He's really good, but not at following orders. And he has no problem killing people. Of course, it's part of our job, to subdue the population, but not to kill for petty reasons like he does. He almost caused a rebellion a few years ago. He hasn't been sent on a mission since."

I can sense by the way he hesitates that there's something more.

"He could have picked anyone. Why me?"

"I'm the one who cleaned up his mess..."

Oh. So it's personal. "Then we'll just have to clean up another mess for him..."

✳✳✳

As I enter the training ground, I'm not very confident. Training with two opponents certainly was difficult, but can it compare to fighting a single better one? Also, I've noticed the instructor watching me. And there he is again. He wasn't there for the other challenges, so why this one?

Facing me, I discover my opponent. She's a head shorter than me, with light-brown hair in a ponytail. She doesn't smile or frown. She's concentrating on the coming fight, displaying no emotion.

As soon as the whistle blows, I prepare to shoot the same feeble bolt I shot yesterday. In the second I use to observe her while pretending to concentrate, I notice that she can move while preparing to shoot. Not fast, but she can. Distracted by this, I don't shoot a bolt, but just a few sparks, earning me a few laughs from the crowd. Luckily, my spear's aimed at my opponent, for her bolt seems quite powerful. My spear acts as a shield, and absorbs it.

After that, the fight is a mess. It's mostly moving around, clanging our spears together, and me shooting a few sparks from my spear, as if I couldn't shoot anything else. I manage to evade her but can't create an opening.

The sun disappears and darkness grows. It won't be long before there's another whistle and the fight is declared a draw. Maybe darkness is my chance.

I put some distance between us, and we begin circling each other again. She thinks herself safe. I'll just have to cover for my pretended concentration.

Her steps slow down. That's my chance. She'll have to close her eyes so as not to be blinded by her own bolt. As she closes her eyes, I run to my left and a little toward her, eyes closed. As soon as I hear the thunder, I freeze. She's surprised not to see me where I was before, but as she spots me, she prepares to shoot again, slowing down her moves, convinced I'm still too far away to be dangerous.

My bolt isn't very powerful, just enough to throw her to the ground. I don't try to stun her as I'm not sure I have enough control not to kill her. The whistle blows before she can stand again.

As I turn toward Pyrias, I see Garbos smiling. Not far from him, the instructor turns away and leaves.

Pyrias congratulates me, but once we're alone, his smile fades. "That was dangerous, shooting a bolt like that."

"I hoped people would think I just got lucky."

"But if they think it was just luck, you'll be challenged again."

I smile. "Then, tomorrow, thanks to my trainer, I'll improve greatly and manage to shoot an even better bolt."

He chuckles. "It could work... But you should be prepared for tomorrow."

"Why? Will someone else challenge me?"

"I don't think so. They'll wait a few days this time. But you just won your first Grand Slam."

Why doesn't it sound good when he says it like this? "What will happen?"

"You'll see. Sleep well tonight. You'll need to be rested for tomorrow night..."

Gosh, I hate his wicked smile.

***

When I wake up, I'm glad to see no dead snake waiting for me outside. Pyrias resumes my usual training. As I run down the street, I hear a few shouts of, "Prome," and even, "Miracle Boy." I also notice many people staring at me. I don't know what awaits me tonight, but I'm already stressed.

I'm back to my regular training, and suddenly I appreciate it. After noon, the power training begins.

Pyrias and I have decided that my second attempt should be the good one. The ones after that too. The message has to be clear: I may have had a little luck, but now, I really can do it.

As I shoot a bolt that throws the target to the ground, half of it blackened, Pyrias emphasizes it with a, "You got it! You just needed a little incentive. I should have challenged someone for you earlier!"

Everyone heard that. They'll think twice about challenging me. For now.

Just as the power training finishes, my mood better than it has been for weeks, a hoplite comes to me.

"Follow me!" He turns around and walks off.

Surprised, I look at Pyrias, but he isn't looking at me. He's staring, frozen, at the hoplite.

"I said, follow me!"

"Do as he says," Pyrias says in a low voice, still not looking at me.

I just nod and jog after the hoplite. "Where are we going?"

"Shut up and follow!"

Okay... I don't know what's happening, but judging by Pyrias's reaction, it can't be good.

We reach an avenue, and the hoplite turns toward the center of the agoge. I follow without a word. Soon, our path is blocked by two soldiers.

"I'm bringing him for a hearing."

The two guards step to the side and let us through.

The inner circle of the agoge is nothing like the rest of it, and not just because the tents are an immaculate white instead of red or blue. Instead of the efficient order of the soldiers' quarters, havoc reigns. A wide tent blocks the avenue. We take a side road, but that one is soon blocked too. Turn follows turn, and I become lost in the labyrinth. And nowhere do I see any building that might be from the Last Era.

We stop in front of a tent, and the hoplite shows me inside.

It's an empty antechamber. On the other side is an opening. I walk through it and find myself in a much bigger tent. This one is empty too, save for a long table. More than fifty people could easily sit around it, but presently there are only five, facing me. To the right, I recognize the instructor, but the other two I've never seen before. Judging by their golden cuirasses, they must be high-ranking officers.

Nothing could have brought me here, except one of my secrets. Either they know I'm not here to become a soldier, or they know that I can use any weapon. My hands are moist and my stomach churns.

"Trainee Prome." So the instructor still knows my name. "You've been accused of cheating during a challenge. What do you have to say about it?"

CHAPTER TWENTY-SIX

"What?" Why is he talking about a challenge? It's not about—

"Did you or did you not cheat during a challenge?"

Ooh, so it's just because of a sore loser? I smile inwardly. Against this accusation, I can defend myself. "I know nothing about cheating. I was challenged, and I won fair and square."

They all stare at me. Obviously, this isn't over yet.

"Did you pretend to be unable to shoot a bolt to mislead your opponent?" This time it's the officer in the middle questioning me.

I ponder my answer. They are high-ranking officers. I'll give them what they want to hear.

"Yes, I did." I stare back at them.

"So you recognize that you cheated. We'll take a decision according—"

"No I don't." I cut him short.

Looking at his displeased face, I understand he's not used being interrupted. He's about to retort, but the instructor speaks first.

"What don't you do?"

"I don't recognize having cheated."

"Why is that?"

"Because I didn't cheat. My trainer forewarned me about the challenges, that one might come soon. Although I'd learned how to shoot a bolt, I decided to downplay my ability." A little truth. "Even my trainer didn't know about it." A little untruth, but I wouldn't like to put Pyrias in a bad situation.

"Why did you do that?"

"To gain an advantage. If your opponent underestimates you, he'll make a mistake. When I fight, I fight to win, whoever my opponent, whatever the situation. I'll use any tactics necessary. And if my opponent falls for a simple trick like that one, he's just a fool. I don't expect my opponent to fight fairly, and so I ready myself for any trick on his part. That's how fights are won, aren't they?"

The leftmost officer seems outraged. The others, on the other hand, maintain a neutral expression. As I look at the instructor, I catch a fleeting trace of a smile. I relax a little.

The officer in the center speaks again. "Trainee, go back to your quarters. We'll let you know our decision on the morrow."

As no one speaks nor moves, I turn around and exit the tent.

I'm crossing the antechamber when Malia comes in, carrying a tray of refreshments. She wears the gray dress of the slaves. She immediately signals to me to keep quiet. I slow my pace. Once we're near each other, she stops.

"I found the entrance," she murmurs. "Find a way to come back with Garbos. I'll know about it. Look out for me and be ready."

Before I can ask her how she is, she walks past me and enters the main tent.

✳✳✳

"They didn't kill you on the spot. It's a good sign. Death sentences are always pronounced immediately. They might even end up punishing Urgeios. You're really blessed by the Gods!" Pyrias slaps me on the back, laughing.

I still have doubts about the outcome, but seeing him so cheerful washes away the tension I've felt all day.

"Come, let's go training. I'll go easy on you for the rest of the day. You earned it."

Even before we reach the training ground, I can hear trainers shouting and kicking at their trainees. I'm very lucky Pyrias chose me.

✳✳✳

As much as I dislike having to side with Garbos again, I need him. And I'm not sure Malia would proceed if I showed up alone. "We have to find a way to get in."

"Don't think I haven't looked for one." Garbos takes a bite of bread and swallows it hastily. "The avenues are guarded, and there's no other way in. There's a wall surrounding it. It's concealed by tents, but it's there. And it's completely smooth, like the walls from the Last Era. There's no way we can climb it."

"And the guards will never let us through. I could always try to stun them, but it would alert everyone. Once we find the box, we'll need time to find what's in it. We need to get in inconspicuously."

"And we'll need to get out," he adds.

"Yeah, that too." Getting in will be difficult enough, if we ever manage to do it. I'll think about getting out later.

"There's something else. I overheard two soldiers talking. One phalanx will leave in five days. They'll travel to the north. I didn't hear the specifics, but there's trouble out there. You know what it means?"

"Thanks to our suggestion, they'll take Malia with them... We have four days to find a way in. If we don't, we'll just barge in. I hope we won't have to do that."

"Hmpff," he says through a mouthful of bread.

✳✳✳

"I thought you were going easy on me today?" I fall onto my mat, exhausted.

Pyrias smiles. "I did. After your Slam, I should have pushed you to display your abilities more. We'll do that tomorrow."

"Great," I grumble. I take off my amulet and look at it. How can we get in? I lie down, still clutching it in my right hand.

"Don't sleep, you should get ready!"

"What for?"

I notice a hubbub outside, getting louder.

"For that."

"What's—Fuck!" I had completely forgotten about the hazing or whatever that was waiting for me...

Two soldiers barge in and grab me. They drag me into the middle of a howling crowd. Pyrias follows me with a smile on his face I'd be more than happy to erase with a good punch.

Someone pushes me. I bump into a soldier, who pushes me back into someone else. Whenever I try to stop, someone pushes me.

Suddenly everything stops. Pyrias comes to me with an amphora and gives it to me. "Drink."

The liquid stings my nose as I smell it. Alcohol. Strong.

I take a prudent sip and cough. My throat burns.

"Drink! Drink! Drink!" The whole crowd repeats the word like a litany.

"I can't drink that!"

Pyrias smiles. "You'll have to. All of it. If you don't do it, you'll get help..."

Three soldiers come closer. Before they reach me, I lift the amphora and try to swallow as fast as I can before I throw up.

***

A lurch of my stomach wakes me up. I only have time to roll on my side before I throw up.

"Congratulation, you survived your krypteia."

Another wave of nausea. It takes several minutes of vomiting for my stomach to settle down. Eyes still closed, I bring myself to a sitting position. My head hurts like hell. I keep my eyes closed. If I open them, I'm sure my head will explode.

"Drink that."

Pyrias puts a small amphora in my hand. I smell at its contents and almost barf again.

"Drink it. It will help."

"I'd prefer some poison to kill me quick."

Pyrias laughs. "If a chimera didn't kill you, no poison will." He brings the amphora to my lips.

The stinking liquid doesn't taste as bad as it smells. It's thicker than water, both sweet and sour.

I stop after a few gulps and hesitantly open my eyes. The world doesn't spin around me. "What happened?"

Pyrias laughs again. "Don't you remember last night?"

I want to shake my head but stop just in time. "Honestly, I don't remember anything after you made me drink that stuff."

Another laugh. "Too bad. We all had quite some time." I must look horror-struck, as he quickly adds, "Don't worry, you behaved. Now get dressed or you'll be late!"

I look down. I'm completely naked. I don't even have—

"*My amulet!*" I look around in a frenzy.

"Relax, it's here." Pyrias hands it to me, and I put it back around my neck. "You left it in the tent yesterday. I kept it for you."

The rush of adrenaline has somewhat cleared my head. I pick up my tunic from the foot of my mat. It's not white, it's red. "Sorry, Pyrias, this is yours."

"No. It's yours. You've passed your krypteia. You're not a hoplite yet. Not until the Stratigos promotes you. But you're not a trainee anymore. Now, up!"

"What about the year of training?"

Pyrias snorts. "You'll still train, but let's say you took a shortcut."

Pyrias makes me drink more before we go for our morning run. For once, he runs with me. The fresh air and the movement finish the process of putting me back together.

"Sir, why are you running with me?"

"Call me Pyrias from now on. Even when we're not alone."

"What? Why?"

"I told you. You're not a trainee anymore."

A few strides later, he adds, "Last night wasn't quite the end of it. There's a bit more waiting for you today."

I wonder if punching him to force him to tell me what's coming is against the rules, now that I'm not his trainee anymore...

***

We're all lined up on the side of the training ground. Facing us is the Stratigos, just as Pyrias told me. He's the same officer who interrogated me yesterday. At his side is the instructor.

"Trainee Prome! Come forth!"

Pyrias pushes me slightly to make me move.

When I stop in front of the Stratigos, he addresses me with a loud voice that everyone behind me can hear. "Trainee Prome. As of today, and by my authority, you have reached the grade of hoplite. You will stay with the trainees to train and supervise them until their final test. After that, you will take the lead of those who pass."

A soldier approaches, carrying something I can't identify. "Don't move." He moves around me, fixing something on my torso. As he retreats, I see a bronze-colored leather breastplate.

Behind me, cheers erupt. When they die out, the instructor orders me to go back to the ranks.

I look at the faces of those around me. Garbos seems ecstatic. A few paces away, Taeros scowls. I bet he won't like taking orders from me. Too bad for him.

As soon as I'm back among the others, the instructor gives the order to resume the training, and the crowd moves away.

"I can't believe it!"

I look at Pyrias. "What?"

"Do I have to call you sir now?"

I blink in surprise. "What?"

"Didn't you hear the Stratigos? You'll lead the next lochos!"

I shake my head. "No, I'll just lead the trainees who pass the test."

"And what do you think that will be? The next lochos! He has officially named you lochagos, though technically you're still a hoplite until the test. He gave you your breastplate."

"What does it mean?" I should have learned the military ranks by now, but I never planned to stay and didn't care.

He shakes his head. "Hmpfff. It means you're an officer. You outrank me. You'll have to wear your armor at all times from now on."

"Does it also mean more challenges?" I'm sure beating an officer-to-be is a great way to move up.

Pyrias laughs. "On the contrary. No one will want to be on your bad side now." He claps me on the back. "Come on. You might outrank me, but I'm still your trainer."

***

It feels strange to talk to Pyrias like I would to a friend. Although he's still my trainer, as I outrank him, there's a gray area about how we should address each other. For now, I just drop the *sir*, and he doesn't *sir* me either. It's incredible how so little has changed so much. No hierarchy anymore. We're a bit like two friends training together.

My training changes too. Pyrias doesn't just teach me new moves. He also asks me what I think of such and such a trainee. *Is this one good? What is that one doing wrong? What would I do differently if I were her trainer?* For now, I don't intervene in their training, but analyzing the others like this changes my whole perspective of the agoge.

I really see my fellow trainees for what they are for the first time: boys and girls giving all they have to become part of the only group that accepts them.

I remember one boy from my first days here. He was dressed as a poor ceramist, but even I could tell he was too strong, too big for such a job. The young blonde girl over there was probably an orphan, doomed to a life of begging. They've all escaped a life that would have killed them by coming here. They gave all they had and got stronger. The agoge is their last hope. It's not perfect, but it's enough to belong.

And their trainers... I knew I had it good. I just didn't know how good. That tall boy beats a poor girl as if it could improve her aim. This one can't talk, he can only shout at his trainee... But they're just the same as their trainees. They're just doing their best to prove their worth. It's not their fault if they reproduce the way they were taught.

There are a few exceptions, of course: trainees and trainers who sneer at the others, like Taeros. They don't fight to belong. They don't train to improve. They do it to be able to kill. I can see it in the way they hit their adversaries, humans or not. The strikes are mean, deadly. They don't care if they injure their opponent, and once the fight's over, they don't look back.

Taeros stares back at me and spits. He couldn't have made it clearer: lochagos or not, he'll never take orders from me.

* * *

I wonder what Pyrias's story is but don't ask him. I don't want to embarrass him. I've never felt this close to him before, though. "Pyrias, I know you think the Gods have plans for me..."

"They have," he interrupts me. "How else could you be able to do all this?" He points at my spear and his sword.

"Maybe they have." I won't change his mind, and it might be easier if he believes it. "But if anything happens, don't try to protect me. Do what's good for you, even if you have to slander me."

He stares at me, only the white of his eyes visible in the darkness of our tent. "Why do you say that? I'd never—"

"I know. But no one knows what the future brings. If you have to do it, just do it. Okay?"

"Okay."

I know by his tone he'll do it, though reluctantly. I wish I could trust him and take him with us, but that wouldn't be doing him a favor. If I don't belong in the army, he does.

Chapter Twenty-Seven

Two days have passed, and neither Garbos nor I have found a way to get to Malia. Tomorrow, the phalanx will leave with Malia, and I feel cornered. The only thing I can think about is bolting my way to her with my spear. It sounded crazy when I went to bed yesterday. Now it just sounds desperate. And that's precisely what I am.

Desperate.

If it comes to it, I'll wait for the camp to fall asleep. That's when I'll be most likely to succeed. But until then, I have to play my role. Training is excruciating. I just can't concentrate on it. This morning, Pyrias sends me sprawling to the ground so many times, even with simple moves I should have blocked easily, that he gives up the hand-to-hand combat. Instead, we spend the day seated in the dirt in a corner of the training ground. He traces lines and crosses in the dirt representing combat maneuvers. We both pretend I'm listening. At least, if someone looks at us, he'll just see a tactics lesson.

"Prome, follow me."

I stare up at the soldier towering over me. Obediently, I stand and follow him. We're out of the training ground when I ask him where he's taking me.

"The instructor wants to see you."

I stop dead in my tracks. I can't believe what he told me.

He stops and turns to me. "Come!"

"Wait." I have to think fast. I won't have a second chance. I need to get Garbos. "Wait for me a second. I'll be right back!"

I run off to the training ground. Garbos is shooting arrows. I run to him. "Garbos! Come with me."

Garbos looks surprised but puts his arrow back in the quiver.

"What do you think you're doing? Keep shooting!" His trainer, a tall girl with black hair, scowls at me.

"I need him right now."

She stares at me defiantly. "He's my trainee."

"And I'm his lochagos!" I retort with as much authority as I can. It seems to shut her up. "Follow me." We walk off before she can recover.

"Where are we going?"

"The instructor asked for me. It's now or never. I hope my new status can get you in with me."

We reach the soldier who came for me. "Who's that?"

"One of the trainees."

"The instructor wants to talk to you. Not to him." He frowns, unhappy.

Time to call another bluff. "Yes, he wants to talk to me. And I'll need this trainee to discuss an important point with him. I wouldn't want him to wait while you run back to the training ground. That would be wasting his time. I doubt he'll like that."

He glares at me, undecided, and eventually nods.

When we reach the inner circle, Garbos and I have to leave our weapons with the sentry. It's a drawback, but a minor one.

We make turn after turn, but there's no sign of Malia. The soldier takes us to the same tent I was brought to before. As we reach it, I look around one last time.

She's not here.

Garbos and I enter the anteroom.

"Wait for me here," I whisper. It makes me nervous to leave Garbos alone. I'm giving him the best opportunity ever to betray me.

I have no other choice.

✻✻✻

"Now there's a last point I'd like to discuss."

I sigh inwardly. The instructor has been droning for an eternity about my role as a lochagos. It took all my willpower to pretend to listen. I don't expect to stay long enough to get the job, and even if I did, my mind keeps wandering to Malia.

"I've heard certain rumors."

This certainly gets my attention. "What rumors?"

He clears his throat. "You won one of your challenges in a... most unusual way."

His hesitation gives me the creeps. They judged me once. They can't do it twice, can they? "I already explained that I purposefully hid my ability to fire a bolt. I thought it was—"

"I'm not referring to that fight, but the one against the swordsman..."

Shit. How much does he know? Could it be Pyrias?

"Your opponent stunned himself with his own weapon."

I nod. My throat tightens.

"The rumor has it that you *used* your opponent's weapon against him."

I give a nervous laugh. "How could I do that?"

He leans toward me. "You tell me."

"Is it even possible?" I try to put on my best incredulous face. I hope he can't read my face like Malia does, or I'm toast.

"It's unheard of, not necessarily impossible."

I notice a furtive twitch in his right brow. He doesn't know. He's heard about it, but he doesn't believe it. Not yet.

I laugh again. This time, it sounds more genuine. "If I could use both weapons, it would be an incredible advantage on a battlefield. I wish I could, but I can't. I don't know who started the rumor, but I have a pretty good idea why."

"And why is that?"

"Ishar isn't stupid enough to stun himself by mistake, but he definitely isn't the sharpest knife around. He made the worst decision possible at the worst moment possible. He had me in his grip. He could have subdued me. He chose the wrong option. Too bad for him. I don't blame him for stunning himself. I blame him for making the worst decision possible. In a real fight, it would have cost him his life. But trying to divert the blame is just as unacceptable."

The instructor leans back and smiles. "You spoke like a true lochagos. I agree with you; it's unacceptable. I'll sanction him for that."

Now I feel bad. There's only one sanction here, and Ishar certainly doesn't deserve it. "Please don't. If he passes the final test, he'll be under my orders. I'm sure I can make a good soldier of him. He can't use his brain, but he certainly is strong."

The instructor stares at me silently for a couple of seconds. "It's your decision. You may go."

I exit only too willingly. In the anteroom, Garbos is still waiting for me. He heard everything. I don't bother to fill him in.

As the soldier escorts us back, I scan every side alley in search of Malia. It's our last chance to find her, and each step I take brings me closer to losing her. Another two turns and we'll see the exit of the inner circle. I can't let the chance pass. There won't be another one before tomorrow.

I check around us. We're alone. "Sorry."

The soldier turns around, surprised. "What for?"

"This." I unsheathe his spear and stun him. "Quick, Garbos, help me."

We pull him into a narrow alley. "If we stay here, someone will see us."

"I know." I listen through the fabric of the tent. Nothing. I lift the bottom of the tent. Without looking at the inside, we both go in, then pull the unconscious soldier inside.

"Prome?"

"What?" I don't look at Garbos. I take the soldier's sheath and search to see if he has anything else we could use.

"Prome! Look."

Garbos stands near me, facing the inside of the tent. I turn around and stare at a wall.

The tent isn't a tent. It's just a prop to hide the smooth, gray wall. We've found the Last Era building.

"It's..." I can't believe I'm finally seeing it. "We have to find Malia. She knows where the entrance is."

"Are you sure it's safe to go out there?" Garbos points at the soldier. "What if he wakes up?"

"I don't think anywhere is *safe* for us. But you're right. Help me gag him."

We use the soldier's own clothes to bind him. Once it's done, I take a peek outside. "Come on, Garbos."

I don't want to look for her anywhere and risk getting lost. We retrace our steps toward the tent in which I met the instructor. This path is where Malia will look for us.

"Hide! Quick!" Garbos lifts the fabric of a tent and pulls me inside. As soon as the fabric falls back, I hear footsteps outside.

As we wait for them to disappear, I look around. This is another false tent hiding another wall. "How many buildings are there?"

Outside is silent again. Before Garbos can say anything, I step out, stride to the next tent, and then enter it. I'm out and running to another one before Garbos comes in.

I stop, facing an umpteenth wall. The streets haven't been designed as a maze. They just twist and turn between the buildings. Judging by the number of turns, the place must be full of small ones scattered haphazardly around. Whenever there's enough space, it's occupied by a real tent.

"What are you doing here?"

Garbos and I both turn with a start and discover someone entering the prop tent in which we're hiding.

"By Hades, Malia! You scared me to death!" My heart beats furiously.

"Prome found a way to get in. We were looking for you!"

I recover enough for my mind to spin into motion again. "You told me you'd find us, but you weren't there. We had to improvise."

"I was kept busy by the cook." Judging by her expression, she despises the guy. "How did you get here?"

"I was training—"

I cut him short. "No time for this. I stunned the soldier. We bound him, but we probably don't have much time left. Can you take us to the entrance?"

"Do you have your amulet?"

I slip it out of my tunic.

"Good! Follow me."

We follow her through more twisting alleys, hiding when we hear footsteps. The place is almost empty. It's making me nervous.

"Where's everybody?"

Malia doesn't slow down. "The tents are all props, even those that don't conceal anything. All the officers and their staff live in the main building. We're taking the rear entrance."

She leads us through more alleys, then stops in front of the entrance to a tent. She takes a look inside and then shoves us in. We face another wall, but this one has a door. She motions to us to stay silent, and we enter.

Inside, the air is cool, almost cold. We follow a narrow hallway, lit by those strange tubes of light. For once, they all work perfectly. As we advance, I hear voices coming from the end of the hallway. I grab Malia's arm and point to my ear, then to the voices.

"Mess hall," she articulates soundlessly, "wait for me." She moves forward and disappears through a door. The voices are suddenly louder. Someone shouts, but I can't understand what they say. Where did she go? We should have stayed together. I have to go after her!

I signal to Garbos to stay here, but before I can move, Malia appears again, carrying a bag and a bow with arrows. She opens a door to a staircase and we go down one level.

More hallways, another staircase. Here, some lights are broken.

"We should be okay now. They seldom come here."

"How far is it?"

"We're almost there."

The hallway turns to the right. At the far end is a metal door with a small black box by its side. Malia stops in front of it. "Open it."

I try, but it's locked.

"With your amulet!"

"Oh." I take it out and put it on the black box.

Nothing.

"Are you sure it's the right door?"

"I don't know, but it's the only locked one I've found."

I notice a crack on top of the box. I put the amulet in it. Immediately, it emits a low buzz and the door opens. I take the amulet back, and we enter.

"Close the door behind you. It will slow them down if they come after us." *If* is a big word. I seriously doubt we'll be able to come out through here.

We've entered another hall. It has a single door at the other end. I don't need the amulet to open it. We walk into a square room. In the middle is a single table with a black cube on it.

I look at Malia. "Ready?"

She nods.

We all walk to the cube. I'm about to put my amulet on it.

"Stop!" Garbos's shout makes me jump.

"Are you crazy? Don't shout like that! What's the problem with you?"

"It's not the right cube."

CHAPTER TWENTY-EIGHT

I blink and look around. "What do you mean *it's not the right cube*? It has to be the right cube! It's the *only* cube." I move my amulet to it again.

Malia grabs my hand to stop me. "Listen to him. Why is it not the right cube, Garbos?"

"It's just... I don't know. I've been in several rooms like this one. This one doesn't feel right."

I can't believe it. He's showing his true colors at last. "It feels exactly as it does! I opened the door with my amulet and we found the cube. Locked door, amulet... It's always been like this!"

"I know, but it feels wrong, and—"

"I don't care how it feels, we have to see what's in the box and then leave as soon as possible!"

"Prome, listen to him." Malia turns to Garbos. "What's wrong?"

"I don't really know. It just... feels wrong." He walks to a bookshelf. "There isn't even a single book about the Gaia Protocol."

"Don't you see what he's trying to do, Malia? He's just preventing us from getting the info we need to save your mother! He's a spy! He's—"

Malia slaps me, hard.

"Why did you do that?"

"Because you're an asshole. He's helping us! I don't know why you're so prejudiced against him. He saved your life when the chimera poisoned you. Without him, we'd never have reached the agoge!"

"It's just an act! He wants us to find the box before turning us in!"

Malia clenches her fists and looks at the ceiling, grunting. "First you say he doesn't wants us to find it, then he wants us to find it! You're not even making any sense, Prome! Listen to yourself!"

"I... Okay. But how can you explain how he shoots arrows like he does? Why can he use the power when you can't?"

"Because he trained. Others can use the power. Because I can't doesn't mean everyone who can is a traitor!"

"Yes, it does!"

"Then *you are a traitor!*" she shouts back.

I can't answer that.

"Garbos, can you give us a minute alone, please?"

"Sure," he answers feebly, and leaves through the door.

"We should keep an eye on him!"

"Cut that out, Prome. He's not a traitor. So what's the problem with you?"

"With me? *He* is the problem!"

"Come on. I know you better than that. When you react like this, there's usually a better reason."

I think twice about what she just said. "Listen. I'd like to be best friends with him. I really do," I add as she makes a face. "But I can't trust him. There's been too many warnings, even if he saved us a few times."

Malia sighs. "Can you at least give him a break for now?"

"I'll try, but—"

"Malia? Prome?"

We run outside. A boom echoes through the hall.

"I think they raised the alarm." Garbos stares at the other door.

Another boom.

I grab his shoulders and shake him out of his trance. "What happens if it's not the correct room?"

"I don't know... They—"

"Listen!" Malia isn't looking at us anymore.

I don't hear anything. "What did you hear?"

"Nothing. They stopped banging on the door. Maybe they've found the guard and are just testing all the doors to try to find us."

I return to the more pressing problem. "Garbos. What will happen if we use this cube and it's not the right one?"

"We won't find anything. They'll know we're here and come after us."

Okay. For now, they don't know where we are. We can afford to lose a little time. "Let's say it's not the correct room. How do we find the right one?"

"I don't know..."

I shake him again. "Think!"

"I don't know. It's probably like the one in the Dead Steppes. The room must be hidden."

"Okay, so let's look for it!"

We rush back to the room and search the walls, toppling the shelves that are in our way.

"There's nothing here!"

Malia freezes. "Wait! Remember in the Dead Steppes. The mechanism wasn't on the wall."

I rush to the table and look underneath it. "There's nothing there. Where would they hide the mechanism?" I lean on the table and look around. In front of me is the door through which we came. The rest of the wall is bare, nothing on it. Same with the walls on my right and behind me.

On my left, the only opening is an empty recess, too small to hold more than four people.

I take a closer look. It's the only part of the room that has no apparent use. Two thin lines show where the threshold is. They run up the sides of the entrance and meet on the ceiling.

I cross the lines and step in.

Inside, the walls are perfectly smooth. I put my hand on one. It's cold to the touch. I knock softly on it. It rings like metal. Intrigued, I put my ear against it to try to hear something.

A loud beep erupts, and the walls begin moving in, to close the entrance.

I try to block them. "Malia! Garbos! Quick!" I manage to stop the walls, but they still try to close.

"What did you do?"

"I don't know. The walls are different in here."

"Let us in!" Garbos gets in, closely followed by Malia. "Okay, let go, now."

"Are you sure?"

Garbos nods.

I look at Malia. I promised I'd be nice. Time to prove I can do it. I remove my hands and feet and let the walls close.

The ground vibrates and gives a little jerk.

"I think we're moving." *Garbos and the obvious...*

I can feel the ground vibrating. "Where are we going?"

"We're moving down."

"How can you tell?"

Garbos scratches his left ear. "The air pressure is changing. I can feel it."

The question is what's below us? I can read it in their worried stares. They certainly read it in mine, too.

Nothing happens.

The ground vibrates. No one dares to speak.

I count the seconds.

One.

Two.

Three.

My heart's pounding expectantly.

Twenty.

Twenty-one.

I keep counting, but each second seems longer than the former one. Pressure blocks my ears. I pinch my nose and blow air in it until my drums pop.

The room jerks. I jump as much from the sudden move as from Malia's startled shriek.

We stare silently at each other, waiting for something to happen.

The wall opens on a pitch-black room.

"Do you know what's out there?" I ask Garbos.

"No."

The darkness in front of us attracts us as much as it repels us.

"Do you want to go first?"

"Hn-hn."

From the corner of my eye, I can see him shake his head twice. Okay, it was cowardly of me to ask, but I'd really like not to go.

I take a deep, long breath. Malia grabs my hand. I take a step, and a second one. Our arms are stretched out; only our fingers are entwined. I stop breathing, release her fingers, and walk out of the room.

Something crackles above my head and a light appears. That first light triggers a chain reaction. Right and left, lights appear, one after another. A few seconds later, the place is bathed in white light.

I take another step and stare in awe. I'm in a huge room. In front of me, a long table runs the length of it. On it, dozens of cubes. But something else roots me to the ground. On the other side of the table, the wall is one huge window. Behind it, a pipe four times as tall as I am runs as far as I can see to my right and left. It's made of polished metal. Along its side, cables bigger than my arm run everywhere, and every few dozen paces, the tube is circled by other smaller pipes and cables. The only opening is right in front of me. Most of the pipe is filled with tiny copper cables and dark-gray pieces of metal.

I feel a hand slip into my left hand.

"That's *it*," Malia whispers softly.

"Yeah." I gently squeeze her fingers.

She lifts her hands and puts them on the glass, as if touching it would make everything more real. "Gaia," she whispers.

She squeezes my hand.

I look at the hand in mine, and then up the arm at Garbos's face. He's staring at the machinery, smiling, a tear rolling down his cheek.

I snatch my hand away. *What's he thinking?* Immediately, he turns to me. His eyes widen, as if he's just realized what he's done.

"Sorry," he mutters, looking down.

I glare at him.

"Prome!" Malia barks.

I'm surprised to see my fist clenched, ready to strike Garbos.

"Come."

She grabs me by the arm and pulls me away from Garbos. When we're out of earshot, she turns to me. "What are you doing?"

I'm thrown off by her hostility. "I... I didn't do anything."

"You were about to punch him!" she snaps back.

"He took my hand and..." I can't put into words what he's done and why I resent it so much.

"Come on, Prome. He likes you. Can't you be nice to him? He's never had friends."

I snort. "He probably comes from a rich family with enough money to buy our whole town... I won't feel sorry for him."

Malia glares at me, her face red with anger. "You don't know him. You don't know that his family sent him to school to get rid of him. You don't know that he was everyone's punching bag because of his clumsiness. You don't know that he never had any friends. And you especially don't know that, since he met us, he doesn't feel alone for the first time in his life!"

I can't believe all this. "How do you know all this?"

"I talked to him. You would know it too if you hadn't ignored him or treated him like a foe. You've acted like an asshole since you met him. Now act like a man and talk to him!"

"I won't—"

"Yes, you will!" she snaps back. She grabs my arm so hard it's painful and turns me around to make me face Garbos.

I look at him and immediately feel ashamed. He's still looking at his feet. He's so different from when we met him. The fat has disappeared, replaced by muscles that show through his clothes. He also looks older, almost adult. And yet, he's still the same shy kid, afraid to move.

I can't help but pity him.

And then I look at his hands and the urge to hit him boils in me. How did he dare touch me like this? I feel nauseated. I glower at Malia. "He's a freak and a traitor!" I shout.

I hear a pained squeak and see Garbos turn around. He runs to the end of the room and disappears through a door. I only glimpsed his face, but it was enough to see the tears.

I didn't mean for him to hear all this, I...

Shocked, I turn to Malia.

She's staring at me with a face I have never seen before. Her mouth, her eyes, her breathing... Her whole face shows only disgust.

She doesn't say a word. She turns, walks to the other end of the room, and leaves through another door.

CHAPTER TWENTY-NINE

For a few seconds, I feel numb.

Then everything comes crashing down on me. A lump blocks my throat, ice-cold shivers run over my skin. My knees buckle under me.

I did it! I pushed away the only person who was always at my side, the only one who never abandoned me. And the worst part is that I understand her. The lie I told. Garbos's face: the tears, the hurt... It's all etched in my mind and in my heart. Malia's right. I can't find words strong enough to describe how I treated him. I had to be cautious, but it doesn't excuse what I did. He followed us. He helped us. And when he eventually found the dream of all Technologists, I ruined everything just because he shared this moment with me by holding my hand. I can still feel the warmth of his soft skin on mine.

I feel a tear escape my eyes, followed by many others.

***

I have no idea how long I've been kneeling on the ground, crying, but when I stand again, my knees protest the sudden move. I don't mind the pain. I've earned it. But it won't atone for my acts. I know what I have to do.

I walk to the end of the room and open the door through which Garbos ran out. It leads onto a hall.

There's a door to my right, but I disregard it. It leads to the room behind the glass. I would have seen him if he had gone through that one.

A few steps farther, the hallway turns left. The right wall is just a row of windows and glass doors. Behind them, small, white rooms with tables and equipment the like of which I've never seen. And cubes. At least two or three per room.

Garbos is nowhere to be seen.

Along the left wall, several doors reveal dark, empty rooms. I slowly open the last door at the opposite end of the hall.

The place is brightly lit. Rows and rows of shelves filled with neatly stacked books cramp the room. An aisle leads to a faraway door on the other side of the room. I start toward it, looking right and left between the rows of shelves. This is the sort of place Garbos would like. He must be here somewhere.

About halfway down the aisle, the shelves make place for a little square space with a table and a few chairs. Ignoring them, Garbos is seated on the floor. His back is turned to me, but I guess he has an open book on his lap.

"Garbos," I say softly.

No reaction.

I take a tentative step forward. "I'm sorry."

Still nothing.

I walk to his side and get a better look at him. My heart shatters, and the lump in my throat comes back.

Indeed, he has a book open on his lap, but he's not reading. The pages are drenched by tears that keep flowing.

I'm at a loss. I don't know what to do or to say. Malia would know. But no thanks to me, she ran away too. She would know for sure. She always does. She's always been the kind one, the one who comforts crying little kids. She's always been the one to go to them, hug them, and speak the words that soothed them.

I've never been as good as her with words, but there's something I can do.

Cautiously, so as not to frighten him, I kneel in front of Garbos.

"I'm sorry," I croak again.

Without thinking, I hug him.

I hear him sob, and he hugs me back.

"I'm sorry," I repeat again, and again, with a voice broken by tears.

Now comes the real pain, the price for my acts. It's not a physical pain, but it hurts more. His arms crush me. His sobs pierce me to the heart. His tears burn me like hot iron.

For the first time, I forget to hate him, and let myself like him. I tighten my hug, and I cry.

The pain gradually recedes. His face on my shoulder doesn't weigh me down anymore. The crush of his arms become a cuddle. His body emits a soothing warmth against mine.

Nothing has changed and everything has changed. Suddenly, I'm the one being comforted.

When we break our embrace, our tears have dried out. When we pull apart, he stares at me, and I see in his eyes, what he's craving; what would heal him completely. But I can't kiss him. Even if I crave too, I just can't. I called him a freak to hurt him.

"I really am sorry." I've probably said it a hundred times, but I need to say it once more.

"I know. I'm sorry too. I shouldn't have—"

I brush off the end of his sentence with a wave of my hand. "I've been a jerk. And I'm not speaking just about today. Can you forgive me?"

"Hmm." He nods.

✳✳✳

Finding Malia isn't very hard. The door she went through leads to what must have been private quarters, with dozens of individual bedrooms, and more doors leading to yet unexplored places. We find her sitting on a bed, a book open on her lap. She understands as soon as she sees us together. She runs to us and hugs us both.

I can't quite look Malia in the eyes. I didn't tell Garbos what my true feelings are. And I definitely can't tell Malia. I've already hurt Garbos; I don't want to hurt her. I can't choose between them.

"And now?" Malia asks.

The three of us are back in the first room, staring blankly at the huge pipe behind it.

I shrug. "We have to find out if this is the Gaia Protocol."

"And if it is?"

"We try to find out how it works…" I take my amulet out and move it toward a box.

"Wait!" Malia stops my hand. "They're probably already looking for us. But once we activate a box, they'll know where we are. We won't have much time."

In the cities, it didn't take the guards long to find us, every time we used a box. And being directly under the agoge certainly won't help us. "Do you have a better idea?"

"We try to discover everything we can about the place."

Malia and I stare at Garbos. "And how do we proceed?"

"I'll search in the library," he answers tartly.

Malia smiles broadly. "I found a few handwritten books in the rooms. I'll check those." She immediately runs away.

Without another word, Garbos leaves too.

"Okay... What do I do?"

No answer from the empty room.

I look around. There are thirty boxes in this room, all identical. I can't find a single detail to show which one we'll need to use, if any.

With nothing more to do, I go exploring. If I want to find something useful, my best chances are behind the door in the library. As I cross it, I see Garbos, sitting at the table with a dozen books spread on it, and many more lying open on the floor around him. He's absorbed in his readings and doesn't even notice me.

On the other side of the door, I discover a staircase going down. Six long flights of stairs and a thick metal door later, I enter a different world.

The light isn't white, but a dark orange, turning all colors to different shades of brown. To my right and left, the room is so wide I can't see the end of it, and the ceiling is twice as high as in the other rooms. Everywhere, a mayhem of cables and pipes twists and turns everywhere.

In front of me is a small cubicle. I try to open the door, but I can't. Surprised, I look around the door and find a metallic rectangle on the wall. As I press my amulet against it, I hear a click. This time, the door opens.

As soon as I enter the room, a bright white light goes on. The room is mostly empty, save for a large table in the center. There is no window, no other furniture. I can't see the color of the walls or of the table. They are plastered with wide sheets of paper covered in drawings. One, hanging on the wall to my right, catches my attention. The agoge is easily recognizable: a large circle with tiny rectangles in it, as if seen from above, without the soldiers' tents. I wonder what a map of the agoge is doing in a Last Era building. Have the soldiers come here?

Except that it's not the agoge. I can see it now. The rectangles are too big compared to the circle, and misplaced. They should be in the middle, but they are on its border. There's also a line touching the circle.

The drawing next to it has two circles: a huge one with a small one touching it on the inside. In the small circle are tiny dots. I look at it and then at the first drawing. Having them next to each other, it's easy to tell the circle from the first drawing is the small one from the second drawing.

On the other drawings, I see so many rectangles and lines crisscrossing, that all meaning is lost to me. Even the few words I see don't help me understand.

I check all the drawings on the walls, without getting any information from them. At least, none I can understand. I turn to the pile on the table. I shuffle through the sheets, but none makes any more sense. My hopes rise when I see the word *PROTOCOL* written in red at the top of one, but *SAFETY* attached to it crushes them. The rest of the document is just as unhelpful as all the others. It shows what looks like a building, with thick red lines everywhere. Even the rest of the title is cryptic: *Emergency Containment*. Why would they prevent someone from going out?

I give up. I won't find anything here. Plus, I feel tired and hungry.

The library is empty. Books are spread everywhere, but Garbos is nowhere to be seen. As I enter the main room, he runs to me, jumping with every step, shouting my name...

"Prome, we found it! We found it!" He hugs me for a second, and then starts jumping again, shouting, "We found it!" over and over again.

"Whoa. Calm down! What did we find?"

"The Gaia Protocol!" He shakes a book in front of my face. "It's here! We found it!"

"What did we find?" asks a voice behind us.

I let out a sigh of relief. "Malia! He thinks we found the Gaia Protocol, but I can't calm him down long enough to get an explanation..."

She flashes me a wicked smile. "Who wants to eat something?"

We both stare at her, goggle-eyed. "You... you found some food?"

She pulls a face. "No. But I brought some. What do you think is in the bag I brought? Come, I'm hungry too. Without the sun, I don't know how long we've already been in here..."

We follow her sheepishly to what used to be living quarters. She shows us several halls connecting with ours. "These lead to bedrooms. Over there is the common room."

She opens a door to a wide room equipped with chairs and tables, several sofas, and lots of objects whose purpose I can't even guess. One of the tables is already set for three with plates full of food. Garbos and I run to the plates under Malia's amused gaze.

Once we've cleaned our plates, conversation resumes.

"So, you found out what the Gaia Protocol is?"

Garbos nods. "Yes and no. I found a book in the library about it, but it was very technical, and I didn't understand all of it. It seems this whole place was built for the Gaia Protocol. All the buildings, everything. A consortium of Last Era countries decided to build it after an experiment made in some place called CERN. Something unexpected occurred that they wanted to investigate. Don't ask me what it was. They had to build that huge tube to complete their experimentation."

"What did they find?"

"I don't know. I haven't found it yet." He rises. "I'll go back and try to find it."

"No, you won't!" Malia grabs him before he can leave. "I don't know what time it is, but it's certainly late enough to sleep."

As soon as she pronounces the word *sleep* my body feels incredibly tired, as if I haven't slept for days.

"There are rooms with beds just over there. Have a good night."

***

As tired as I am, sleep eludes me. I'm thinking about Malia and Garbos. I can still feel where Garbos touched my hand. And when he hugged me in the main room... I became happy just because he was.

I've never had such strong feelings for anyone before.

Even for Malia.

Of course, we've spent most of our time together. And when we're happy or sad, we hug each other. I know that everyone who knows us in our city thinks we'll marry each other someday. We've never talked about it, but I think Malia does, too. And until recently, I never really thought about it. It's what's supposed to happen. It's... natural. And Malia and I would be happy together.

Except that when I think of kissing someone, it's not her lips on mine. It's not her touch that sets my skin on fire. I love her, but not like that.

The hug with Garbos... It had an intensity the ones with Malia seldom reach. But it was a mistake too. His tears, if not Malia, convinced me he's no traitor. But if I allow myself to love him, I will be the traitor. I will betray Malia.

Chapter Thirty

"So the only way to find more about the Gaia Protocol is to make that huge pipe do whatever it's supposed to do?"

Garbos nods. "I didn't find anything else I could understand in the books."

"And how do we discover how it works?"

"We'll have to use a box." His tone is almost sad.

We both know what that means. The soldiers will know where we are and what we're doing. And with the agoge above us...

We hear running footsteps, and Malia rushes toward us. "I found something! Look! This is some kind of logbook written by one of the Technologists who worked here." She spreads the book open near a box.

"It's not about the Gaia Protocol. It's about the Purification. It's written that they built this place to work with your CERN thing, but before they could use it, the planet was attacked without warning by aliens pretending to be Gods. The CERN was the first place attacked and destroyed. After that, all the scientific buildings were targeted, beginning with the biggest, until there were no laboratories left. Doctor Gerbier—he's the one who wrote the logbook—thinks that the attack was triggered by the experiment in the CERN. That whatever they found was a threat to the aliens, who decided to invade Earth. As this facility was never used, the Gods didn't attack it. But most of the *scientists*—"

"That's what Technologists were called during the Last Era," adds Garbos.

"Well, as most of them were in CERN when the Gods attacked, most of them died. This building was deserted for fear it would be targeted soon."

"And?" I ask.

"And that's all."

"You mean they discovered a weapon so great that it caused the Gods to come back, but never created it?"

"That's what the book says."

"But... They could have fought back! They could have—"

"I know. But they didn't get the chance."

We all stay silent for a while, thinking about what could have happened if they had built the weapon. There would be no monsters lurking around the cities, waiting to kill us. The huge buildings would still be standing, with lights everywhere. We'd still be in our city. My mother would still be alive, and Malia would be with hers...

I feel hatred like never before for those Gods without mercy. Through gritted teeth, I make a vow. "May it take one day or my whole life, I'll create that weapon and destroy the Gods!"

Malia flinches at my words. Despite all we've been through, she still has some of the student left in her.

"Malia! It's our best hope of saving your mother. If we want to save her, we have to build that weapon and then go after the Gods. There will be no turning back. If you don't want to do it, I'll do it alone. You can leave now; I won't begrudge you for it. Same goes for you, Garbos. What's your decision?"

Surprisingly, Garbos is the first to answer, with a voice full of determination. "I'm with you."

I give him a smile, and we both turn to Malia.

"From what I've discovered about the Last Era and their technologies, not everything was bad. It wasn't all about killing each other. If the Gods lied about this, they probably lied about other things too. I won't let Mom be imprisoned or killed for a lie."

She sounds like she's trying to convince herself, but I'm impressed nonetheless. For the first time, she's questioning what's written in the Book of Gods. I give her a comforting hug.

I turn to Garbos. "It's your call. How do we proceed?"

Stone-faced, he points at a nearby cube. "We use one of those."

"Do you know what to do?"

"No. But we're in the control room. These cubes must control everything. I'll have to search through them to find the Gaia Protocol and start it."

"I hope you'll find it fast. We won't have much time." I take the amulet from around my neck. I look at Garbos and Malia, to see if they have any last-minute questions.

None comes.

I touch the cube with my amulet. Immediately, it emits a beep, and a picture of buildings appear, floating, above the cube. The picture was taken from above, but I recognize the canyon immediately.

Garbos immediately begins moving his fingers on the table, and the screen changes.

"Can we help you?"

He shakes his head. "Malia can use another cube and search too."

We move to the next cube.

Another beep, and the same picture appears.

Malia moves her fingers over letters that have appeared on the surface of the table, in front of her. The picture fades and words appear. Malia is a fast reader and everything changes before I can read much. I soon give up trying to follow what she's doing.

Not being able to do anything makes the wait even worse. I start another cube, just to have something to do, but I can't even get past the picture.

BANG!

The sound comes from the small room that brought us down here. It's an explosion, though a distant one. A few seconds later, there's another explosion.

"Garbos, Malia, you'd better hurry. They're trying to get in."

They don't answer but move their fingers more frantically. I come back to look at what Malia's doing.

"What's that crap?" She sounds perplexed.

On the screen, a long list of words has appeared. At the top of the screen, *Emergency Containment* blinks in red.

"Malia, Wait!"

She freezes, staring at me.

"I saw that on a map, downstairs. I think it was the building. Wait." I run out to get the map. When I return, out of breath, I push a cube to the side and spread the map on the table.

Garbos throws an eye on it and immediately gets excited. "Look! This here is the building seen from above. This is the building from the side. The red lines follow the outline. This, here, has to be a door. Here too." He looks at us and calms down. He traces lines on the drawing, explaining that it's a building seen from above, and here from the side, following the walls with his finger.

Now that he's explained it to me, it seems so obvious I wonder how I didn't see it earlier. I look around. "We must be here!" I point at a large room, almost at the bottom of the building. Even the moving closet is on the map. The shaft above it is closed by several red lines. Several other red lines circle the room where we got in it.

"Malia, can you activate it?"

She blinks. "Aahh... I think so." She moves her fingers quickly and a blinking red sign appears.

ATTENTION! WARNING! ACHTUNG!
EMERGENCY CONFINEMENT
ACTIVATE?
YES/NO

She looks at us.

"Do it!"

A deafening siren goes off, and all the lights become red.

I put my hands on my ears. After several minutes, everything becomes quiet. We stare at each other, stunned. After another minute, the red lights blink and become white again.

"Wow. What was that?"

"No idea."

Garbos walks back to his cube. He stops dead in his tracks about halfway, in front of a wall. "Prome? Malia?"

We turn to him. "What?"

He points at the wall.

I just shrug. "What? It's a wall!" When he doesn't immediately move, I add, "Malia, tell him it's—"

Malia is just as transfixed as Garbos.

I blink, look right and left, and it hits me. There shouldn't be a wall here. There should be the small closet! I look at the map again. There is indeed a red line between the room and the closet.

"It's the confinement," I say triumphantly. "The place is completely sealed off. It should keep everyone out."

They both shout out, "Yeah!" at the same time and go back to their search for the Gaia Protocol. I strain my ears but can hear no more noises from above.

Time slows down. They're both active, but I can't do much. After a while, I decide to go back to look at the maps. We'll have to find a way out eventually.

Once in the room, I look at all the drawings with brand-new eyes. I see buildings and rooms and not just meaningless lines anymore. But even understanding them, these drawings don't help me much.

I look at the ones hanging on the wall, with the circles. These two are so completely different, they intrigue me. Little rectangles in a circle. If they represent buildings, it could be the agoge, except that it didn't exist then. But they have to be buildings. So what's the circle?

I walk back up. Before entering the control room, I stop in front of the door I haven't opened yet. I do it and face the giant pipe. It fills most of the hall. I can't see the end of it, left or right. The hall and the pipe are not straight. They curve so slightly it can only be seen in the distance.

I go back to look at the drawing, and can't believe it. The circle is the outline of the pipe. It's so huge; it would probably take a day and a half to walk the whole circle. Except for these buildings and a tiny one on the opposite side of the circle, there's nothing to notice.

"Prome?" Malia's standing in the doorway. "I've been looking for you. Garbos found something."

✳✳✳

"And you still don't know what will happen?"

Garbos answers with a shake of his head. We all look transfixed at the words hanging in the air above the box:

INITIALIZE GAIA PROTOCOL
YES/NO

"Go on."

He moves his hand, the *YES* blinks once, then another question appears.

USE PRERECORDED SET OF VALUES?
YES/NO

"I'd better say yes. We don't know anything about those values."

He moves his hand again and everything disappears.

A few seconds pass, but nothing happens. The doubts I've managed to keep under control until now come back, stronger than ever. "Did it work?"

"I don't know."

"Did you break it?"

Malia shoots me a murderous glare, but I don't care. My doubts are turning into a visceral fear. "Did you break it?"

"No! I... I... I don't know?" Garbos's voice rises to a treble squeak. He moves his hands frantically in front of the cube, fruitlessly. He shoots up and inspects the cube. "It's not broken, the light's still there..." His voice quavers with the same fear that's gripping me.

"My cube's broken too." Malia stares, appalled, at her cube.

We glance at each other, unable to say or do anything. I feel pain in my right hand. I look down and realize that my fingers are clenched around something. As I unclench them, I see the amulet.

"Garbos, let me see." I brush him aside.

With a trembling hand, I put the amulet on the box.

Nothing.

I take it off and put it back again.

Nothing.

I stare at it blankly. It's never failed me before.

I take a step back, away from my crushed hopes.

Beep.

I keep staring at the box, each and every muscle in my body tensed to a painful point.

A word appears, blinking, above the cube.

ERROR

CHAPTER THIRTY-ONE

Garbos immediately starts working again. Other words appear and disappear, too fast for me to read them.

Malia and I wait for him to tell us anything, but he keeps working. It's as if he doesn't notice us.

Without warning, he turns to me. "Prome, put your card on all the cubes!"

"What?"

"Put your card—your amulet, on all the cubes to start them!"

I'm surprised by his tone. It conveys an authority, an assertiveness I never suspected he had. I hurry along the room, doing as he required.

The last one hasn't beeped yet, when Malia asks Garbos, "Should he do the same with the boxes in the other rooms?"

Garbos throws a glance at the door, as if he could see the boxes through it. "It can't hurt."

It doesn't take me long, but when I come back, Garbos is reclined in his chair, Malia doing the same next to him.

"Did you fix it?"

Garbos smiles. "It didn't need to be fixed. It just needed all the boxes to work. I started the initialization again. Look."

I look above the screen and see a green bar with a percentage under it that eventually changes from 0.1% to 0.2% as the bar grows longer.

"It will take a while," he says.

"Why did you call my amulet a card?"

Garbos swallows the piece of dried meat he was chewing. "Because that's what it is." He bites his meat again.

He says it so naturally, as if I everybody knew it. I feel a remnant of my old hatred toward him. I take deep breaths to calm down. "What kind of card?"

He looks up, surprised. "Don't you know?" Seeing me nonplussed, he looks at Malia. "And you?"

Malia's face reflects my own ignorance.

"Okay. Story time. When the Gods came back, and during the following decades, the Gods hunted all technologies ruthlessly, to totally and utterly erase them. The Technologists tried to save what they could, but many things were lost or destroyed. Time didn't help. Among those things were cards, like the one you have. They were the control keys the scientists from the Last Era used to hide the technologies from the Gods. They tried to hide the cards too, but most of them were destroyed. In fact, we were pretty sure there was none left, though we kept looking for them."

"That's why my mother immediately recognized it?" Malia interjects.

Garbos nods. "Yes. For all the Technologists, they are the cornucopia, the access to all lost knowledge."

The irony of it seems lost to him. I look at Malia. "The Technologists put so much effort into the search for the cards, that they forgot what they gave access to…"

Garbos looks down. "Yeah. Kind of."

"Do you think what we'll find will help us save my mother?"

He looks up at Malia. "I hope so."

"Then let's sleep. It looks like whatever's happening won't reach a hundred percent for a few hours, and we don't know when we'll be able to sleep next."

✳✳✳

I'm woken up by a low rumble. It's barely audible, but lasts long seconds before stopping. I dress quickly, and run to the common room. Malia and Garbos arrive at the same time.

"Did you hear that?"

"We all did."

"What do you think it was?"

We all stare at each other, unable to answer that question. I'm not sure I really want to know the answer. "I don't know, but it can't be good for us. Let's go to the boxes and see the progress. The sooner we leave, the better."

Malia takes her bag and we all run to the boxes.

99.7%

The green bar is still there, its progress almost complete, with just a tiny blank space at the end of it. Just enough to set my nerves on edge. "Can you speed up the process?"

"No. We have to wait."

We stare nervously at the number. Minutes pass, but it doesn't change. Sitting immobile is too much for me. I stand up and begin pacing the room. Malia throws me an angry glance, but I have to move.

Another rumble.

I start counting.

One...

Two...

Three...

I reach twelve before it stops.

We exchange nervous glimpses. We stay silent, too afraid to say out loud what we all noticed: it was louder this time.

99.8%

I hear a sigh of relief, but I can't tell if it comes from Malia, Garbos, or me. Maybe from all of us. Yet the wait is not over.

99.9%

I pace the room again, trying not to look at the ominous number. Is there anything else to think about?

Don't look! Think.

What will happen next? We'll launch the Gaia Protocol and get whatever weapon it creates.

Good.

And then?

Garbos will find out how to deactivate the confinement. We go back up and barge through everyone waiting for us with the weapon. If it's powerful enough to frighten the Gods, it should be enough to kill their soldiers.

99.9%

Then we go to Parthenos and save Malia's mother.

Another rumble.

What if we can't go up again?

For no reason, I get the picture of a circle in my mind. It's stupid. A circle won't help us out.

Twelve again.

99.9%

Circle.

I stop dead in my tracks, close my eyes, and slow down my breathing. In... Out... In... Out... In...

"Yeahhh!!"

I open my eyes and see Garbos and Malia staring at the writing above the box. The green bar has disappeared. Instead, it asks us another question.

INITIALIZING COMPLETE
LAUNCH PROTOCOL
YES/NO?

Another rumble.

"Do it, Garbos!"

All the lights turn red and a loud female voice announces, "Gaia Protocol initiated."

A loud noise comes from behind the windows. We stare at the pipe in front of us. The two parts move together to close the gap between them.

A deep hum fills the air, rising to higher tones. It takes a minute to stabilize. Above all the boxes, numbers are displayed, changing constantly. Some go up, others down. I don't understand any labels. One is called C and is currently at 0.9999952147287 and rising. But as it's in the middle and bigger than all the other numbers, I follow it, guessing that when it reaches 1, something will happen.

0.99999695498561

0.99999829548715

0.99999900267454

The rising slows down as it gets closer to 1.

0.9999999997638

Another rumble. This time, I can hear it above the hum. From behind us, where the closet used to be, comes the sound of falling rocks. When it finally ends, the rumble is over.

"Give me the card!" Malia snatches it from my hand and brushes it against the wall frantically. "It doesn't work! We're trapped!"

"The confinement is still active. It can't work." I don't believe it myself. If there's been a rockslide, we are trapped. "For now, we have to wait. Once we have the weapon, we'll see how we get out. One thing at a time. Okay?"

She nods and looks back at the numbers.

0.9999999999975

There's no sound except the hum. We don't speak, don't even move.

0.9999999999992

I can feel my heart beating.

0.9999999999997

I hold my breath.

1.0000000000000

All the numbers disappear. In their stead, a few words blink three times before disappearing too.

SPEED OF LIGHT REACHED
COLLISION

A few seconds later, every cube in the room displays an avalanche of numbers, diagrams, and drawings. On the other side of the glass, the two parts of the pipe slowly move away from each other. We wait impatiently for them to reveal the weapon inside.

Through the tiny slit, I can see the other side of the room. As it grows wider, I see nothing.

The two parts of the pipe stop moving. I wait for something else to happen, but seconds go by and nothing changes. In the pipe's opening is only emptiness.

I turn to Garbos, angry. "What? Is that all? We did all this for nothing?"

Garbos doesn't move, eyes stuck to the emptiness in front of us. "I... I..."

A silent tremor shakes the room. A reflex makes me look up at the ceiling. "They're coming after us. Malia, get your bag, quick! Garbos, disable the confinement."

They both obey without questions, Garbos working on a box and Malia going back to the common room. I rush to my room and retrieve my weapons and breastplate.

"Why are you wearing that?" Malia asks as she sees me in full armor.

"Whatever's waiting for us, it can't harm us to be ready."

I run back to the control room before Malia does. I take out the amulet and brush it against the wall, without much hope. As expected, the closet doesn't open anymore. I haven't seen any exit through the living quarters, and the only way through the library leads down and not up. I know that all the soldiers are waiting for us up there, but it's nonetheless a blow.

Garbos stares at me. "Will we die here?"

Yes. That's what I think. That's honestly the answer I want to give but can't. I can't let him down like this. And I can't let Malia down. We have to do something, even if it's just an illusion to keep their hopes up.

Malia comes back with her bag. "Can you open the closet?"

I don't have time to think. I look at the pipe and go for the only solution I see for now. "No. It won't open. Come."

I lead them out of the room for the last time.

"Where are we going? The exit is—"

"There is no exit there anymore." I cut Malia off. "It won't open. And even if it did, they'd kill us once we reach the surface."

CHAPTER THIRTY-TWO

I open the door and we stop, facing the huge pipe. The hall in which it stands is well lit. It seems to be straight, but far away, on both sides, its curvature is revealed.

"Come on. There should be an exit this way."

Malia gapes at me. "Should?"

"Yeah. I saw it on a map."

The ground shakes, harder than it did before. All the lights blink and go out, leaving us in almost total darkness. A single light still shines in the opening of the pipe. I look at Garbos, who walks toward it.

"Malia! Prome! Over here!"

We both run to him, curious to see what he found. Inside the pipe, right in its center, is a small marble, no bigger than the nail of my little finger, but just as bright as the sun.

"Do you think that's the weapon?" Garbos asks, hopeful again.

"I don't know. Let's try. Garbos, you created it. Try it."

He looks at me with a wide smile and reaches for the light. Malia and I take a careful step back. He lifts his hand with the light in it, and holds it like this for a moment.

"I can't do it. Prome, try."

He puts the marble in my hand. It feels smooth, slightly warm, and heavier than I expected. I close my fist around it and concentrate, but it feels just like a regular marble, not like a weapon ready to answer my will. I try to trigger it anyway, to no avail.

"I can't do it either. It doesn't work like the spear. Malia. Do you want to try it? Maybe you can do it."

She stares wide-eyed at me, then takes the marble. Soon, she hands it back to me. "I can't do it either."

"If we can't use it, then we'd better move. We'll find a way to use it later." I hand the marble back to Garbos.

He shakes his head. "No! I don't want it. You can have it."

"But you created it..."

"Yes, and what good did it do? I don't want to touch it."

I can hear resentment and disappointment in his words, and I can only sympathize. All his life, he's been told about a weapon that would rid us of the Gods. And now that he found it, it can't be used.

I give it to Malia instead. "Lead the way. The exit is a short day's walk away. I'd rather be out of here when they find a way in..."

✳✳✳

"Malia, do you have a lace?"

She hands me a long, thin strip of leather. I knot it around the marble, like a cage, and hand her the improvised necklace. "It will be easier to carry this way."

The stop is also an excuse for a very short break. We've been walking for hours without stopping. That and the disappointment of the weapon weigh on our spirits. At least the marble gives us light to see the way.

Poor compensation.

The darkness around us takes its toll too. From as young as we can remember, we've always been taught to fear it, that monsters lurk in it, waiting for careless prey to come to them. We try to walk soundlessly and barely whisper to each other.

Hours later, we're still walking. There is no change in the pipe or in the walls. Everything looks just the same as when we started. I begin to wonder if we haven't passed the exit, without seeing it. Or if it even exists. The light from the marble seems to grow dimmer too, but that's something else I don't want to consider. If it comes to it, we'll make torches with whatever we can find.

The tremors are our biggest incentive to keep walking. They come more often. They don't even seem to grow feebler with the distance, rather the contrary. I wonder if we've passed the midpoint and are heading back to the control room.

In front of us is a recess in the wall. Another one like the ones we've seen every half hour or so. It doesn't bring us hope anymore, just the fear that a monster hides in it.

We approach it cautiously. As I round the corner with my spear ready to strike, I discover only emptiness.

Emptiness and a wide, gray door.

"Malia! Garbos! Come on, we've found it!"

We all push the door to the side to reveal another hallway and, at the end of it, stairs.

Malia starts running, and I'm all too happy to follow. Our enthusiasm is soon tampered by the innumerable flights of stairs that force us to slow down to a panting pace. Surprisingly, Garbos doesn't seem to suffer as much as we do. As I say that aloud, he cracks a smile.

"At school, I always keep—kept," he corrects a bit sadly, "forgetting things, and I had to run back to my room to get them. Between that and Veron, who made me run up and down the stairs between his office and the secret room to get his own material, I've had quite a training."

What seems an infinity of stairs later, even he is showing the strain. We finally reach the top landing and enter a short hallway. At the other end of it is a dark-gray door.

"Do you think it's the exit?"

I shrug. "Your guess's as good as mine."

As much as we wanted to reach it, we all suddenly hesitate to open the door. We've grown accustomed to this Last Era building. It somehow feels familiar, even safe. Or, at least, safer than whatever may be waiting for us on the other side of the door.

"Let's eat something and then get some rest. The door will still be there in a couple of hours, and I don't think the guards have managed to get in yet."

As if in agreement with me, a new tremor shakes the ground.

***

My right hand is on the knob, ready to open the door. With my left one, I try to take Malia's hand, but my fingers find nothing. Surprised, I look at her, and notice she has deliberately taken her hand away. I wonder what it means, but let go for now.

"Put the marble under your shirt. I don't want anyone or anything to notice us."

With a slightly trembling hand, I open the door.

On the other side, everything is dark until light appears around Malia's neck.

"Put it back!" I shout back.

I wait for my eyes to grow accustomed to the darkness. It's not as dark as I first thought. Two rugged walls line a narrow path. I can't see the ceiling, but the reverberation of our footsteps tells me there must be one high above our heads.

We don't walk for long before the walls disappear and we emerge from the mouth of a grotto in the side of a small, rocky hill, and face the desert, illuminated by a half-moon.

"What's that?" Garbos begins to climb up the hill.

"Garbos! Wait!" We both climb after him.

We reach him, crouching at the top, just as a flash lightens the sky.

"Look!" He points in front of us as the rumble of thunder reaches us.

What I see doesn't make sense. In the distance is a gigantic cloud that just sent out a dozen lightning bolts at the same time. The cloud itself is illuminated by misty blue lights.

Another set of bolts shows me dark shapes on the ground.

"That's—"

"Yeah, that's the agoge," Garbos answers me.

And then the horror of the situation dawns on me. The Gods have gone to war again. Zeus is attacking the agoge in an attempt to destroy us.

I can only stare as more lightning and thunder fill the air.

A hand shakes me softly. "Prome! We have to leave!" I turn around. Malia and Garbos are ready to move.

I can only nod. Was Pyrias still there when the first lightning struck? Is he still alive?

"Where should we go? What are we going to do?"

Garbos's questions bring me back to our present situation. I look around and see the same questions in Malia's eyes. But, without knowing it, she has given me the answers.

"We'll walk back to Parthenos! Whatever that marble is, the Gods fear it. We'll have several days to learn how to use it. And if we don't, we'll trade it for Malia's mother." I hug Malia. "I promised you we'd save your mother, and we will."

I look up in search of the northern star. "Let's go."

✳✳✳

When the sky begins to lighten, the agoge is just a spot far behind us, but Zeus is still attacking it. Only the resolve to save Malia's mother holds me together. I can't stop thinking I've sentenced Pyrias and all the other guards to death. If I hadn't found that amulet, they'd still be alive.

Something else is burdening me. We've been more or less retracing the path we used to come here for several hours now, and I haven't seen any sign of Nemeos.

"Over there!" Malia points to our left, at a rocky outcrop. "We'll find a hiding place so we can rest."

I look back at the agoge, under the attack of the ominous thundering cloud above. "We should stay hidden today. We're still too close to the agoge. We'll be too easy to spot."

"But if they come after us?"

"I don't think they will. They're still trying to destroy the buildings. They must still think we're inside. We'll be safe hiding and resting. At least for today."

Hiding among the rocks is easy enough. We eat some of Malia's food and soon fall asleep.

***

The sound of a distant explosion, followed by a violent earthquake, wakes us with a start.

"What's that?"

"Come down!" I grab Garbos's arm and pull him back down just as the blast reaches us.

Even protected by the rocks, we fear for our lives, so strong is the wind. It carries dust and sand, getting into our mouths, and threatening to choke us. Pebbles of all sizes fly everywhere, colliding on the rocks around us. For an eternity, we're in hell.

Just as suddenly as it started, everything stops. We cough and spit to clear our mouths and lungs but are otherwise uninjured.

I creep out to look at the agoge and gasp at the sight. Instead of a tiny dot in the distance, there is a crater so huge I can see it easily from where I stand. Above it, Zeus's cloud is higher than before. It still glows blue but doesn't send out lightning anymore. Slowly, it starts moving toward us.

"Do you think He saw us?" Garbos asks while we go down to our hiding place again.

"I don't think so."

We watch, squeezed against the rocks, as Zeus flies above us. He doesn't stop, and a few minutes later, we're smiling stupidly at each other, simply happy to have escaped and be alive. Garbos grabs Malia and me in a bear hug. His joy is infectious, and I hug him back, laughing.

"How far ahead are the Dead Steppes?" I ask when we calm down.

Malia thinks twice and answers, "About a week's walk."

"But they're not quite on our path," Garbos adds. "If we walk slightly to the North, we should avoid them altogether and maybe reach the road from Gallia to Parthenos."

"Without horses and water, we'll never cross the Dead Steppes anyway. Lead the way."

∗∗∗

Since the second day, we've been walking by day and sleeping by night. We make better progress, and the danger of the agoge and its soldiers is now far away. We've been walking for four days in a desert, eventually reaching a more fertile country.

Until now, we've met no monsters. I suspect the marble is responsible for that, but it's just a wild guess. I'll probably never know, as each night its light has grown weaker. It won't shine much longer. It has grown, though. I had to untie and retie the lace around it almost every day. It's now as big as my thumb. We all wonder if it's an egg, but a shining egg is unheard of. Could it be a man-created monster? I hope so, because all our attempts to use the marble as a weapon have failed.

The green land spreading in front of us is a relief. We'll find water. And we're getting closer to the road.

"Prome?"

When he wants to ask me something, Garbos always says my name first, as if to warn me, so that I don't spear him or something. From anyone else, it would exasperate me, but I somehow find his shyness cute.

"After you've saved Malia's mother—"

"After *we*'ve saved Malia's mother," I correct him.

"What will I do? I mean, I've always—"

A low grunt coming from a little spinney puts us all on guard, ready for battle.

There's a rustle of leaves.

The biggest lion I've ever seen comes out of the spinney with bared teeth. It's as tall as I am. Its tawny mane looks like dancing flames. It approaches menacingly, then roars so loud my ears ring.

It starts walking toward us again, ready to strike.

CHAPTER THIRTY-THREE

We're all ready to strike too, with arrows and bolts, when my eyes meet the lion's.

"Wait! Hold your fire!"

They seem familiar. The size, the fur. This is a Nemean lion... I put down my spear and take a step toward it.

"What are you doing? Are you crazy?" Malia shouts at me.

"No. I think it's Nemeos."

"What? It can't be. It couldn't have grown that much. Come back!"

"Malia, shut up! Don't do anything. Don't move."

I walk cautiously, arm stretched out in front of me as a peace gesture. "Nemeos?"

The lion stops and grunts.

"Nemeos. It's me. Prome."

He walks to me, and we stare at each other. I was wrong. He is now taller than me, and I have to look up. His fangs are still bared and he emits a constant growl. Without warning, he roars once more and circles me.

"Don't move," I order again.

He sniffs at my arm, where the chimera injured me.

"It's okay. They healed me. Look." I show him my arm with the scar on it.

The next second, I'm pinned to the ground under his huge body, as he slobbers my face with his rough tongue.

"Prome! Are you all right?"

I recognize Garbos's alarm, but I can't stop laughing long enough to answer him. And when I manage it, my first words are for the friend I just found again. "I'm sorry, Nemeos. I didn't expect us to leave you alone for so long."

At last, he lets me stand.

"You remember Malia and Garbos?"

Nemeos lazily walks to them. Malia pats him, but Garbos looks like he may faint.

"It's okay, Garbos. He won't hurt you."

"I... I know."

I pat Nemeos on the flank, but he ignores me.

"Nemeos? What's up?"

Without looking at me, he jogs away, ignoring my calling his name.

I watch him disappear again. I can't believe he would leave me so soon after we're reunited.

Malia puts her hand on my shoulder. "He's been living alone for a while, now. Look how he's grown. He can take care of himself. Even if he doesn't stay with us, I'm sure we'll see him again. Now come on, we have to go." And she pulls me away.

✳✳✳

I spend the rest of the day looking for him, hoping he'll be back. When the day grows old, I can't shake off the feeling I'll never see him again.

We settle down against the trunk of a fallen tree, the only shelter we can find. Malia takes out the marble, but its light is almost gone now. She hands around food, and I eat in silence. Malia and Garbos chat happily, trying to include me in their conversation, but they soon give up. I'm still brooding over Nemeos's departure.

While chewing on a piece of dried meat, I hear the faint, rhythmical thumping of a running animal. I stand up and look around. In the distance, I see a large animal running. As it gets closer, I recognize Nemeos, carrying something in his mouth.

When he reaches us, he puts down my old spear and Malia's sword.

Garbos looks at him, amazed. "He kept everything."

"Yes, and now we have a small arsenal." I hand Malia her sword.

"No, I'm using a bow now. I feel more comfortable with it."

"Take the sword anyway. You never know when you might need it. Garbos, you should take the second spear too."

Later, when we lie down to sleep, Nemeos settles down next to me and puts his big paw on me. His familiar warmth and protectiveness let me drift into the best sleep I've had for ages.

✳✳✳

I'm surprised to see a low sun when I wake up. I feel well rested, and ready for the day. Malia and Garbos are already up and ready.

"We didn't want to wake you. Here, eat that, it's getting late." Malia throws me a piece of dry bread and a little piece of meat. "We'll have to hunt today to replenish our rations."

"Speaking of hunting," Garbos adds, "don't you find it strange we haven't met a single monster yet? I mean, in the desert, with the explosion and all, I understand. But here?"

I watch Nemeos stretch and shake his mane. "They're probably afraid of a full-grown lion."

Garbos throws a look, between relief and worry, at Nemeos.

I hide a smile and swallow the last of my meal. "Come on. Time to go."

Not long after we start walking, Nemeos goes wandering. When he comes back, he has a big, fat rabbit in his mouth, which he gives to me. At noon, we build a small fire and eat it. With such a hunter at our side, our journey is suddenly much more enjoyable. After that, Garbos doesn't stay away from Nemeos as much. I'm sure that, tomorrow or the day after, he'll have accepted him completely.

***

In the early afternoon, we reach the edge of a large wood. The trees are sparse enough for us to walk through it easily, and the bright green leaves and birds' songs make pleasant scenery. Yet we're all much more subdued.

We know what a forest means.

We know that monsters or beasts lurk in it.

And even if we haven't seen any during the past few nights, tonight won't be the same.

We all walk silently, much closer to Nemeos. Malia and Garbos have their bows poised, ready to shoot. I have my spear in one hand and a sword in the other. As much as we'd like to be out of the forest, our progress is much slower.

Nemeos stops with a low, guttural grunt. We look at each other, unsure of what to do. I signal to them to be silent and move forward, hiding behind trees or bushes. Malia and Garbos do the same, but Nemeos seems much more reluctant to follow me. It doesn't take me long to discover why.

A stone's throw away from the bush where I'm hiding is a small clearing with a nest in the middle. There must be more than a hundred eggs, each one bigger than my head, in it. From the side of the clearing, seven enormous snakelike heads watch them.

Another hydra. I had always been told there was only one, but this is already the third I've see. Why are they multiplying like this? Could it be that because of it we haven't seen any other monsters yet?

My questions are stopped by the sudden jerk of an egg, soon followed by another egg. A few seconds later, a cacophony of bangs and cracks rings out as they all move, bumping against each other.

A head appears from an egg, then another. Dozens of the same two-headed lizard-like creatures scramble out of their egg to stand atop the broken shells, unmoving, absorbing the sun, and staring at each other.

It's eerily peaceful. All the newborns lie in the sun; the mother doesn't move. Even the air is still, soundless.

Without warning, a green-streaked baby jumps on his nearest sibling and tears off one of its heads. The severed head flies in the air while its twin emits a high-pitched scream. It falls among the other babies, but none moves. The injured hydra keeps wailing as the headless neck suddenly splits in two and each new neck grows a new head.

The wailing stops. Instead, all three heads hiss and spit at its attacker. It jumps on it. It bites off both its opponent's heads and eats them. With all its heads severed, the victim lies dead on the ground. The winner screams out in victory, then looks at its siblings, as if taunting them.

Once again, the whole nest is silent.

And then all hell breaks loose.

They all jump on each other. Heads fly while new ones grow. The ground is red with blood, and there are dead bodies everywhere.

And the mother watches the bloodshed without moving.

As the number of deaths increases, the fight loses intensity, until it stops altogether. There are only six hydras left, all with five heads, except for the green-streaked one, which has four.

Its five siblings jump on him at the same time. When they move back, the body is just a mass of torn flesh. No heads are left on the body. The murderers glare at each other.

The mother screeches once, then turns and walks away.

The babies keep staring at each other for a minute, then all run in different directions and vanish in the forest.

"That was... sick." Malia shivers.

"I never want to see this again." Garbos looks like he's about to throw up.

"Neither do I. Let's move."

***

That night in the forest, despite the presence of Nemeos, none of us sleeps well. Nothing attacks us, but in the morning, we're eager to be on the move again and leave at first light.

***

"One more day in that forest and I would have gone mad!" Garbos undresses quickly and jumps into the small lake where Nemeos is already bathing.

I can't help but stare at him for a moment. He's lost a lot of weight since we first met in Kurea, and grown lots of muscles instead. I'm tempted to brush his iron-hard stomach with my hand.

I catch Malia looking at me and feel my face going red. I try to hide my confusion. "Look at them, playing like a kid and a puppy..."

Malia smiles, but she's still staring at me. Eventually she looks at them. "We should join them too. I could do with a bath." She sniffs. "And you definitely need one!"

I don't need more incentive, and soon we're all four swimming in the cool water.

When we come out of the water, laughing and out of breath, the sun is setting. Garbos lights a small fire to warm us.

"Its light is gone." Malia holds the marble in her hand. "Look."

She hands it to Garbos, who holds it in front of us. "Not quite. There's still some of it left."

Now that it doesn't shine anymore, I can really look at it. It's full of thousands of tiny specks of light, but that's not the strangest part of it. I've never seen anything like it. It's indescribable. It's transparent, but I can't see through it. And its surface is so smoothly rough...

"Do you know what it is?"

Garbos shrugs. "I didn't learn anything about the Gaia Protocol that told me what its purpose was. I don't even know if the scientists who created it knew it."

"But I thought you knew it was a weapon?"

He looks down. "We inferred it was a weapon. But we never knew for sure. All we knew was that the Gods didn't want us to find it."

I sigh. "Great. You don't think we would have liked to know that earlier?" I walk a few paces away and settle down for the night, turning my back to him.

***

Midmorning the next day, we reach a road.

"See? I told you we'd reach it," Garbos exults.

I'm still grumpy about yesterday. "You sure it's a road leading to Parthenos? I'm just asking. After all, you could forget to tell us it leads somewhere else!"

Malia glares at me, but Garbos feigns not to hear the sarcasm in my voice and answers with an extra-cheery voice, "No, it's the one! I'm certain of it. If we had horses, we'd reach Parthenos in three or four days."

He keeps on chatting merrily, at first with me, and then, when I don't answer, with Malia. It's going to be a long day…

As usual, Nemeos walks away to hunt. I call after him and follow him. Making my escape gives me time to think about the marble. It's not a weapon, but if Zeus himself left his temple—something unheard of since the end of the Purification—and destroyed the agoge, it's certainly something he fears. What doesn't fit is that he came alone. If it's that dangerous, he should at least have come with one or two other Gods.

If we want to exchange the marble for Malia's mother, we'll have to do it somewhere safe. A place where Zeus won't dare use his destructive weapons. There's only one such place. We'll have to do it in his temple. The problem is how to go where no human has ever entered.

When we come back with two rabbits, both caught by Nemeos, I can see from afar that Garbos is sitting, unmoving, in front of a small fire. As soon as he spots us, he becomes animated. When we reach Malia and him, he immediately starts ranting about our prizes, and never stops talking.

By the time the rabbits are cooked, I can't stand it anymore. "Stop it! You don't have to do that!" I look at his crestfallen face and take pity. "I'm sorry. You didn't know what we'd find. I don't hold you responsible. I'm just frustrated we didn't find anything better than that stupid marble."

Garbos looks down and fumbles with his fingers. A lonely tear runs down his face. "I'm sorry."

From the corner of my eye, I glimpse Malia, and her face reminds me of the fight we had under the agoge. Shame hits me.

I soften my tone. "It's not your fault. Besides, we have the marble, and I really think it's the key to freeing Malia's mother. Without you, we wouldn't have gotten it."

He still looks like he's about to cry. I feel the urge to hug him tight, to save him those unnecessary tears, but fight it back. I must not do it. Not now. Not ever.

CHAPTER THIRTY-FOUR

Everything was too perfect. We got out of the woods without being attacked. We reached the road. We spent yet another night with no sign of any monsters, and Garbos was acting normally again. We were walking at a good pace with high spirits.

But we got careless. A horde of maybe forty cavalrymen is coming toward us. We saw them too late, and now we can't try to hide anymore. At least Nemeos is safe, having gone off to hunt.

"They're all bowmen. If we can get close enough before they shoot, we'll have a chance to kill them before they kill us."

Garbos scrutinizes the approaching group. "There's no officer. We still have our trainees' outfits. Maybe we can confuse them."

I smile at him. "We have better than that. Malia, give your bow to Garbos and stay behind us. Garbos, you stay at my side. Don't say a word, either of you. Throw all the extra weapons in that little bush.

They both look at me as if I've just lost my mind, but obey. I only keep my spear.

"Trust me on that one." I give them another smile and turn to face the horsemen.

As they come closer, they ready their bows.

"I hope you have a plan."

I hear doubt in Malia's voice, and I can't say I don't have doubts too, but I shush her anyway. It's too late for another plan. A moment later, we're surrounded; forty arrows pointing at us.

"Put down your weapons! I don't know where you got them, but you'll be sentenced for that!"

I take a deliberate step toward the speaker. "Soldier! What's your name?"

He sneers at me. "My name is of no concern to you. Put down your weapon!"

I raise my voice. "Do you recognize this?" I theatrically tap my breastplate and turn around so that everyone can see me.

"You stole a lochagos' breastplate. That will only increase the charges against you!"

I shoot the biggest bolt I can, just over his head. The crash of thunder is so loud, even I am surprised. I wait a few seconds for my ears to stop ringing, staring at his stupefied face.

"Who are you calling a thief? I am a lochagos, and this breastplate is rightfully mine! Point your arrows away!" I turn around again, pointing my spear at each one in turn and am happy to see them comply.

He stares suspiciously at my spear and Garbos's but, after my display, doesn't dare do anything about them. "I'm sorry. Finding a lochagos, a soldier, and a slave here is unexpected."

This is slippery ground. I prefer to cut the discussion short. "You heard what happened in the agoge. We were nearby, and our horses fled in fright. We've been traveling for days, now."

He doesn't look quite convinced. Before he can utter his doubts or ask an embarrassing question, I order him curtly, "Give us three horses. We need to be back in Parthenos as soon as possible."

As he hesitates, I point at him, then at two others. "You, you, and you. Get down from your horses. You'll ride with other soldiers. Now! You!"

Finally, I get them moving. They follow my orders swiftly. When I send them away, we have one horse each and food to last us to Parthenos.

As soon as they're out of sight behind us, Nemeos joins us. The horses whinny, but as Nemeos doesn't threaten them, we manage to calm them down easily.

"We're lucky he didn't come back earlier."

I smile at Malia. "I don't think we're lucky. I'm sure he stayed hidden, ready to strike if they attacked us. Didn't you, Nemeos?"

He answers me with a satisfied roar.

✳✳✳

Two days later, Parthenos is in sight.

"How will we reach the temples?" Garbos asks.

I look up at the acropolis. I don't have to think twice. "There's only one way. The stairs."

We all look at the thin white ribbon on the cliff's side.

Malia sighs. "But they're guarded."

"Yeah, I know."

"And how will we get to them, then?"

I've been thinking about it for a while now. My lochagos trick won't work there. "There's only one way."

"Which is?"

"We smash through," Garbos answers.

Malia laughs out loud, then looks at me. "Seriously, how do we do it?"

"As he said. We smash through."

We stare silently at the city.

"Do you think they put more guards on duty?"

That point is bothering me too. "I hope they're too holier-than-thou to think they could be in danger, but we'd better reconnoiter the place first. We'll sneak into the city this evening as mounted soldiers, find other clothes, and take a look at the guards. We'll come back tomorrow night.

***

Nemeos doesn't want me to leave him alone again, but it's unavoidable.

"Listen. We're going away tonight, but we'll be back tomorrow." Maybe I'm imagining it, but I see disapproval in his eyes. "We'll have to attack some guards to get to the temples, and we have to see how many there are in order to devise a plan. We'll be back tomorrow night. I promise. Just stay hidden, okay?" I hug him tight.

When I release him, he tilts his head, then turns around and leaves.

We hide our weapons and my breastplate.

"Okay. Time to go."

***

The ride to the city is uneventful. As we reach its outskirts, stress builds up. Even in the dark, our clothes can still betray us. Luckily, we reach the stable and tether our horses without being seen. Once in the streets, places where we can hide are numerous.

There are more patrols than I remember, and we try to avoid the main streets.

"Wait here." Garbos runs away, into a side alley.

"Where did he go?" Malia whispers.

"No idea."

The alley is dark enough to be safe for now, but I feel the shadow of the old distrust I had for him clawing at my mind.

A few minutes later, he's back with a bundle under his arms. "A linen maid lives nearby. I got us some clothes."

I pat him on the back. "Well done. Now, let's go to Artemis's temple to hide for the night.

***

The temple is just the same as when last I came in. It's full of trash, and it stinks, but as soon as I see the statue, I feel calm and I wonder why. No God has ever had any effect on me. Until I came here.

"Prome?" Malia takes my hand. "Time to sleep. We should be safe in the corner over there."

***

The streets are bustling with the usual crowd. We mix in, but stay alert. There are way too many soldiers to relax. Things get worse when we reach the agora at the foot of the stairs leading to the acropolis. Half the agora is completely closed off by hoplites. On the roofs around, bowmen watch the agora and the surrounding streets.

We prowl the city, searching for another way through, but we all know it's useless. When the afternoon grows old, we walk back to the temple in silence.

We hide in the corner, waiting for the night to come. Garbos draws a map of the agora and its surroundings in the dirt. We all look desperately at it.

"Smashing through is still the plan?"

I sigh. "There's another possibility..."

"Which is?"

"We wait for things to calm down." Even I don't believe that will work.

"It could take months," Malia says ruefully.

"Yes."

"My mother could already be somewhere else, or dead. We can't wait."

"Then we don't have a choice." I hunch closer to the map. "Which is the easiest way?"

Garbos points to a street east of the agora. "If we go through there just before sunrise, the street should be almost empty. We can use the horses for the surprise."

"And if we cross a patrol on our way?" Malia objects.

"I don't believe we will. It's not a big street, and goes through the stinkiest parts of town."

"If we cross one, I'll get rid of them with my spear before they raise the alarm," I add.

Garbos follows the street with his finger. "With the element of surprise, entering the agora through here, I will be able to shoot at the sentinels on the roof before we reach the guards. Malia and you will have to open a path."

"This will protect our backs, but it won't get us through the lines of soldiers."

We try to find other ways, but by midnight, we have no better plan, and still no way to break through the guards, except for my spear. We walk back to the stable through narrow streets, hiding at the tiniest sound of a patrol. We untie our horses and ride back to our camp.

✳✳✳

Our breakfast is morose. Nemeos wasn't here when we came back, and is still absent this morning. I feel like a complete failure. I can't keep a friend, and I can't get us through to our destination.

I draw another map of the agora absentmindedly. "There's no way we can do it. It would be suicidal."

They don't answer. I can see in their eyes that they're thinking the same. Malia pinches her lips together. "No, we can't."

I can hear defeat in her voice. Tears aren't far away. "I'll do as Garbos said."

Garbos snaps his head up. "What? But I thought you said we can't go—"

"I'll do as you said. Make a rush to the agora and shoot a path through the guards with my spear."

"You just said it would be suicidal." Malia looks at me as if I've just gone crazy.

Garbos puts a hand on her arm. "He doesn't plan on us going with him." He turns to me. "Do you?"

"No. I'll take my spear and a sword. If I keep shooting, I'll have a chance to get through."

Malia shoots up. "Are you crazy? How can you say that? They'll kill you!"

"Maybe." I shrug as if it was just a very remote possibility. "But I have to try. And I don't want you two to get killed too. If you turn away, you can be safe and find another way to free your mother. If I get to the Gods, I'll try to strike a bargain."

"But Zeus will kill you!"

"Not if he wants the marble. You'll keep it safe. You'll be my best chance to stay alive."

"No!" they both shout at the same time.

I sigh and stand up. "Sorry, but it's the only way I can see. If you don't want to help me, I'll go alone. But I certainly won't let you die on the agora." I take my spear and a sword. "I'll go now. From here, you'll see me climbing the stairs. If you don't see me when an hour's gone, take the horses and ride back to Kurea. Veron will hide you."

Without waiting for them to answer, I walk to the horse, deaf to their protests.

I'm about to straddle my horse, when all of a sudden it whinnies and jerks to the side. The three animals paw the ground nervously, emitting nervous neighs. I catch the reins of mine, but it rears up, freeing itself, and runs away. Malia and Garbos didn't even get the chance to reach their horses before all of them disappeared into the distance.

"What happened?"

We all have weapon in hand, ready to fight.

From the nearby wood comes a grunt. Nemeos appears, and stops at a safe distance.

I lower my spear. "Sorry, Nemeos, you just surprised us. We didn't mean to—"

I ready my spear again as another shape comes out of the wood. It's a boar, even bigger than the one that attacked me a lifetime ago. A second one emerges. They stop at Nemeos's side. Behind them, other beasts keep coming.

"What should we do?" Malia's voice quavers.

I have no answer. I watch, mesmerized, as the monstrous pack keeps growing. Soon, nine monsters face us: Nemeos, two boars, a two-headed dog, a hind and a deer, both with golden antlers, a black horse with fire coming out of his nostrils, a fox, a ram with fleece the color of gold, and, surprisingly, another Nemean lion.

All are of gigantic proportions, and only the fox is smaller than Nemeos.

Nemeos approaches casually, closely followed by the others.

"Prome?" Garbos keeps aiming at all of the monsters in turn.

Facing us is probably the deadliest army on earth. And it's walking toward us.

CHAPTER THIRTY-FIVE

Even from just a few paces away, I can't feel any danger coming from Nemeos. He stops in front of me, then places himself at my side. I stare at him, then at the other beasts. None shows us any animosity.

"Put down your weapons. I think Nemeos brought these animals here to help us."

Nemeos brushes his mane against me as if in approval. I can see Malia and Garbos have doubts, but they obey.

I pat Nemeos. "Is that what you did yesterday and tonight? You gathered some friends?"

Garbos answers me. "He's probably been gathering them since we went into the agoge. There aren't that many beasts in the area."

"And there shouldn't be more than one hydra either," I say, thinking about the nest. "I wonder how long the beasts have been following us. No wonder no monsters attacked us."

"Speaking of attacking... you're not planning to go alone anymore, are you?"

I smile at Malia. "No. The plan just changed. Nemeos brought us the army we needed to succeed."

All the beasts fall still and look at us.

"We don't have horses anymore, though. Nemeos, do you think we could ride you and two of your friends?"

The deer and a boar come closer. I can't explain why, but I'm convinced they understand me perfectly.

"Thank you. We'll approach the city at night. At first light tomorrow morning, we'll charge through the streets to the agora. Garbos, you'll shoot the sentinels on the roofs. I'll blast us a way through the soldiers while the beasts attack them from the side as a diversion. Malia, you'll protect our side with slashes of your spear." I see she's about to object. "They won't know you can't stun them. We'll be safe as soon as we step on the stairs. Even the soldiers aren't allowed there, And I doubt they'll risk staining them by shooting arrows at us." I turn to the beasts. "As soon as we're safe, break the fight and flee the city."

"Not much subtlety..."

"Not much time for it either."

✳✳✳

Hours pass sluggishly, but eventually night comes. Thinking about what will happen in the morning keeps sleep away. When it's time, I feel relieved to get moving.

Riding Nemeos is a first, but it feels just right. He's grown so much he probably doesn't notice my weight anyway. Malia appears to enjoy her ride on the deer, but Garbos looks much more nervous on the boar.

Nemeos and I take the lead, walking fast. Malia and Garbos follow. The other beasts are last. For such a large pack, we are surprisingly noiseless.

The sky is still dark, but the city will soon wake up. We must hurry up. Thanks to the darkness, we reach the first houses without raising the alarm. But once in the streets, the risk of being seen is much greater, especially as the sky is already getting lighter. Garbos takes the lead, and we start running.

Turning a corner, we fall upon a patrol. They don't have time to shout. Garbos has already shot three of them. Nemeos crushes the last soldier. I glimpse Malia stopping by the dead soldiers briefly.

We keep running. Soon, the air begins to stink. We hurry along the street, passing tanners' and dyers' houses. Some of the windows are already lit.

"Prome! We're getting there!" Garbos shouts out.

The street turns slightly to the right. The agora is just after the turn. We'll see it soon. I stop.

"Everyone get ready for a fight! Malia and Garbos, just behind me, left and right. I'll shoot us a path through the guards. Beasts: keep as many of them occupied as you can, far from us." I get ready to shoot bolts with my right hand and turn on the sword in my left one in case a soldier comes close. "Let's go!"

Nemeos starts running at top speed.

As we reach the turn, I'm surprised to glimpse Malia with a bow. So that's why she stopped by the dead soldiers. Garbos and Malia aim their arrows at the roof, but two sentries fall down to the street before they shoot. The hind managed to climb the building and is taking care of them for us.

The sight of the agora as we reach it makes my heart drop. The gate preventing access to the stairs is closed, and no wonder. In front of it are five rows of soldiers waiting for us. As the beasts emerge from the street behind us, some of the soldiers glance each other with fear in their eyes. I'm the first to react and shoot bolt after bolt through them.

I shoot the biggest ones I can, but all the guards are armed, ready to neutralize us with their own weapons. I hit nothing, but on the plus side, the reverse is also true. With a spear and a sword, I can absorb all the bolts sent at me.

Malia and Garbos are luckier. Their arrows fly and hit the guards.

"Arrows," Malia shouts out to me.

Fuck! My spear can't do anything about arrows. I can't shoot the soldiers to create a path and the arrows at the same time.

Nemeos runs in twists and turns. A few arrows barely miss me. I shoot bolts at the archers. I'm pleased to see explosions among them.

With no chance to break the line, Nemeos and I turn left to run full circle.

I survey the area. Malia and Garbos are still following me. The other beasts are attacking the lines from each side, but with a full and organized formation, the guards hold their ground.

As we face the guards again, I see they have a new tactic. Each archer is protected by a spearman. I won't be able to shoot them anymore.

"Why are you grinning?" Garbos asks me.

"Because I know how to open up a way through."

"How?"

"By aiming poorly." I wink at him.

I don't aim at the soldiers anymore. It would be useless. Instead, I shoot at the ground, as close to their feet as I can.

My first bolt is a success. The explosion is powerful enough to throw the nearby guards to the ground. I keep firing as fast as I can. The line is breaking in its middle, and I can see the sides weakening. The beasts are tearing through the ranks.

"Malia! Garbos! Now or never!"

We all run straight toward the gate. The guards are in complete disarray. A few arrows fly toward us, but their aim is poor.

My bolts open a path. I shoot at the gate, but it holds. Nemeos roars. Garbos's boar goes first and rams into it with such force that the gate is sent into the air and crashes into the side of the cliff.

We reach the first steps of the stairs and stop. We're safe.

I step down from Nemeos. Beside me, Malia does the same, and I hear Garbos do it too, clumsily as ever. Our three beasts run back to their friends, and, hopefully, out of the city.

Time for the last climb. I turn around and freeze.

Garbos is sprawled on the stairs, four arrows jutting out of his abdomen.

"Garbos!" I run to him. I touch his face, but he doesn't react. A lump grows in my throat. I look at the arrows. I can't risk pulling them out. Instead, I pat Garbos's cheeks to soothe him.

He doesn't react. "Garbos! Come on! Talk to me!"

Everything is getting blurry as I try to shake him back to life.

Malia takes me in her arms. "He's dead," she whispers.

✳✳✳

I don't know what happened. I break down. I've spent most of our time hating him, and now that he's gone... I miss him so much already. My whole world is crumbling.

Malia pulls me away. "Come on, Prome, we have to keep going. For my mother, and for him."

Garbos's death fills me with such hatred for the Gods, I run up the stairs without getting tired. When we reach the top of the stairs, what I see only makes me want to kill all the Gods. Everything is made of pure white marble: the flagstones of the wide avenue, the gigantic statues of Gods and Goddesses lining it, the temples on each side. Everything is pristine, luxurious. Peaceful. Garbos is dead, and every statue is a reminder that no God cares.

I'm blinded by rage. I walk up the long avenue, straight to the temple at the end of it. It's the biggest of all temples.

Zeus's.

Malia is hard-pressed keeping pace with me. She's talking to me, but I don't listen to her. I walk up a few stairs and enter through a door of inhuman proportions. Inside, the temple is empty, save for a single statue. It reaches almost to the roof. My head barely reaches above its feet.

Zeus is sitting on his throne, his bolt in his right hand. The statue is made of marble, gold, and silver. The details are so fine, it looks alive.

"*Zeus!*" I shout.

No answer.

I lift my spear and shoot a bolt at the statue's head. The nose explodes, and pieces of stone clank noisily on the ground.

Several people appear from behind the statue. I hear other footsteps behind me. They're all dressed in white, with gold jewelry. Some are taller than me, others smaller. They look like regular humans. Not even menacing ones. I recognize two of them. They have the same faces as the statues in their temples. A tall, blonde woman and a dark-haired man with eyes as blue as the sea. Artemis and Poseidon.

I snort at them. *These are the Gods everyone fears?*

A man steps forward. He has the same face as the statue I've just destroyed. "How dare you come here? No human has ever dared such an affront."

"I don't care what other humans have done or not." I cut him short. "You imprisoned my friend's mother and you killed my friend!"

The Gods look at each other uneasily.

"Yes, I'm human and I dare talk to you like this!"

Zeus laughs. "I'll just have to kill you and your whole city for your crime! Seize them!"

All around us, the Gods approach.

Suddenly, the noise of a running animal followed by a roar stops them. Nemeos unceremoniously knocks one of the Gods down as he rushes to me. He stops at my side, baring his teeth and growling at the Gods.

"Lion!" Zeus shouts. "I created you! Leave this place right now!"

Nemeos snarls at him and walks around Malia and me, growling at every one of the Gods. Artemis turns to Zeus. "He's no longer yours to command, I fear, Father."

Zeus's face is distorted by spite. "How can you say that? I'm its creator and master!"

"No! You created it using technologies you don't fully understand. It seems he found a new master, and I believe I know the reason."

She turns to me. As she looks at me, she smiles. Her face exhales purity and calmness. "I don't think you came here without a reason." Her voice is soft and polite.

I turn to Zeus. "I order you to release my friend Malia's mother!"

Around us, the Gods burst out laughing.

A God with jet-black hair addresses Zeus. "At least, he has guts." He turns to me. "Who are you to give us an order?" He looks at me the way a parent looks at a young, unreasonable child.

I turn to Malia. "Show them."

She takes her necklace off and holds it in front of her for the Gods to see the marble. All the Gods look at it, shock registering on their faces.

"How did you get that?" Zeus roared.

"We created it."

"Liar!"

I glare at him. "You know it's the truth. Why would you have destroyed the agoge otherwise?"

All the Gods stare at him. Questions burst out.

"Is it true, Father?"

"How could they?"

"Is it real?"

Zeus silences them with a sign of his hand. "Yes, I did destroy the agoge, to destroy the abomination underneath. But even if I was too late, it doesn't matter. They didn't create it themselves! And I'll kill them for their impudence!"

"No, you won't! They did create it, with human technology. Our laws are clear!" Artemis turns back to us, still smiling.

At my side, Malia stirs. "Excuse me, but what is it?"

"See?" Zeus's face is crimson. "They don't even know what they did. How could they claim anything?"

Another woman steps forth. She looks older than Artemis but is just as beautiful, with wavy long black hair. "Let us all be judges, and not just you, Zeus."

Artemis bows to her. "Thank you, Hera." She turns to Malia. "My dear child. What you hold in your hand is a universe. And, according to the Gods' law, you are now Gods too."

CHAPTER THIRTY-SIX

"I can't let this nonsense—"

"Oh shut up, Zeus!" Hera cuts him off curtly. "We all know history. You created life on one planet using the technologies you stole from the Titans. They created a whole universe using a technology created by their own ancestors."

Zeus glares at her but doesn't answer.

Hera turns to another Goddess. "Themis? You are the Goddess of justice. You know the laws better than any of us."

The young Goddess bows politely. "The universe the girl is holding cannot be ignored. The laws are quite clear. These two humans are now Gods." She bows again.

Hera faces Zeus. "Then the matter is settled. Any action against them might cause another war amongst Gods. We can't risk it. Aphrodite, please give them their attire."

I'm blinded by a flash of light. When I reopen my eyes, I gasp. Malia's dressed in a pristine white dress trimmed with gold. She looks just like the other Goddesses. I look at myself. My tunic is also pure white. My breastplate is made of pure gold. I'm also wearing a suit of armor, complete with arm and leg protection. Even our weapons are now made of gold.

"Thank you, Aphrodite." Hera turns to us. "Now that your status has been settled, none of the Gods will harm you. You are free to go wherever you want." She turns around to leave. The other Gods follow her lead.

"Wait!"

They all freeze and turn back to me.

"We didn't come here to become Gods. I don't care about that."

Zeus doesn't look pleased by my tone. "Why did you come here, then?"

He glares at me, but I hold his gaze. "I want Malia's mother. I want her freed."

For the first time, I see a strange flicker on his face. It's over before I know what it means.

"Agreed. We'll have her sent back to your village." Zeus turns away.

Such haste to get away from us. But we're Gods too, now. I've waited too long to get even with them to let them go this easily.

"I'm not finished." All my life, I've been waiting for this. I won't let them walk away this easily.

All the Gods freeze and turn to me stiffly. Zeus is glaring at me as if he's about to kill me. One of the Goddesses at his side, on the contrary, looks almost frightened. I haven't said anything yet. Why should she be frightened?

Artemis gives me a small nod, and it all becomes clear. We're Gods now. Their own laws forbid them to hurt us.

Laws.

A hand grabs mine. "Prome, what are you doing?" Malia whispers.

I ignore her. "I demand that you leave this country right now, and never return!"

All the Gods look at each other, shocked. Only Zeus keeps a stone-hard face.

"What makes you think you can make such outrageous demands?"

"Because we're Gods. And as this country is ours, I claim it back!"

Whispers erupt around us.

Zeus smiles nastily. "I'm afraid this isn't something you can demand. Now I demand that you leave right now and never come back!"

My hatred for him flares. "Then I'll get the other Gods to declare war on you!"

He laughs, then glares at me. "Beware your words! You're a God, but even among Gods, fools are not welcome."

I feel my lips move despite myself, distorting my mouth into a humorless rictus. "Your soldiers killed my friend at the bottom of the stairs. If we are Gods, so was he. You broke your own laws. You already started the war."

"Father!"

"Zeus!"

"It can't be."

Everyone is shouting.

"Silence." Zeus's voice thunders.

He glares at me, but I don't look down. I won't ever let a God have his way with me again.

"Themis?" he asks without looking away.

"Father... I..." The voice is hesitant.

I keep glaring back at Zeus.

"Speak!"

"He's right, father," Themis says sheepishly.

We glare at each other in silence for an eternity.

"What if I bring your friend back to life?"

I swallow hard. Can a God really do that? "Then you can stay here if you want, but you'll stay in Parthenos. You won't intervene in people's life in any way. The soldiers are not yours to command anymore!"

The Gods look thunderstruck. Their silence and ashen faces confirm that this claim is rightfully mine to make. I stare at Zeus triumphantly.

"Hades! Do it! And you!" He points at us, and Nemeos gnarls. "Don't ever come back here. The country is yours, but Parthenos is still mine. Law or no law, if you ever set a foot in it again, I'll kill you myself!" He storms away and disappears behind the statue's pedestal.

The other Gods look at each other, unsure of what to do, before following him without a word. Only Artemis smiles weakly to us before going.

A moment later, Malia, Nemeos, and I are alone.

"Do you think he'll do it?"

I look at Malia. "Do what?"

"Free my mother, leave the people alone, and resurrect Garbos?"

I look at her wide eyes and can't help laughing. When I stop, I feel much better. "I never thought you'd be the one doubting the Gods, and I the one trusting them. Yes, I think he'll do it. We've become what he fears most. What he tried to prevent us from becoming. His equals. Come, let's go."

I take her hand and lead her out. We walk down the avenue, Nemeos in the lead, and down the stairs.

About halfway down, someone appears in the distance. He's too far away for me to recognize the face, but he wears the same white garments we do.

I walk faster, then break into a run.

Out of breath, I stop a step away from Garbos, who's alive and scared-looking.

"Prome! I'm so glad to see you! What happened? I got shot during the fight, and then I lost consciousness... Prome?"

I look at him through flowing tears. My heart is bursting with happiness. I put a hand on his face, to make sure I'm not dreaming.

His skin is so soft.

I take one step closer and then kiss him.

"Finally," Malia says behind me.

I turn back to her, appalled to have kissed Garbos in front of her.

"Don't look at me like that," she says, smiling. "I've known you were in love with him for a long time."

"When?" I mumble. "I mean... I'm sorry."

"Don't be. It's okay. I love you, but not like this. It took me a while, but I figured it out."

Still in shock, all I can answer is, "How?"

She laughs. "I've known you with better communication skills..." She smiles almost sadly. "I noticed how you looked at Garbos, even when you said he was a spy. You never looked at me that way. And although I should have been, I wasn't jealous." She sighs. "I'm happy for you. Just promise me you won't forget me."

I take her into a hug. "Of course I won't."

✳✳✳

When we reach the bottom of the stairs, the soldiers are still recovering from the battle, taking away the injured.

We step onto the agora, and all the soldiers turn to us. Some are ready to attack us, but none do. They all stare at us, unsure of what to do. I look at Garbos and Malia, and smile. Even if no one has seen a God for eons, there is no mistaking what we now are. As we walk closer to the first soldier, he suddenly kneels, soon followed by the others.

We cross the agora in an eerie silence, everyone kneeling before us.

The High Inquisitor, surrounded by a cohort of hoplites, emerges onto the agora and stops, looking at the scene. All of the soldiers kneel, except for one who draws his sword and marches on us.

"You! I'll kill you!"

"Shut up, Taeros!" I shout loud enough for everyone to hear us. "Zeus doesn't command the warriors anymore. We do!"

"How dare you blaspheme in front of the City of the Gods?" snaps the High Inquisitor.

I sneer. "The Gods have recognized us as their equals." I refuse to call myself a God, especially now that I've confronted some. "From now on, the soldiers will answer to us! As for you, your services won't be needed anymore."

The High Inquisitor's face contorts with outrage. "Blasphemy! May the Gods throw their wrath upon you and all those who listen to you!"

"Enough!" I shout and shoot a bolt into the sky. But this one is different. The sound is louder than any thunder I've heard before, ant the bolt is the color of gold. It flies higher and higher into the sky, without fading. Suddenly, it explodes into thousands of stars that fall back to earth. For a moment, it looks like the whole city is caged in a golden dome.

The people who had followed the High Inquisitor fall on their knees.

Only Taeros moves, and launches himself at me. Before he can take more than three strides, two soldiers tackle him to the ground and disarm him. As they lift him up, held tightly, I recognize that Pyrias is one of them.

"I challenge you!"

Pyrias and the other soldier try to gag Taeros, but he resists them.

A challenge. The soldiers' way. I remember what Pyrias once told me. If I want to discourage further challengers, I need a spectacular win.

"Release him!" I order Pyrias.

"What are you doing?" Malia is horror-struck.

"Don't worry." I give my spear to Garbos. "Keep it for me a minute, please, and lend me your bow."

Garbos looks surprised, but hands me his bow anyway, with his quiver.

"I'll just need one." I take one arrow and prepare to shoot.

Taeros starts running again toward me. I aim at the sky and release the arrow. The arrow flies straight, then turns at a right angle to race toward the ground and plant itself in front of Taeros's foot. He stumbles upon it and falls.

I unsheathe my sword and walk to him. "Move away!"

The kneeling soldiers around us stand and step back.

I turn on my golden sword, ready to stun Taeros. It emits a soft, warm light.

Taeros looks at it for a second, and I see hesitation in his moves. I just have to wait for him to attack.

I don't have to wait long for his first and last attack. He doesn't even feint, but attacks me frontally.

I block his sword with mine. As they touch, my sword flashes, and Taeros's sword breaks cleanly in half.

Taeros stares at me, wide-eyed.

I wait for him to launch another attack. Instead, he falls to the ground, stunned.

"Kill him!" The High Inquisitor's voice is high-pitched with fear.

None of the soldiers moves.

"Arrest him for blasphemy!"

I turn around and see Malia pointing at the High Inquisitor.

Five soldiers rush to obey her. They take the High Inquisitor and Taeros away. The other soldiers line up in front of us, and kneel.

I recognize many soldiers with whom I trained at the agoge, other trainees like us. I walk over to Pyrias, who still kneels.

"Don't do that, Pyrias."

"But you're a God. I'm sorry for talking to you like I did." He bows lower.

I laugh. "The Gods made me their equal, but I'm still Prome. Stand."

He obeys but doesn't dare look at me in the eyes.

I sigh. "Many things will change. For now, I'm putting you in command. Don't kill anyone anymore. Rebuild the agoge and spread the word that Technologists aren't criminals."

"As you order."

Leaving Pyrias in charge is the best solution I can think of. He will be fair and obey the no-killing order.

***

Five days later, we reach our city, Malia and Garbos on white horses, me on Nemeos. Waiting for us at the gates, a large crowd is assembled. At the front of the crowd, Archelia is smiling.

Malia dismounts and falls into her arms, crying.

"Gods can keep their promises."

I smile at Garbos. "Did you doubt it? I gave them good motivation for that."

He laughs, then looks at Malia and her mother with sad eyes.

"What are you thinking about?"

He shrugs. "I guess it's over now."

"What is over?"

"The three of us. Our adventures..."

I smile at him. "I doubt that. We still have things to do, and I doubt even being Gods will help us." I enjoy his surprise before dismounting. "Presenting my love to Archelia. Come."

Garbos smiles at me, and my heart swells. "Do you think we'll have our happily ever after?"

"Our what?"

"In some of the books I read, there's a Prince Charming, and he saves a princess from a dragon or whatever, and the story ends with *and they lived happily ever after.*"

"Did you just compare me to a Prince Charming?" I laugh.

Garbos reddens. "Well, more to a God Charming, I guess." And he joins in with my laughter.

"I don't know about ever after, but what I know is that you make me happy, and I don't want to spend a minute of my life without you."

We stare at each other, too shy to kiss in front of the crowd. The kiss will have to wait, and for the first time in an eternity, I'm really looking forward to what will happen later, unafraid of monsters or Gods. Just impatient to be alone with the one I love.

About the Author

Alec Nortan is a French social services worker. Though he learned English at school, he chooses this language to write in. His works are gay-related fictions, varying from young adult, science fiction, or fantasy adventure, to romance.

Facebook: https://www.facebook.com/alecnortanbooks
Email: alecnortan@gmail.com

NINESTAR PRESS, LLC

www.ninestarpress.com

www.ingramcontent.com/pod-product-compliance
Lightning Source LLC
Chambersburg PA
CBHW050024180626
46810CB00002B/563